# Creepy Campfire Quarterly
## #2

I0457453

Edited by
Jennifer Word

# Creepy Campfire Quarterly
## #2
Compilation Copyright © 2016 EMP Publishing
www.emppublishing.com

Cover design by MaxMaster © 2016 Jennifer Word

ISBN: 0692688528 (paperback)
ISBN-13: 978-0-6926885-2-6 (paperback)

Printed in the United States of America

# CONTENTS

# INTRODUCTION

You have in your hand a collection of some of the best grim & creepy, spectral and supernatural stories my friend and editor Jennifer Word could gather for your entertainment. Campfire Stories. In a perfect world, you'd be sitting in the dark, listening, rather than reading. Someone would be on a log—maybe with a flashlight highlighting the hollows of their cheeks and eyes; skull-faced or perhaps jack lantern orange, depending on the voltage in the batteries. The trees and tall grass would be rustling and whispering, hiding any of those things that might be watching you just outside the rim of a dying campfire.

Now, there are real and immediate things to be considered, sitting there in the woods, in the dark. Mosquitos, wood ticks, ragweed, poison ivy, snakes, and, for all I know: Bobcats and Bears. But, you're not thinking of them. Your mind is on the guy with the hook, or the ghost lingering about the body, buried somewhere very near to your campsite. You've heard the story, or one very much like it before, but *this time* it has that certain ring of authenticity, and later that evening, when you have to leave your pup tent to use the bushes, you remember every word of it, and it seems an endless, eye rolling walk back to the safety of your tent and sleeping bag.

OK. Chances are, you are not in the woods right now, but in your apartment, or between classes, or waiting to be called at the DMV. Yet, you have obviously bought, borrowed, or stolen (in descending order of approval) this book, anticipating the same sort of shiver. Why do we share this fascination with scaring ourselves?

Let me offer one possible explanation.

When I was a kid, each summer, my parents shipped me off for two weeks to Camp Ihduhapi—a place where mostly City and Suburban kids would live in cabins named Boone or Crocket, Chippewa or Sioux, to sleep in bunk beds, and where the Counselors would toss your wet swimming trunks on the roof if you left them dripping off the bed posts. The highlight was always the overnight camping trip to the island in the middle of the lake. It was kind of swampy and marshy. You canoed out there like mini-voyagers, set up your tents, grilled hot dogs for supper, and of course, built a big fire so the Counselors could scare the crap out of little kids right before bedtime with tales of the island's resident ghost: *JACK SIMMONS.*

Maybe Jack wasn't really a ghost. Sometimes he was more of a monster, depending on who told it, but the gist was always that he had been a former counselor (not a particularly nice one, either) who had died on one of those trips by getting sucked down in a hidden pool of quicksand. He still walked the night, draped in weed and rotting flesh, seeking vengeance on the campers who disturbed his rest. If he could, nothing pleased him more than to pluck you from your tent by the ankles and drag you off to join him eternally in his grave of green slime. Of course, about 2:00 a.m., you could expect one of the Counselors to run screaming through the camp dressed in something like a sniper's Gillie Suit.

It's been fifty-six years since I first heard the story, but I remember every word vividly. Obviously, I see it from a bit more sophisticated perspective than I did as a nine-year-old boy. I now realize the YMCA was not going to charge my parents a substantial sum and then send us all off to a quicksand-ridden island to face suffocation and death at the hands of an undead former employee. Lawyers are scarier than ghosts when it comes to that sort of thing. I doubt very seriously there even *was* a Jack Simmons, and certainly no camper-eating pond of goo. Yet, you couldn't have convinced me of it back then, and even now, there's a small part of me that resists it. If it wasn't real, it should have been!

So, no—your toys and dolls don't come alive at night and stalk your room while you're sleeping. No monsters hide under your bed waiting to pull you under, should an arm or leg dangle within reach. That misshapen form in the shadows is not some minion from the outer depths of night, but only all the clothes you piled on the chair rather than hang them up. Your neighbor probably isn't a Vampire, and that kind-of-spooky woman down the street wasn't made by her husband in the basement. But, wasn't it a different and more thrilling world when you thought they might have been?

And that's why I think we still cling to the scary story—the things long gone from our experiences—if not our minds and imaginations. It's boring to become an adult and the top of the intellectual food chain. We need a good vampire, werewolf, or supernatural being to keep us not only humble, but to maintain that healthy "What If?" instinct that kept us so interested as children. It's the same reason we go to the thrill parks…so we can experience what it feels like to plunge hundreds of feet in uncontrolled free fall and still expect we shall get off the ride without being spattered like an egg. To put it another way, while I'm sure we are all glad not to run into a

# Introduction

Tyrannosaurus Rex or a Saber Tooth Tiger on the sidewalk, doesn't a part of you rebel that it's not possible? That's why we read books and watch films where it is.

You all know this without my telling you, but reinforcement among like minds is a good thing and, I hope, a comfortable means of slipping into the stories that follow. So, now, go on to the important stuff...all the authors waiting to share with you the "What If's" that ran from their imaginations to their fingertips, to your eyes. There's no reason not to expect that you'll be pleased.

And, Jack...if you're still out there after all these years...I still believe in you, Buddy!

James E. Coplin
Mesa, Arizona
2016

# COLD COMFORT

## James E. Coplin

Bobcat Clements could only imagine how cold it was. Whiskey froze solid when it was 30 below and Bobcat had chewed as much as swallowed the last swig of the bottle some time ago. Since then the wind had picked up considerable. Even over its howl, he could hear the trees pop and snow was so frozen it crunched beneath his snowshoes like broken glass.

He believed himself some miles north of the Otter Creek Digs but between the dark and caught in the blizzard, was confused at his direction. The land sloped up and down, the patchwork of timber un-navigable without moon or stars. There was a frozen haunch of moose in his possibles sack but no shelter to build a fire. Despite his wolf skins and fur cap he felt the heat of his body being sapped like a cat drawing breath from a sleeping child; legs heavy as iron, each step lagging the other like a reluctant dog.

He'd trapped and prospected too long to fool himself. He needed shelter and there was none. He was a dead man.

The easiest thing to do would be to just lie down and close his eyes. It would be a kind death. He'd go to sleep and the snow would encase him like a warm grave and maybe if he were lucky, someone would come across his bones at spring melt to lay him out proper.

He was staring at nothing when he noticed a dark shape within what seemed a small clearing. It stood against a bank of snow cut partially into a hillside with a roof and chimney.

It was almost hidden but there it was – a miner's or trapper's shack! Halleluiah and Praise Be! Bobcat Clements wasn't a praying man but unless he was seeing visions, this was a miracle. For all that, it was some queer. He knew all the land within fifty miles of Otter Creek, every cabin and shack, but he'd never seen this one. He must have been off his reckoning far more than he realized. At any rate, he struggled up and towards it with the will of a drowning man who spies a spit of land in the distance.

He could see no light behind the cracks of the shuttered windows, no smoke rising from the chimney. The rough timber door was banked with snow and it was clear it hadn't been opened for some time. No fresh prints led to it or around it. It was deserted. Bobcat dug away at the drifts blocking the door and eventually forced it back on the sagging hinges.

"Anybody home?" He called into the darkness but received no answer. He pushed his way in. The fireplace was cold but there were logs and tinder piled on the grate. With shivering fingers, Bobcat set his flint to the dried timber and it caught, the room taking shape in the flickering light.

There was a planked table and shelves along the timber and earth walls; a tin of coffee and a battered blue pot with all the provisions a trapper might need living far back in the wood. Traps and skins lined the walls, and, tucked in the corner with a kettle stove by its side, was a cot and straw mattress piled thick with covers and furs. The fire had already made a small circle of warmth and he stood rubbing his frozen fingers in front of it. He couldn't make out the why of it but the fact remained. He was saved.

There were beans and some pots, some venison strips all cut out and ready, and while they simmered, he poked about some. It was then he noticed that the blankets on the cot didn't look right. There was a shape under them. As he lit one of the lamps, he saw frost twinkle on the wisp of a beard that lay over the covers, a night-capped head almost buried in the goose down pillows. He pulled back the covers and there it was; the long, lean body of an old man, stiff as a frozen board and just as dead - long since deceased.

Bobcat poked the body with his numbed finger. "Died in your sleep, hey Partner?" The eyes were closed, body was hard as wood, mummified by the cold and tanned the color of leather. He wore a thick flannel nightshirt that reached to his knobby knees, the skinny shanks of his legs ending in bare feet.

Outside, the wind howled about the cornice, the snow pelting the shutters like icy claws tearing at the planks. Inside, the warmth had spread, the frosted crystals beginning to thaw on the dead man's face and hands. The smell of venison stew and wood smoke was like a live thing probing every corner of the cabin. Yet, Bobcat had one task to tend to before he could appreciate dinner and a bed.

He gingerly reached down and placed his arms under the old man's hips and shoulders. He lifted and was surprised just how light the body was. It was like lifting a sack filled with straw.

"Another kindness on your part, Grandfather." he said, as he carried the stiff body towards the door. "Sorry to put you out, but I'll be needing that bed and blankets more than you and don't hanker to share. You'd be feeling the same, I'm sure."

Clements maneuvered the body through the door, wind tearing at him and flapping the old man's nightshirt like a stiffened sail. He struggled through the snowdrifts, plowing his way, until reaching a knot of fir trees some 30 yards away. Far enough, he reckoned. He pitched the corpse unceremoniously into the snow and gave it no further thought. By the time he walked to the cabin, it was already half-buried.

*Funeral enough,* thought Bobcat, as he shut the door against the wind and the night.

When his belly was full of stew and biscuit, he brewed coffee and sat at the table, warming himself and basking in his luck. This was a fine cabin and even when the storm broke, he saw no reason to move on. He'd sit the winter enjoying that fine bed and eating the well-stocked provisions, warm and cozy, instead of shivering in some mining camp tent at five dollars a week, waiting for the diggings to thaw. Yep, luck had at last come to sit on his shoulder, and right now, the world looked pretty good to him.

He threw wood on the fire, filled the shuttle full of coals to get the barrel stove going and eased himself gratefully between the covers, settling down into the depression left by the bed's previous occupant. That part didn't bother him one bit. Safe and warm, he listened to the wind battering at the cabin as if frustrated at losing its prey. "Not this time, Old Man Winter," he taunted, and by-and-by, fell peacefully into dreamless sleep.

Sometime during the night though, he stirred uneasily and frowned in his sleep. He was in that drugged spot between deep sleep and consciousness, where the dream world and the real are hard to decipher between. He felt himself fingered by cold wind, lifted and floating upon it. The storm had reached in and grabbed him, gathering itself like Old Man North, to lift him solid and bear him away. He couldn't wake. He couldn't stir a finger, yet he accepted the sensation without concern. It was a dream and he allowed it to carry him along.

He was shivering; so cold. Something was tickling his face like a coating of spider web but it stabbed like needles. His eyes struggled to open but they seemed crusted shut. And he was so stiff. His bare feet felt like they were submerged in ice water and he reached to pull the covers tighter. All his fingers scrabbled at was air and with that, he became fully awake. His eyelids snapped open with a tearing sound like sheet ice parting.

He bolted upright. Some distance off was the cabin, the light from the dying fire red through the cracks and spilling out the open door. He was freezing. Struggling to his feet, he chaffed his arms, shaking out the stiffness and his confusion. This was real. Somehow, he was outside without any idea how he got there.

No matter how, he had to get out of the cold. He plowed back through the snow, realizing as he did that the spot he'd been laying on looked familiar. It was where he had deposited the dead trapper earlier that evening. Where was he? The snow-covered mound where it should have been was no longer there. But something else was.

There were prints overlaying his, bare feet walking a staggering line as if fighting to carry a load. As he followed them to the cabin door, they turned to melted splotches, crossing the threshold, receding into the dark shadows and across the planked floor. They ended in the dark corner where the bed sat tucked against the wall.

"Whoa, Old Hoss!" He shivered again and this time with more than the cold. Maybe he had never found the cabin at all? Maybe he was still dying in the cold and this was all a death delirium? Yet, there was his pack and rifle leaning where he'd put them. His boots were sitting by the bed and his coat and clothes piled beside. As they thawed, his frost bitten toes felt like he had hot coals between them and he'd never heard of that being part of a hallucination.

Nor would he have made up the thing he stared at. The bed was once again occupied; the covers pulled up to the whiskered chin, beads of melting snow dripping on the edges and a contented smile turning the corners of the dried-out lips. Knobby brown fingers grasped the bed covers as if just finished nestling down beneath them and gratefully settled in. It was as if he had never been disturbed.

This was more than could be said about Bobcat Clements. He was a hard man and took most things as they came without being shook. But there and then, standing only in his woolen long johns, bootless and without his pack, rifle or provisions, he fled into the night.

He didn't look back, hardly felt the wind that was sucking the warmth from him and freezing his blood. He ran and it's hard to say how far he made it. He wasn't seen that spring at the Otter Creek digs or any of the surrounding camps. There was a pile of bones found by some passing Tanguit Indians later that spring. They might have been Bob's. The wilderness was littered with nameless remains each spring and not a lot of attention was given them. They were left undisturbed, for the foxes, wolves, and ravens to pick and scatter.

But some in the wilderness make their tombs where they lay and can be damned particular about being disturbed.

# MONSTER GARAGE SALE
## Morgan Griffith

Emma Collins was headed to her Mom's antique shop when the sign caught her eye.

## Monster Neighborhood Yard Sale

The opportunity to pick up something with resale value for the shop was too good to ignore, especially since Emma had bailed on movie night last week. She turned onto Damask Street; found a parking spot under a jacaranda tree, and walked toward the first house.

Halloween was a week away. Like any kid-friendly neighborhood, more than half of the houses were decorated with store-bought cobwebs, cheery inflatables and Styrofoam grave markers from the local Halloween shop. There was always one house that outdid the rest. Emma shielded her eyes from the glare of afternoon sun through dark clouds. At the end of the cul-de-sac, a realistic spider the size of a Volkswagen was suspended over the patio. A life-sized witch with rotting teeth was poised to greet trick-or-treaters by the front door.

Skeletons clawed at windows.

She browsed a table at the second house, marked "odds and ends" as the wind gusted, sending brittle leaves skittering along the driveway. A signed, Baccarat paperweight sat on a gold pedestal. It was highly collectible, but evidently the seller had done their homework. It was priced accordingly with little chance for resale profit.

"Have a nice day, dear," the woman called, as Emma moved on to the next house.

Most of the homeowners were in costume, sparking weird connections in her obsessive brain. Catwoman hawked baby clothes; a strikingly real Furiosa had a damned fine book collection, and a Walking Dead Carol (who also sold cookies) tempted her with the complete Buffy series.

*Why is it that when you're shopping for someone else, you find the best stuff for yourself?*

Emma was making her way closer to the spook house. She strolled hastily through the next one, keeping one eye on the strange, shirtless dude slathered in yellow paint, who wore Minion goggles. Beneath his tables of grimy and busted CD's were boxes filled with naked and limbless, and sometimes headless Barbies. Without a closer look, she could see they were stained.

*I don't even want to know.*

Thunder pealed, rattling old dishware and used back scratchers. Emma hurried on, one house removed from the giant spider. The air smelled like rain.

Sellers with tables out front all scrambled to drag stuff back into houses before the storm began. The next guy was either psychic or lazy, having propped his merchandise up on card tables in the garage. He nodded to her from his beach chair.

Emma debated. The temperature had dropped several degrees. A shiver spider-walked up between her shoulder blades. She should go, empty-handed or not. It was probably going to pour any minute.

Beach chair guy was sizing her up. He'd really gone the extra mile with his costume. Not. A Raiders football jersey and cap, with something dark smeared under his eyes. He was cute though. College aged with slight stubble.

"You've come this far," he called to her in a friendly tone. "A shame to miss a great deal. I have some unique things, and I'll be happy to lend you an umbrella."

When he flashed a casual smile at her, Emma forgot about her mother and the impending rain. She passed under the overhanging garage door and approached four tables crammed with items, sneaking sideways glances when she thought he wasn't looking.

Thunder rattled shelves above a jewelry-making station against the wall. Emma's gaze trailed over the snarl of items that seemed to have been haphazardly thrown onto tables. There were dishes and female clothing, some of which was definitely from a fashion savvy teen. A crowded box of supernatural romance novels stood beside pink barbells. Jewelry. An odd wrongness scratched vaguely on the outskirts of her brain like a buzzing fly.

"My Mom and sister were called out of town at the last minute. They had already gone through all this stuff, so I agreed to man the tables," he explained, as if reading her thoughts.

Emma tucked her purse under her arm to hold up clothes.

"Some of these things are really cute."

The beach chair creaked as the fellow started to rise and then changed his mind.

"You're welcome to use the bathroom inside to try them on."

"I wish," she told him. "A shame they're not my size."

Football Guy rubbed the stubble on his chin thoughtfully. A sudden barrage of rain hit the cement driveway. Emma turned to watch.

"It's probably just as well. Place is a mess. I'm in the middle of making props. I know Halloween is only a week away, but I thought I'd try and give the house next door some competition."

Emma whipped her attention back to him.

"I'd love to get some decorations for my Mom's shop. Are you selling any?"

"Most of my stuff is gory. Ever work with that fake blood? A bitch to clean. I tried wearing a barbeque apron but it still went everywhere."

He held up his palms to show her red streaks and splotches.

She pointed to the bottom half of his jersey.

"On your shirt, too."

"Damn!"

He jumped out of his chair, pulling at the fabric to look.

"The price you pay for the scary stuff, I guess," he shot her a sly smile. "I think I have a few smaller items that might do for your Mom's shop. Pumpkins and stuff. C'mon inside."

"Oh, I really should be going," she instinctively backed a step away from the tables.

"How about if I bring them here?" He waved an arm at the interior house door. "I can give you a better deal than the stores."

Emma hesitated but nodded, visualizing her mother's smile at cute decorations.

"Be right back."

The sky was surprisingly dark as the rain intensified, drumming a metallic beat in storm drains and on awnings against the house. A glance at her watch shocked her.

"How is that possible?" she muttered, moving toward the door into the house.

"Excuse me?" she called out. "I'm really sorry, but I have to go…"

No answer.

"Hello?"

The door hadn't shut all the way. With her fingertips, Emma pulled it toward her, revealing an inch-by-inch view of a shadowy kitchen. A severed arm lay on the tile floor against the base of a center island. Dark blood was partially congealed in a pool beneath it. Farther down, propped against the splattered wall like an oversized rag doll with head resting on its chest, was a body. An unmoving body, one of whose legs had been hacked off beneath the knee. Emma saw ragged, very *real* bone. Light from a connecting room shone in a large pool of blood. Footsteps had walked through it, trailing off until out of sight.

There was blood everywhere.

Sudden rictus froze Emma's face as she stared open-mouthed. Her eyes throbbed, mirroring insanely random words slashed in blood on the kitchen walls. Shadows curtained a walkway leading to the rest of the house.

The metallic blood smell was overpowering, assaulting her face with sickening heat. She gagged, and clamped a shaking hand over her mouth.

*OhmyfuckingGodthisisreal…*

Emma let go of the door. It made a small *click* as it fell back in place. She turned and bolted, jamming her thigh into a table. Glass and ceramics and jewelry clattered like a thunderclap in the garage. She almost fell into it. As she regained her balance, her right hand found and closed around a silver letter opener. A muscular hand grabbed her left arm.

Violently jerked back, Emma was thrown into a wall. The stench of him was rancid as he pinned and pressed himself against her. Thready drool mixed with blood dripped from his chin. Grinding his teeth, he forced her legs apart. It gave her half of a second to free her arm and plunge the letter opener deep into his ear.

Into the torrent of rain she ran, into the flooding street, past sodden yards with deflated Halloween monsters. Only a short time ago, those yards had been clustered with people. Her legs ached as she reached her car. Emma trembled uncontrollably, stealing a frightened glance back as her freezing hand pawed frantically through her purse for keys.

The garage door had been lowered. The house glowered in darkness.

***

Emma's pulse thundered in her ears as she drove, still shaking. Her mother was watching the news on a portable TV in the shop when she arrived. They sat on hold with the police, as images flashed, of cops in rain gear swarming a neighborhood. A grim-faced reporter followed a close-up of a soggy, cardboard yard sale sign. The camera zoomed in on a dark house.

"This is what we know so far. The victims haven't been identified pending notification of relatives, but two women, a mother and daughter who lived in the house, have been brutally murdered.

11

"While a neighborhood yard sale was ongoing, an unknown assailant entered the house, killed both women, and continued running the sale inside the family garage.

"Three additional women, ages ranging from twenty-two to fifty-one, were lured inside and also killed. Police are still on the scene, and the killer has escaped and is at large. A massive manhunt is currently underway..."

# PUT HER BACK TOGETHER

**Vincent Salvati**

## I

Her eyes fluttered as she pulled herself out of unconsciousness, struggling to understand. Slowly, the memories came drifting back to her, and so did the panic. Her heart rate quickly increased as the perspiration surfaced on her brow. She couldn't tell where she was, exactly, but it was dark. She remembered back to the dumpy, disheveled man in the parking lot who asked her for the time. She remembered looking down to her wrist, but she didn't remember anything else.

She moved her hands and realized she wasn't bound, and her feet moved as well. Though she couldn't see a thing in the dark room, and she still felt a bit groggy, she decided to get up and make a go of it. Just as she stood, Max punched her dead in the face, knocking her back over the chair she had been sitting in. The pain was excruciating. Her jaw and the side of her face were broken, probably shattered.

Max wouldn't take long now. He had just been waiting for her to wake up. Before she could move, he was on top of her. He slammed his fist into her stomach so she couldn't breathe or fight, and then another to the face. She thought she was going to vomit from the pain but Max wouldn't let it get that far. She felt the sharp slice as the knife entered her chest. And felt it cut down her body. Then she felt no more.

## II

Max took the can of Chef Boyardee out of the cupboard and cut through the top with the rusted can opener. He poured the thick, orange contents into a pot and turned the flame on medium. He took a can of beer out of the cooler that sat between the peeling Formica table and the refrigerator that had stopped working a year and a half ago. He never got around to moving it out, or getting a new one.

The phone on the wall rang and startled him. No one ever called on that number. After three rings, he picked it up.

"Hello?"

Max listened to the silence as it expanded.

"Hello?" he said a little louder and more pronounced, which made the silence seem even more engulfing when it returned. He could tell the line wasn't dead, but at the same time, there was nothing.

"I don't know who this is but you better cut it out," he growled into the phone. Just as he was getting ready to hang up, he heard a voice.

"Max," was what it simply said.

Max did not answer but returned the silence. And then after a few more seconds, he heard the same voice.

"Max."

"Who is this?" he demanded.

"We know what you did."

"Who is this?" louder.

"We know what you did. Put her back together." And with that, the line went dead.

Max stared at the phone and felt the weight of it, and then slammed it back into the cradle from which it came.

"Fuckers," he mumbled.

## III

Max woke to the loud banging on his front door. He got up off the couch, stepping over the eleven empty beer cans that had helped him sleep. By the time he got to the door, the FedEx truck was pulling away. On his front porch sat a medium size box. He hadn't ordered anything, but brought the box inside and closed the door – and sun – out of the room. The box wasn't heavy but well packed. He tore through the outer tape and started pulling the packing out, and then stopped. He slid the packing to one side and took a step back.

It was the girl's hand.

He knew for sure it was hers because he recognized the lime green nail polish and the heart shaped ring on her index finger. Max was surprisingly calm for a man who had just received the hand of the girl he recently killed. He realized how calm he was and slowly, the panic began to set in. Who was the call from? How did they know? How did they find her body?

There was an envelope in the box as well. Max opened it and slid a square of paper out. He unfolded the note and read it:

## PUT HER BACK TOGETHER.

He opened a bottle of Scotch, poured a generous amount and swallowed most of it immediately. He quickly walked down the basement stairs with the hand. He had a spot behind some loose bricks where he would keep things he didn't want anyone to find, ever. He stashed the hand there.

IV

Max's shift at the warehouse started at 8:00 p.m. He didn't mind working overnight or the extra cash he got for doing it. As he approached the freeway, he could see the traffic backed up. By the time he got through the bumper-to-bumper, he was running late. There was no way he was going to make it by 8:00, even at the speed he was going, which turned out to be just enough to get a cop's attention. In the rear view he could see the lights and he knew it was for him. Max pulled the car over slowly and put it in park. Cops made him nervous. He knew he was good, but he also knew no one was perfect. And with the recent turn of events, he was very unsteady now. The cop took a good while before he got out of the car. Then he slowly walked up to the driver's side window, which Max already had rolled down.

"Evening, officer."

"License, registration, and insurance, please."

"Sure thing."

Max pulled out his wallet. He fumbled a bit but then slid his license out of the plastic sleeve and his insurance card from another compartment.

"Here you go," he said, handing them to the cop. "Registration is in the glove box." He leaned over and popped open the compartment door and went to reach in when he saw something he did not expect. He began to sweat, his body felt like it was on fire. But he knew the cop didn't see anything from that angle. He just needed to be calm. He reached in, his hand brushing the ear lobe, grabbed the registration card, and closed the small door.

"Here it is, officer."

"Thank you. I'll be back in a few minutes."

Max felt like those few minutes took a couple of lifetimes. Eventually, the cop returned.

"So, where are you heading so fast?"

"Sorry, officer, I'm late for work. I got stuck in that traffic on the freeway. I guess I didn't realize how fast I was going."

"Well, slow it down," he responded, and handed back the paperwork.

Max drove the rest of the way at the exact speed limit. When he got to work, he pulled into the far end of the parking lot where there were no other cars, and slowly opened the glove compartment door. He was hoping what he saw did not really exist; hoping he was going crazy. But there it was, illuminated by an LED bulb. He looked closer and realized something even more shocking, if that could be possible. The human ear did not belong to the girl from the other night. He recognized it and the small, black and white peace sign earring. He had killed this girl two months ago. But it looked so fresh. How could it be?

He had done enough contemplating for the time being and knew he had to get into the warehouse. The ear would keep until the end of his shift.

V

Max sat on his couch for a long time, holding the girl's ear in his hands. He stared at it and remembered every detail of the girl, every scream and moan, every anguished call for help. He also thought deeply about his new situation, but couldn't make heads or tails of it. Eventually, he carried it to the basement and placed it with the hand.

Just as he put the last brick back in place, the phone rang. Max ran up the stairs as fast as his thick legs and slow heart would allow. Out of breath, he answered on the fourth ring.

"Hello."

Again, the silence followed.

"What do you want?" Max asked in his best fake-calm voice.

More silence. Max leaned against the old refrigerator and steadied himself, waiting.

"Max."

"Yes?"

"Put her back together."

He heard the click of the line going dead.

"What the fuck does that even mean?"

# VI

Max was working the night shift again. He knew he should get some sleep but there was no way he was sleeping that day. He sat and thought and drank most of it away. And in the end, was no closer to solving his puzzle.

At 7:30 p.m., he pulled into the parking lot. There was no way he could be late again, so he made sure he had enough time. His plan was to sleep during his lunch and breaks. That should get him through the night. Since he was early, no one else from his shift was there yet. When he got to the lockers, he was alone. He sat on a bench near his locker and put his head in his hands. He was worried and nervous. He had no idea what was going on, but someone was messing with him.

He stood up and walked to his locker. He turned the dial on the combination lock to the right, and then back to the left, and then to the right again. He easily slid the handle up and the locker door glided open. He felt a rush of vomit try to escape his body, but he forced it back down and slowly closed the door so no one could see the foot hanging there.

Panic once again took over. Max operated well under stress, always did. Outside, he was calm. Except for the thin layer of sweat that covered his entire body, Max seemed just like he always did. Inside, he was angry and scared. But he thought fast. He had to act before anyone else came into the room. He briskly walked over to the large trashcan with a black, plastic bag in it. There were only a few pieces of trash – an empty coffee cup, a pretzel bag. He pulled the bag out and emptied it into another can. He swung the locker door back open, grabbed the foot and tossed it in. There was an exit right near the room. He quickly – but without drawing attention – made it through and headed back to the parking lot, where he finally did throw up, next to his car. He tossed the bag in the trunk and walked back into the building.

He washed his face in the men's room and went back to the locker area. It was getting close to start time now and some of the other guys had arrived. Max was so glad he showed up early. He would work an hour, say he didn't feel well and go home. He headed back to his locker, which he had neglected to lock before his hasty exit. He pulled it open again and where the foot had been hanging, there was now a folded note. Max was pretty sure he knew what it said. Without removing it from the metal box, he unfolded it enough to see the words:

## PUT HER BACK TOGETHER.

He looked around the room at about eight guys getting ready for work. Who could be doing this? Some of the younger guys liked to play pranks on each other, but never on him. And none of the guys here even knew where he lived. Exhausted from lack of sleep, and stressed out, Max felt another wave of nausea coming on. He secured the locker and headed back to the men's room. He made it to the stall and locked it just in time. When he was done vomiting, and walked to the sink, his supervisor was standing at the urinal.

"Wow, you OK there, Max?"

"Feeling a little under the weather," Max replied. "Must be that bug going around."

"Sounds like you need to get some rest. Why don't you head home before you get the rest of the crew sick?"

"Yeah, probably a good idea."

"Feel better."

"Thanks," Max said as he left the men's room and slowly walked to the main entrance.

In his mind, he scrutinized every co-worker he passed on the way out. He sat in the car for a few minutes and then drove the speed limit back home.


## VII


It was dark and the neighborhood was quiet. He popped the trunk, grabbed the bag and walked up the front porch. Once inside, he removed the foot from the bag. Again, shock filled him and his eyes were wide with surprise. Not the girl from the other day and not the girl from two months ago. But he remembered this one, too. It was about two years ago. He recognized the tattoo of a vine that wound its way around her foot and up the ankle. The vine went further up the leg but he didn't have that part. It was a pretty clean cut. He remembered how it traveled up the back of her smooth calf and into the gully behind her knee.

The phone rang and startled Max back from the daydream he was in. He dropped the foot and jumped up. He marched to the kitchen and pulled the phone from the wall.

"What the fuck you do want? If I catch you, I am going to kill you, too!"

Max waited for an answer he knew would not come. Instead, he listened to the silence again, but only for a second, and then went into a bigger rage.

"Why don't you come show yourself? You think this is funny? What is wrong with you?"

And then, more silence. Max was getting scared again. His tone changed.

"Listen, if you want something from me, just say what it is. Please, I don't know what you want from me. Please, tell me."

And more silence.

Then, the voice.

"Max."

"Yes?" Max pleaded. "Tell me what you want."

"Put her back together."

Click.

He slammed the phone back into the cradle and lost it. He went into a rage like never before. Max grabbed a chair and tossed it into the living room, where the foot still sat on the floor. He flung his arm across the small countertop next to the stove and everything went spilling onto the dirty linoleum floor. A coffee mug shattered, a box of cereal spilled and utensils bounced around. Max then turned and threw a punch, with all of his weight, into the non-working refrigerator. It rocked back and bounced off the wall, and as it tipped forward, the door flew open, and out fell a naked body. Max stood there staring down at the slumped over corpse. Finally, he reached down, grabbed her shoulder and pulled her back so her face was visible.

He dropped her back to where she was, stepped to the sink and vomited. He had killed his sister twenty years ago; yet, she looked the same now as she had on that day. Max turned back to look again, in hopes he had imagined her, but she was still there. He bent down to examine the situation and noticed one of her feet was missing. He bent her back and noticed a hand was missing as well. He laid her head back against the open refrigerator door and took in the rest of her body. He brushed her soft hair out of her face and saw the missing ear.

At that moment, the phone rang, followed by a loud knock on the door. Max didn't know what to do. He had body parts in his house from multiple kills, his twenty-year dead sister was sticking out of his refrigerator, and someone was stalking and haunting him. He decided to ignore the door for the moment and grabbed the phone.

"Hello!" he screamed.

"Put her back together!" the voice demanded.

"Why are you doing this?!" Max yelled.

"Put her back together!" again it demanded.

Silence. Max took a deep breath.

"Put her back together! Put her back together! Put-her-back-together! **Put-her-back-together!**" The voice just kept repeating itself and demanding.

Max hung up the phone and rushed into the living room to retrieve the foot. He tossed it into the kitchen with his sister, and then moved to the window to see who was at the door. But the banging had stopped and there was no one there. He went to the door and slowly opened it. Tacked to the door was another note. Max ripped it from the door and tossed it on the floor, knowing quite well what it said.

Again, the phone rang, and the banging on the door resumed. He threw open the door but no one was there.

Another note was tacked where the last one had been.

He slammed the door and immediately, the knocking started again. He flung it open and again, no one was there.

Another note hung on the door.

He slammed it again and the banging resumed. The phone was still ringing. He answered.

"What? You made your point!"

"Put her back together! Put her back together!"

He hung up the phone and stood there staring at his dead, mutilated sister. A sadness poured over him. He tried to remember her alive but could only remember the day he killed her. Her screams echoing in his head – along with the ringing phone and banging door – was driving him crazy, or crazier than he already was. He collapsed and held her body close to him and sobbed. He began screaming, trying to stop all the noise, but it wouldn't go away. He took the phone off the hook, but did not listen to it and let it hang.

*That will stop the ringing*, he thought. But it didn't. After a few seconds, it began ringing again, even though it was off the hook. Max just stared at the impossibly ringing phone. He slowly reached for it and held it to his ear.

"Put her back together! Put her back to…"

Max dropped the phone again and it immediately started ringing. The banging at the door was getting louder and so were his sister's screams.

## Put Her Back Together

Max walked into the bedroom, opened the drawer to the side table, and took out his pistol. He checked the barrel for a bullet and put the gun to his temple.

# INNER DEMONS
**David Neilsen**

I lie flat on my back in my padded cell and stare at the insides of my eyelids. I wish I were dead. More than dead – to have never been born. Ending my life would not be enough to rid me of this nightmare. For that, I would need to be unmade.

The sound of a key in the lock scrapes across my frontal lobe and I clench my eyes even more tightly shut. *I do not want to see. I refuse to see.*

"Manage to off yourself yet, Kyle?" asks the overweight attendant with a snicker.

*I will not look. I will not look. I will not look.*

"Dr. Kastor's coming 'round in a bit, so I need to make you presentable. Sit up, will you?"

*If I do not look, I will not see. Nothing bad can happen if I do not see.*

"Can't sit up? What, your straightjacket's too tight? Hold on," grumbles the attendant. His thick hands shove themselves under my shoulders and lift me into a sitting position. "Christ. You really did a number on the back of your head, didn't you?"

I shiver as a cool cloth pats down my grimy hair in a pointless attempt to wash out the dried blood. This contact with another human being is so agonizing, so torturous, that visible spots of pain sparkle under my eyelids.

Which remain fiercely closed.

"You know, they ain't never had nobody hurt themselves this much in one of these padded rooms before," babbles the attendant. "You're a damn freak of nature."

*He does not know. He does not understand. I will not look. I cannot look.*

"Damn, this nasty crap won't come out. Hold on."

Suddenly, a flood of liquid ice rains down upon me and the physical torment of the freezing chill overwhelms my discipline. I cry out in shock and surprise and involuntarily open my eyes.

*And I see.*

### *Oh God, I SEE.*

\*\*\*

"You're mad."

"On the contrary, Dean Templeton," I assured my esteemed guest. "We have been very scientific in our methodology. You are welcome to examine the data for yourself."

Arthur Templeton, Dean of Rothschild University, frowned, refusing to accept what I was telling him. "23 percent? How is that even possible?"

"But you have it entirely backwards," I pressed. "The question is not what would allow man to use a larger percentage of the brain matter already existing within his skull, but why does he not do so already?"

Templeton frowned yet again, a facial feature of his with which all of us at the University were quite familiar. In an attempt to head off what he assumed would be the Dean's next line of questioning, my youngest assistant, Marcus Brighton, stepped forward to provide an answer.

"Because mankind was not yet ready for the awesome power which doing so would yield!" he argued. "God has always intended for his creations to grow into their true inheritance, but only when the time was right. When they discovered the means to unlock His secrets."

"You claim to know the mind of God, young man?" asked Templeton, raising his eyebrows.

I moved quickly to diffuse the Dean's incredulity. "No man knows God's will," I admitted. "What I believe my young protégé was attempting to impart was the undeniable possibility that man was meant to harness the fullness of his own intellect."

Rather than another frown, Dean Templeton furrowed his brow in thought and walked past me, and my two assistants, to stand before the odd collection of gears, toggles, and wires seemingly thrown together on the laboratory worktable. "And this...machine...has allowed you to access man's untapped potential?" he asked.

"In rats, Sir," said Dylan Cannonbee, with his usual enthusiasm.

Dean Templeton, however, was not enthused. "Rats? Truthfully?"

"It is standard practice to test new technologies on lower life forms before proceeding with human trials," I explained. "What we have achieved is nothing short of astonishing."

"Rats?" repeated the Dean, his face once again displaying a frown.

"Yes, damn you, rats!" I slammed my fist on the table in an attempt to regain control of the discussion. "And based upon the results of our painstaking research, I assure you that when we hook a man up to the

Solomon Resonator, he will gain use of a full 23% of his brain! More than double that of ordinary men! Think of the possibilities, Dean Templeton! The computing power! The ability to regulate one's natural systems! The sheer volume of memory made available!"

I was both earnest and convincing in my argument. However, the politically minded bureaucrat raised a single eyebrow at my words, as one poorly worded phrase lodged itself within his grey matter.

"The 'Solomon' Resonator? Really, Professor, does your hubris know no bounds?"

"Call it the Templeton Resonator, if you wish!" I bellowed. "I don't care, just allow me to proceed!"

The Dean walked around my Resonator, tracing his finger along the many coils and gears. He stopped in front of Brighton and poked a finger against the young boy's chest. "You believe you are on the cusp of history, do you not, Mr. Brighton?"

Marcus shuffled a look over to me.

"I am not asking Professor Solomon, young man. I am asking you."

Poor Marcus dropped his gaze to the floor. "Yes, Sir," he mumbled.

"I see." Dean Templeton pasted his patented frown onto his face and marched towards the door. "You are wrong. You are all wrong. There will be no history, because there will be no further experimentation."

His pronouncement hit us all hard. Dylan visibly shivered. Marcus dropped his head and played his fingers lovingly along the wires and gears he'd spent so many nights oiling.

Seeing the past three years of my life evaporating before my eyes, I leapt after the Dean, grabbing him by the arm. "Don't be so small-minded, Arthur!" I pleaded. "There's no reason to fear–"

"I fear nothing!" roared Dean Templeton, drowning out my protest. "What have you accomplished, Kyle? Rats ran a maze in record time? Ate more cheese? I have said this project was a waste of the University's resources and you have proven me correct. No more! Your funding ends as of today. I expect you to be out of this room within the hour."

The Dean spun on his heels and made for the exit, and deep within my bowels, I felt the steel bars of scientific ignorance slam shut upon my dreams.

And then the world went mad.

My skull squeezed down to the size of a flea, while my brain erupted with gleeful euphoria. I shoved one or more of my hands over my eyes to keep them from melting out of their sockets as everything around me expanded and contracted at the same time. I felt myself falling, yet could not be certain in which direction. A cacophony of noise assaulted the very blood vessels of my brain. And I became aware of something...horrible. Cruel. *Evil.*

"Burning! I'm it stop sake! God's for it stop!"

The words reverberated around me and through me, though I did not hear them so much as sense them. As if they had not, in fact, been uttered aloud. This horrid, non-vocal sensation was followed by the fetid stench of a rose garden in bloom, which itself was pierced through by a terrible scream.

Something wet splashed against my face, yet, still I held my many, many hands over my eyes. The evil I was sensing seemed to multiply logarithmically until it surrounded every fiber of my being.

"What have! Done God! My you!"

The jumble of words pounded against my frontal lobe in a useless attempt to puncture the veil of insanity currently wrapped around my existence. I was not of this state of matter, not of this version of reality, not of this dimension.

Somewhere deep inside, I knew my Resonator had been switched on. Without even thinking, I knew Marcus had done so, and what's more, I knew how he had jimmied the audio feedback to broadcast the frequency externally, rather than transmit it through the wires and cables as we had done when experimenting on the rats. I also knew without a shadow of a doubt that he had eaten a liverwurst sandwich earlier in the afternoon, that one of his molars was loose, and that his head was going to explode within four seconds.

"Get them me off! Get me them off!"

It was Dylan. There was a level of panic in his cry – and this time, I felt it had been an audible cry – beyond anything of which man ought to be capable. My blood boiled in terror as I saw the words in my mind, saw them dripping with carnal fear, saw the unimaginable horrors causing them to charge hoarsely from my assistant's throat.

It occurred to me that the madness within my mind was settling into a new normal. A strange calm enveloped me, even as I detected the grotesque popping sound of Malcolm's skull bursting forth, unable to contain the mounting pressure within. As the quivering contents of his mind splashed against my face, I comprehended – I'd already experienced this moment but an instant before. And in that realization came the knowledge of time's fluidity, and how that primal force of creation bound me no longer.

"My God! What have you done?"

That was Dean Templeton. I had heard him earlier, but now my mind placed the words in the correct order. I had found equilibrium. I rose to my feet and moved to lower my hands (there were only two at the moment) from my eyes.

"No, Professor!" screamed Dylan, who reacted beyond instantly. Reacted before I even began to move. He had launched himself from across the room, bounding to my side with the plasticity of a rubber ball, and draped his arms over my face. "Don't look! As God is my witness, don't open your eyes!"

And then he was gone, replaced by…more evil. More cruelty. More horror.

I kept my eyes shuttered and backed away.

"Dylan! Marcus! Arthur!" I finally found my voice and called out. That I called out for Marcus, when I knew pieces of his brain were even now dripping off my face, was testament to the chaos of the moment.

"Get them off me! Get them off me!" screamed Dylan, and I knew, as certain as I knew the speed of my beating heart, that his death was imminent.

"The Resonator!" I cried. "Turn off the Resonator!"

Using my memory of the laboratory as a third eye, I rushed across the room, towards the machine. As I ran, a part of me noticed that my feet were not, in fact, making contact with the floor – that I was, for lack of a better word: flying. I did not have time to contemplate the implications of this miracle, however, for a sudden inferno consumed me as I reached the Solomon Resonator. I felt fire on my skin – each individual flame, a separate torture – and recoiled in horror.

"Stop it! For God's sake, stop it! I'm burning!"

I was only mildly surprised to learn those words had been mine.

There was an explosion. Though not part of this reality, it nonetheless threw me backwards against the wall, inadvertently putting out my flames. The impact drew a gasp from somewhere deep inside my physical being, and I lost control of my eyelids for an instant.

It was only an instant.

But in that fractional moment, I went mad.

In the half-second before I landed facedown on the floor and once again eliminated any and all visual stimulation, I spied the impossible. Using, according to my instantaneous calculations, over 32% of my brain's capacity, I snapped a digital image of the room with my mind's eye for later study. Lying prone on the floor, arms covering my head, I took the time for that study.

There had been two Dylans, each one smothered in vibrantly dark, bulbous entities with multiple mouths and rows of jagged teeth. The look on my young assistant's face had been beyond simple terror. It had been filled with loss, defeat, and inevitable horror. I discovered an ability to read his very thoughts through this snapshot of his facial expression, and knew he wished for death even as he struggled to remain alive.

Of Dean Templeton, I had seen nothing in my half-second exposure. I wanted to believe he had already been put out of his misery, but his scent wafted into my nostrils from behind. It was soaked with desperation and fear, and I instinctively knew he faced a most unfortunate fate that did not include the mercy of oblivion.

And then, somehow, in this digital image implanted within my mind, the horrid entities, which had been devouring Dylan, turned towards me. I could feel their hunger as they swarmed forward within my mind, mouths open, teeth bared.

A scream escaped my lips then – a guttural, primal shriek from the core of my being. I feared those nasty things, like I'd never feared anything in my life.

And then a second explosion, this time in the physical realm, and everything stopped.

I felt my own essence shrinking, attempting to regain normalcy. Yet, like an elastic band, which has been pulled too thin, I was unable to fit squarely within the normal reality in which we live. It felt confining. Insufficient.

At some point, I opened my eyes, I do not know exactly when. The bulbous monstrosities no longer appeared to inhabit the room, and I found myself breathing deeply with gratitude. My relief turned to horror upon spying the body of poor Marcus lying on the floor; eyes wide open, and blood seeping from his ears. Turning towards the door, I saw Dean Templeton in a similar state, except no blood was to be seen. But the look on his pale, dead face was the same.

The laboratory was much as it had been before this Hellish experience had occurred, but for one difference. The Solomon Resonator was nowhere to be found. Dylan, too, I realized, was shockingly absent.

Then I heard the scratching, saw the bending of time and space in front of me, witnessed a single *tooth* force its way through the fabric of reality.

I closed my eyes and screamed.

\*\*\*

I force my eyelids shut as the cold water runs down my back and pray they did not notice my lapse. As long as I do not look, they maintain their distance, as well as the illusion that they are unobserved.

There are three of them in the room. Three grotesque, eyeless, oddly-concave beings, dripping some sort of primordial ooze from their many mouths. God help me, did I close my eyes in time?

We all have our demons.

We were never meant to see them.

# THE MONSTER NEXT DOOR

## Howard Rachen

The hairs on the back of Simon's neck stood up as he stared into Emmy's window.

In one corner lurked a shadow, darker than it should have been on the edge of the unicorn nightlight, and it held the distinct silhouette of a man. She clearly hadn't noticed it, curled up asleep as peaceful as an angel.

A simple shadow wouldn't be worth a second glance, except earlier that day when he spotted it blended among the bushes while she played in the yard separating their houses, and that evening it hid on the opposite side of her room.

*I need to get a grip. I'm seeing things.*

Simon put down the binoculars and rubbed his eyes. Maybe he spent too much time at this window, or more likely, his paranoia was getting to him.

\*\*\*

"And would you mind taking a survey to let us know how your customer service experien—" the crusty old man on the other end hung up. Simon logged the call and hung the phone up, putting him in the queue for the next individual. Being higher up the chain, he received the real disgruntled calls. Every call was a restrained fight, and he'd worn out the stress ball that kept him from biting back.

From the office window he caught sight of the school bus stopping at the end of the block. Back in the bowels of the room, no one could see him watching, which was just how he liked it. As soon as the pink-swathed, eight-year-old appeared, he smiled bright and content, his chest fluttering. His gaze followed Emmy as she passed the weeping willow in the Farrows' yard, and then his heart seized in his chest.

There, in the depths of the draping branches…

The work phone rang. Not answering it would mean one step closer to getting himself fired. He picked up the receiver, said, "Hello, hold please – just a moment," and dropped the phone, jumping to the window.

Emmy had reached her own yard, leaving the willow and its empty shade behind.

\*\*\*

After work, Simon made an effort to leave the window alone. Instead, he watched the cartoons he'd DVR'd, the ones with characters Emmy had all over her backpack. Cartoons for boys, because it didn't take a grown man to realize the typical programming for girls stunk. But then, the girl did have a little tomboy in her, never afraid of getting dirty or playing space soldiers with the Thompsons' boy in between princess time.

The need to go upstairs, to look into her room, pulled at him. To see her perfect little self – to imagine brushing her hair. Just an itty-bitty peek.

No, he needed to avoid getting obsessed. Obsession was another step down the road to getting caught. Not him, heck no. He'd die before he went to jail; owned a pistol to do just that, because he'd die in prison much worse.

But Simon only allowed himself to look, and now he was denying himself even that? Denying it to keep him safe. He denied himself pictures, and even talking to those little innocent bunnies, he could deny looking too, if it meant being safe.

Still, something nagged at him. A feeling that things were not quite right, and Emmy wasn't safe. That thought sat in the middle of it all, like a rotting tooth.

\*\*\*

On his way to bed, he allowed himself one glance. *Just a quick one.* Sliding into the dark room, he stopped by the window and took up his binoculars before nudging the blinds down.

Simon's blood ran cold.

There stood the shadow, a full stride closer to the bed than the night before. It defied the nightlight, the illumination warped around it like a stone in the middle of a river.

He went to bed, but lay awake with his rational mind running in circles. If it was a trick of the light, why was it different tonight when nothing else had changed in her bedroom?

\*\*\*

"Sir, I told you that there's nothing I can do. You have to—"

"Why are you doing this? You people, you can't even get it to me, forget on time! What is wrong with you?"

Simon picked up his stress ball and squeezed. He would prefer to hit the old man, the third this hour. While this one hadn't cussed him, he had stayed on the line for thirty minutes. "Sir, you need to—"

"You need to stop telling me what I need to do, son! You...—ah!"

What followed was a series of gurgly half-rasps and things brushing against the phone receiver. "Sir? Sir, are you all right?"

A strained, "Help!" gasped free and there came a muffled crash.

Simon had the man's address on file, and halfway to calling an ambulance, the customer finally breathed out, "Holy God."

"Sir, what happened?"

"I...felt like I was being strangled, like something...I don't know. Maybe it was a...a heart attack."

Simon frowned. "Sir, you should see a doctor then, it could've been a stroke...?"

"That's a good idea. I...goodbye."

He shook his head, took a breath, and logged the finished call. A small part of him, in the back of his mind, was satisfied the wretched old man had hung up and left him alone and suffered, just a little.

\*\*\*

The shadow had moved closer the night before, and now closer tonight, but as Simon stared at the silhouette, a thought struck him.

*She hasn't noticed.*

*You've been cooped up too long. You're seeing things.*

As soon as work ended the next day, Simon left to take his afternoon meal out. Feeling that he was owed a treat, he stopped at a frozen yogurt shop and filled his cup to the brim with coconut-flavored goodness.

When he was only half done, a mother with a little boy came into the tiny place. Simon took his treat outside, rather than have them sit so close. Even being near children was a threat – not just for the temptation, even if he didn't care for boys – but because he didn't want to risk an interaction. Any and every attention a grown man gave a child was suspect these days, and Simon had avoided all possibilities of suspicion and temptation; he'd never touched or coerced or even approached a child with the intent, had never owned any dirty pictures of soft little sweethearts. The only proof of his terrible wants hid in his mind where they were safe, and his only crime came in looking from afar.

\*\*\*

That night, when he checked on her, Emmy huddled under her covers, and even from afar, Simon could see them shaking. No flashlight to show she was reading under there, only the occasional peek at the figment, now another step closer. Then she ran, presumably to sleep with her grandmother, who lived downstairs, and the shade disappeared once she was gone. The next night, it was back and so was she. Simon guessed her grandmother wasn't letting her avoid her bed again. So she hid under the covers, and even from across the street, he was with her there, up all night in that chair, keeping watch over the figure that now loomed over her bed.

He kept guard, for what he didn't know. What could he do, really? Just keep vigil night and day, and now it appeared whenever she was on the property. Emmy had noticed the lurking thing existing beyond her bedroom, too.

Now, when he saw Emmy, his stomach seized in a knot of concern, worried for her and the unknown, anguished by the fear that it would only get worse.

\*\*\*

Simon sat at the window with the pistol in his lap. It brought some sense of comfort to him, a vestigial notion of control, because what he saw made him need every bit. The shadow now lay over the bed, too dark for him to see her anymore.

*Run over there and get her. Run over there and tell her grandmother.*

*Tell her what? A ghost was getting her little girl? A boogeyman? Say anything and she'll want to know why I'm looking in Emmy's window.*

Telling anyone else would just draw the police. Certainly going over there to save her would, and then he would be under suspicion.

\*\*\*

As the week passed, Emmy went to bed later and later, played outside or in her room less and less. When the Thompsons' boy came over, Simon could have sworn – *sworn* – he saw the little girl kiss the other boy, touch the other boy. An alarm went off deep inside him, a great wailing siren that things were terribly out of control, now.

When he saw Emmy's grandmother pull up one day with groceries, he hurried outside. "Do you need help with those?"

"Huh?" she said at her trunk, and he remembered she was going quite deaf.

Saying it louder earned him a, "Thank you, Simon. I need all the help I can get."

He shuttled the bags into the house, and made a show of looking about.

"This is a nice home you have here."

"Thank you! It has been in the family since I was a little girl."

"Good memories here?" he asked, and nodded along at her answers, until he offered, "Anything bad happen here?"

"Eh?"

"You know… Tragedy can stain a house." He had to accept the idea of a ghost, of something. The Internet hadn't been helpful, but that, at least, was one of the few ideas he could find.

"Oh, no. No, things are well. Nothing more than the usual bumps a family has. Like now; Emmy is such a handful, lately."

"Oh?" he said, his heart sinking.

"Yes," the old woman sighed as she began putting groceries away. "Fussy. Arguing more, wanting to sleep with me, cries now and then for no reason – oh, she did that when little Daniel called her names or she would skin a knee, but now, just..." she trailed off. "I tell her there's no such thing as the boogeyman you know, but I can't go up those stairs anymore to show nothing's under her bed or in her closet, like a parent should."

Simon left with a choking grip on his throat.

***

He sat back from his computer and cried. The website listed symptoms of child abuse. It was right there. Someone else would see it too, and ask questions. But even worse, it was happening to *her*. Something was doing this.

Now, he loathed going upstairs to the window, to what he'd see across the side yard. Still, he needed to, *someone* needed to. Even if Emmy didn't know it, someone had to be there with her, *for* her.

Emmy looked as unwilling to go to bed as he was, but it happened as bedtimes do, eventually. This time though, when the shadow came, it was different.

The night had been stuffy and he'd opened the window. Apparently, so had she, because he heard it: *a scream*. Not a full, piercing wail, but a whimpering, sobbing call, pleading.

That was it.

Simon grabbed his gun and was down the stairs, out of the house, and across the lawn. What he was to do never came to him, nor the fear of what questions would come. This couldn't go on, not anymore.

He hit their front door but it didn't budge. Pausing, he tried the knob and it came open at once. This was a small enough town, a nice enough part of the country; no one made a habit of locking their doors. Simon was inside and storming up the stairs.

"Who's there?" called the old woman. "Emmy?"

He burst into her room, and she was there, beneath the blanket of darkness. It had a man's form; he could see the arms and the body, and its head that actually *turned* to look at him.

Staring into the face of darkness, Simon knew – as surely as he knew he was standing in Emmy's bedroom – that the shadow belonged to *him*. Its hunger, its need for Emmy, was *his*. Being this close to it, he could feel the black pit inside himself, where it lived and, denied for so long, it had been born to move independent of him.

Even if Simon never acted, this wretched Id would go forth and do it for him, and no one anywhere would be safe from the evil feelings inside of him.

Simon stuck the gun in his mouth and fired.

He lay there, dully aware, through the ringing in his ears of screaming and banging – blinking up in the dim nightlight glow. The shot hadn't killed him, just moved a world of pain into his mouth. Still, he spotted the shadow before it dissolved over the bed. Emmy popped up, squalling in terror.

He couldn't speak, his lips wet and numb, but when his eyes caught Emmy's, he managed to mouth the word, *"Sorry."*

Nestling the barrel between his eyes, Simon pulled the trigger again.

# GHOST DOG
### Nancy J. Hayden

*July 1, 1916*
*The Somme, France*

Michael woke to a chewing sound. He recognized it immediately and felt his usual unease and revulsion. Rats. Big and bold. Not like the farm rats back home in Ireland that kept to the dark corners and out of sight. These rats weren't afraid of anything except maybe the sound of an incoming shell and a ratter dog. They knew to lie low then. Otherwise, they scurried about day and night stealing the soldier's rations, crawling over men's faces while they slept and biting on unsuspecting fingers and noses.

Michael thought he was back in the trenches so he drifted off again, thinking about the ratters. They were good entertainment, those dogs. They could nose out rat after rat, shaking them so hard the rat was dead within half a second. A good ratter got forty or more rats in an hour but it was hard work, digging out those rats and shaking them. The dogs got tired of so much killing.

Michael had a dog like that when he was a kid – Sally, a black and white terrier. God, he loved that dog. Not because she was a good ratter, "the best in the county," his old man used to say, but because Sally had been a good friend to Michael. Michael being twelve years younger than the next youngest kid, a 'freak accident', his three sisters used to say, didn't have anyone else, really. Their rocky farm was far from the neighbors, and by the time Michael was four, all of his sisters had married and moved away. His oldest brother, the inheritor of the farm, was twenty-two years older than Michael and more like an uncle than a brother.

"Jesus, Joseph and Mary. Are you ready now, Shea?" Michael's friend, Joey, said.

Joey and Michael had joined up together and become best friends even though they argued continuously about joining the British, the goddamn British, Army. *Stupidest thing I ever did*, Michael thought. He, being Irish, was no friend of the Brits, but Joey believed all their bullshit. Thought there was going to be some glory in it for both of them.

"Come on, now," Joey said. "Let's go."

Michael woke up at the impatient voice. He remembered where he was then, lying alone in the mud in No Man's Land, helmetless, looking up into a gray sky. *Must have been dreaming*, he thought. *It couldn't be Joey.*

The rustling and chewing sounds became louder and seemed to come from all around. Michael tried to roll over to get a better look, but he couldn't. He tried to move his head in the direction of the sound, but his head wouldn't move. He focused on moving a leg, an arm, his head. Nothing worked.

*My God, I'm paralyzed.*

Fear gripped him then, not unlike what he'd felt that morning as he climbed out of the trench toward the German lines, or when Joey, a few seconds later, was hit with a machine gun bullet and reeled backwards onto Michael. All Michael's nervousness and panic had hit him like a quick punch to his stomach. He'd pushed off Joey and didn't even glance down when his friend hit the ground. His training and duty kept him moving forward, kept his rifle with its shiny bayonet pointed in front of him, kept his eyes looking straight ahead, instead of at his dead friend nearby. That and all the other men moving forward doing the same. If just one of them had turned back, just one had come to his senses, it might have cascaded and sent them all running back. Surely, that would have been the smart thing to do. Men climbing out of the protection of the trenches and hurrying across No Man's Land, toward the Germans, in full daylight – easy targets for the German machine guns – was madness.

A drizzly mist hung low in the air as Michael's eyes darted back and forth. The rustling sound came closer, as did the rat making it. His mind flailed while his body lay motionless. He shouted out as the black nose and beady eyes moved closer to his face.

"Get back, you bloody bastard." His voice quavered at the thought of a rat eating his face while he could do nothing but watch. "Get back. Get back. Get back!"

The rat hesitated, sniffed the air, and turned toward another man lying nearby. Michael relaxed for a moment, but he knew that wasn't the end of it.

He looked up at the darkening sky. It was getting toward evening and strangely quiet, just some random rifle shots and an airplane buzzing far away. Not like this morning with the thundering explosion of shells, the shouting men, the machine gun bullets whizzing by. He'd been here all day through the thick of it, he guessed, unconscious, since he didn't remember any of it but those first few minutes out of the trench.

He tried to move his body again, a finger, a toe, anything, but he couldn't. He felt the panic rise up in him again.

"Please God, don't let me die being eaten by rats. Let someone find me. Anyone. Even a German with a bullet to my brain would be better. Please God."

More rats rustled nearby, chewing bits of flesh, lapping up blood. There must have been thousands of soldiers dead or wounded that day. The previous eight-day artillery barrage that the British had thought would take out the German front line did little beyond warning them that something big was about to occur. It didn't take out the German concrete bunkers or destroy the barbed wire entanglements in front of their trenches. It didn't disrupt the German artillery or blow up the machine gun nests. All the booming artillery did was rattle the nerves of every British troop and give the Germans time to get ready for the onslaught. And they were ready.

Michael's cousin had fought against the British in the Irish Rebellion in April of that year and been killed. His oldest sister had sent him the news. What a stupid waste, she'd said. My God, wasn't fighting *for* the British Empire even more stupid? Wasn't dying in their bloody war a bigger waste? If help didn't come soon, he'd be dead, just like Joey, just like his cousin. How foolish they'd been to believe the war propaganda, to believe the war would give them an opportunity to make something of themselves. The German soldiers huddled in their trenches weren't his enemy. The British Empire, the British aristocrats and generals, they were the goddamn enemy.

He caught a glimpse of movement farther away. Something slinking like a ghost among the dead.

"Christ, what now?"

The ghost came into the open. No, not a ghost. A big, gray dog. A Red Cross rescue dog! It was nosing around the bodies, looking for the living.

"Hey! Over here. I'm over here!"

The dog ignored him and continued sniffing at the bodies. Rescue dogs never made noises as they moved among the casualties; that would draw enemy fire, but when they found a living soldier, they'd go back and get their masters. They had recently stopped putting the Red Cross emblem on the dogs because they realized the Germans were using the cross for target practice. Yet, Michael knew it was a rescue dog. It had to be.

"Hey. Over here!"

Still, the dog ignored him, although it was heading his way. It would figure it out in a few minutes, Michael thought. Then, something startled the dog and caused it to run off in the opposite direction.

"Wait! Come back. Goddamn it. Come back!"

Michael heard the rat noises again. The nose and eyes of a rat moved within inches from his face. Its whiskers must have touched his cheek, but he couldn't feel it. He couldn't feel it!

"Jesus Christ!" he screamed out. "Get back. Bloody hell!"

The rat moved further down his body and out of view, but he could hear its noises, its chewing. It was eating his flesh, and he couldn't even feel it.

He screamed out into the darkness. "Please God! No!"

Another dog came running toward him then, a small, shorthaired terrier. It looked like a ratter, but they'd never let it out of the trenches at night. It must be another rescue dog. The terrier grabbed the rat that was chewing on Michael, shook her head twice, and dropped the dead thing nearby.

"Thank God," he said. He looked at the dog, felt his panic subside. "Good girl!"

The dog looked around, but she didn't grab any more rats even though there were plenty to be had. Instead, she sat down by Michael's side and stared at him.

"Go on," he said. "Go on. Bring back the medics. Hurry."

The dog eased down, resting her head on her front paws. She lightly closed her eyes, maybe even relaxed a bit, although her ears and nose twitched ever so slightly at the movement nearby. The rats kept their distance even though she didn't move.

"I guess you're not a rescue dog," he said and let out a long sigh. "But I'm glad you came when you did. I'm sure glad you came when you did. You look a little like my old dog, Sally."

The dog opened her eyes and stared at Michael.

"You got her eyes. She had more white than you, a sharper nose, too. She was a good dog though. Just like you."

The dog looked at Michael as he rambled on. It kept his mind off things.

"They said I could name her, but boy was my mum mad when I named her Sally. That's my oldest sister's name. My old man didn't say anything, but my sister laughed when she found out. She liked it, said she was watching out for me now, as a dog. I was four when we got the pup. The dog died a couple of years ago. She was diving after a rat when she got cut on a piece of metal. An infection set in; she didn't make it. The worst day of my life. Well, maybe the next to the worst day of my life. This being the worst."

Michael stopped for a moment. Now that he had this dog with him, watching out for him, maybe this wasn't the worst. Maybe everything was going to be all right. Not like with Sally. Lord, how he'd cried. His father had given him the belt for being a baby. Michael stopped crying when the belt hit. Pride made him never cry or make a sound when he got hit by that goddamn belt, even when he was little. When his father's anger was spent and his own backside was sore and red, Michael walked back to where Sally lay dying, and he cried again. He stayed with her all night.

Sadness descended with the darkness. Michael thought about Joey, too, and that made him feel bad. Who was going to watch over Joey's dead body? Make sure no evil spirits took it over; make sure his soul found a way out of this world. That's what his mum told him, anyway. That's the reason for the wake, she said, to watch over the dead. His mum believed in the wailing banshees, spirits, leprechauns and all kinds of things like that. She'd seen them, too. His father said it was all nonsense. His sister said it was the Potcheen his mum drank that made her see things. Michael didn't know what to believe, but he'd stayed with his sick dog that evening and all night, even after she died. He'd stayed awake, too, keeping watch and listening to the night sounds. In the morning, he'd buried her.

Michael heard something farther off. There was the rescue dog coming towards him, a tall, sleek dog with a long nose. The ratter stood up and faced the newcomer. They sniffed each other. The rescue dog sniffed Michael and sniffed the ratter again.

"Finally," Michael said. "Go on, now. Bring back some help."

The ratter lay back down. The newcomer tilted its head, breathed in the night smells of corpses and explosives and trotted off.

"It won't be long now."

A star shell exploded into the air and for a few moments, Michael's world was cast in an eerie, orange glow. The rats moved into the shadows of the dead lumps that had once been men. The dog lifted her head and looked around. Michael thought he saw stretcher-bearers climbing over the mess.

"Here I am. I'm here, boys. Come and get me."

The dog laid back down as the star shell descended. All too soon, it went out.

"Help!" Michael screamed out in the pitch-blackness. "Help me!"

He was blind for a few minutes before his eyes re-adjusted. Then he could make out the shadowy forms of the corpses again, the silhouette of the dog, but there were no stretcher-bearers coming his way.

"That rescue dog will bring them. Won't be long now," he said to the ratter, trying to convince himself. "Well, it may take a little time. There's a lot of dead and wounded out here. You'll wait with me, won't you, Girl?"

The dog yawned and put her head down.

"That's right. Save your energy for the rats. I'll save mine, too."

Michael started thinking about what would happen when they found him. The doctors could fix him. Yeah. They could do all kinds of things these days. But then he thought about what would happen if they couldn't. He'd be paralyzed, unable to move or do anything for himself. Who would take care of him? His aging mum and father? His sister, Sally, with her third child on the way? That wasn't possible.

"They'll fix me," he said. The dog looked over. "They just got to. I was going to be somebody. That's why I joined this bloody army in the first place. I had nothing in Ireland, no farm, no future. Jesus Christ. They said I could make something of my life."

Then he saw them coming closer. Two men, carrying a stretcher. The dog stood up and made a little yowl sound. Not too loud, but the men heard her.

"Over here. Help me, boys," Michael said, although, a strange mixture of relief and dread filled him. Maybe there wasn't anything they could do.

"Look at the dog, Charlie. I told you it was a dog."

"What the hell's a ratter doing out here?"

"Catching rats, I guess."

"Thank God, you've finally come," Michael said, as the two men put down their stretcher and scratched the dog's neck.

One of the men shielded his flashlight and shined it at the dog, then at Michael.

"Christ," he said. "I know this fellow. Shea. Michael Shea. Good mate."

"Hey," Michael said. He was just about to ask the man his name, when the other soldier cut in.

"Jesus. Look at that. Riddled with bullet holes. Must have died instantly."

"And not even twenty feet from the trench."

"Bloody war."

"Bloody hell."

They scratched the dog again and moved off.

"But I'm not dead," Michael called out to their retreating backs. "I can't be. I can't be!"

The dog came in close to Michael's face, nuzzled him once, and trotted off. Michael lay dazed, staring up into a black sky. *I can't be. I just can't be.* A sob escaped into the night.

"Are you ready, yet?" a familiar voice said. It was Joey's. "Let's get out of here."

Michael held back his sadness, his anger. Pride made him hold back, just as with his father's belt. *I'll go find Sally.*

"I'm ready," he said to Joey. And Michael left his earthly shell to the rats.

# PIGTAILS
## Jack Lee Taylor

"I got to pee," Janet said.

It was the perfect four words to break the long silence in the car. The road trip had now spanned close to eight hours since dawn, and the last two hours were the most arduous for Janet's father as he wrestled pigtail curves across the endless countryside.

Ned Rollins glanced from the driver seat over to his wife. Maggie looked back at him with tired eyes. From behind them, Janet said again, "I got to pee."

"Honey, I asked you if you had to potty during lunch," Ned said over his shoulder. "You said 'no'. Even Mommy asked you." He grunted as he made another sequence of braking and steering toward the oncoming curve.

"But Daddy, I gotta piss bad. Right now! I gotta piss! I gotta piss!"

"Janet Ivy," Maggie said, cautious not to break into laughter. She didn't turn to give the five-year-old her expression of schoolmarm disapproval, not that she was able to do so effectively. Her eyes were kind, a soft hazel against the light of day, and the corners of her small face were round against her short-cropped hair, making her look more pixie-ish than womanly.

Janet started moaning and twisting in her pink booster seat, her small legs locking together. Now Maggie did turn to look at her pig-tailed daughter, feeling the tightness of her spine as she twisted to see Janet's weary face. It was a long, relentless trip; the blurring of scenic green, mottled asphalt and yellow sunlight became a tiresome canvas spread endlessly around them. Maggie sighed and then looked back at Ned. She said, "You've got to pull over."

Ned looked at her with shock. "Are you kidding me?" he said. "Do you see anywhere I can stop on this freaking rollercoaster track?"

"I didn't mean right here," Maggie said. She felt that familiar flush of rage that would kindle into loathing, but she doused the heat inside of her. She looked out the passenger window of the Rollinses' SUV and studied the steep decline below. From her side of the road, the foothill sloped down dangerously into a chaos of thick trees and jagged rocks. She thought, *Why on Earth did Ned's parents choose to live this far out in the country?* She hated every part of this impromptu trip, naturally, because she hated his side of the family – brash hicks who did nothing but cover their ignorance with stubborn pride. Pride in what? Living like hillbillies?

"Mommy!"

Maggie straightened in her chair, going into full maternal alert. She turned back to Janet, trying to find some word or action that would calm her daughter for at least a few more miles until they could reach some type of clearing. Janet looked back at her mother, defeated, and it took Maggie a moment to understand the resignation in her daughter's eyes meant her child's battle was over. Janet's bladder had won.

"No, Janet," Maggie said. "Oh, no!" Through the crotch of Janet's purple shorts bloomed dark liquid, soaking out from her inner thighs; glistening streams ran down her shins and stained her white socks.

"Ned. We've got to stop. She's peeing on herself!"

Ned growled, stifling the expletive under his tongue. He inadvertently yanked the steering wheel out of true and the boat-like SUV swished and screeched in and out of equilibrium.

"What are you doing?!" Maggie shouted. Ned ignored both her and his mistake. He sped up at the last stretch of the latest curve and saw the road blessedly straighten for the next few hundred yards. He said, "Mag, there's nothing we can do about it now. I'll pull over when I can pull over."

Maggie opened her mouth to protest, closed it and looked back at Janet. Her daughter looked away, her eyes reddening with tears. Maggie wondered if her daughter's embarrassment would linger on past this moment, becoming a mental scab bronzed into her worst childhood memories. She let out a long breath, mentally preparing for the messy job of cleaning up both her daughter and the backseat.

"It's okay, honey," Maggie said. "You just had a little accident. We've all done that."

Before Janet could hear the rest of her mother's comforting spiel, the Rollins family came to a stop. Ned grinded the gearshift into "P" and opened his door in quick succession, leaving the SUV rocking to stillness. The heat from outside invaded the AC frost within; the smell of grass and sunbaked vegetation filled the interior. Maggie watched her husband get out without a word. He was a tall, lanky man in shorts looking up at the hot August sky. Above him were bulbous clouds that seemed unnaturally low to the ground. He shaded his eyes with a hand and then turned back to look at the rest of his family.

"Well," he said. "You wanted me to pull over. We're pulled over."

"Don't be an ass," Maggie said. She turned and opened her door and felt it jar back against her arm. There was a dull, metallic thud from the car door rebounding back.

"I can't get out," Maggie said and then looked around, taking notice of her husband's half-hearted parking efforts. Ned had nested the SUV against the right side, edging close to the flat green fields on Maggie's side of the road. She looked through the front windshield and saw the stretch ahead was flat where the road was no longer paring into mountains but laying straight for several hundred yards.

Far ahead, the yellow glint of a sign flickered back, and Maggie was sure it was another of the countless warnings of more dangerous curves to come. She thought of how this area was like some sort of relief zone linking to the next treacherous climb, where, during a time, the old builders of this cursed road had decided to obey the flatness of this part of land.

Maggie needed to get out. She had to clean up Janet, but she also wanted to get out, stretch her legs and walk about. Only her door would not open. There was nothing she could tell blocking her, only a scattering of trees – and something else far beyond the first speck of trees. Some type of boxy thing.

"Geez, you dented the door!"

Maggie jumped back when Ned's large face popped up from the other side of her window, consuming her view of outside.

Janet said, "Mommy, can I get out now?"

"Wait," Maggie said and then to the monstrous face outside, she said, "What do you mean, I dented it? I can't get out. There's something blocking me."

Ned kneeled back down out of view. Maggie heard rustling behind her and saw Janet had removed her seatbelt and was scooting down off of her booster seat.

Ned, his voice muffled from outside, said, "There's a damn rock sticking out right here. We got to move up a bit."

Maggie took this cue and waved her daughter back, "Wait honey, your father's going to move the car up a bit. Then you can get out. Okay?"

Janet grimaced and made no effort to get back in her seat. Maggie let it go, seeing as moving up a few feet wouldn't be worth strapping back in for, and she knew sitting back down in a puddle of urine wasn't something she wanted to force Janet to do.

Ned slipped partially back into the driver seat, his door still ajar and his left leg still hanging outside. He shifted back into drive, his right foot lifting off of the brake to idle forward.

"Maybe we should get off the road," Maggie said.

"Nah, we're okay," Ned said.

"It just feels like we're still in the middle of the road."

Ned said nothing, but the weight of the silence came through to Maggie clearly. They hadn't come across anyone else over the past two hours since passing through this part of Tennessee, and there was nothing else on the GPS map until they reached Ned's parents, which was another twenty miles away.

She looked behind her, past Janet and through the rear window. She saw the road behind them veer left and then disappear behind the massive foothill they had just cleared. She could hear the contented idle of the SUV grow louder and wondered why it grew louder still after Ned had stopped. Then her mind retreated, stifling her voice when she saw a metal face suddenly appear from the road behind them, growing larger and roaring forward. Before Maggie could react, could even interpret what she was seeing, the Rollins family began to twirl.

It wasn't a complete spin in place, and there was no hard impact, but Maggie was disoriented, for now her view ahead was the open field instead of the road. *Janet*, she thought immediately.

"Janet Ivy," Maggie cried. "Janet. Are you okay?"

There was no answer. Two things immediately registered. Both Janet and Ned were gone.

"JANET!" Maggie shouted. She reset her mind through her panic and began to think back in series. She saw a car. No. A truck. Loud.

Maggie stretched through the space between the front seats and saw Janet lying on the rear floorboard, her eyes closed. Maggie screamed and riddled Janet's body with trembling hands, feeling for life and breath.

"JANET! Wake up baby!"

Maggie wanted to pick her daughter up, not caring about internal injuries, but it was impossible to pull Janet through the nook between the front seats, even if she was able to climb over toward the back. She called out for Ned, nearly cursing his name. She peered through the gaping hole of the driver side where Ned had just been sitting.

Through the door-less view was the road leading onward. Maggie half-expected the rusty pickup truck somewhere ahead, parked and idling, perhaps damaged. There was no truck, only the empty road and the letter 'L' lying on it. Maggie closed her eyes quickly, squeezing out tears and sweat, down her face. She turned back to the passenger side door and pushed frantically, not caring that it had once denied her exit. Because there was no longer anything blocking her side now, she easily spilled out onto the ground. She pushed herself up and groped for the rear door, feeling exposed to the road now behind her.

Janet remained nestled on the floorboard, her still face pointed up. Maggie reached in and then broke her fast-forward motions and slowed the moment her hands cupped her daughter's face. She was afraid to move the girl. She put her cheek close to Janet's upside-down face, feeling for the feather-warmth of a child's breath mixing with the humid air.

"Please, Janet," Maggie whispered. "Baby, please wake up." And with a rush of blissful relief, she felt her daughter cough into her face. Without the trained grace of a paramedic, Maggie fished her daughter out of the car. If there were broken bones, if there was anything wrong, it would have to wait.

Maggie hoisted her daughter against her chest and then staggered out toward the open field. Janet stirred in weak sobs, never fully awakening. Maggie shushed her, pushing back her own guilt for another moment. It was her fault, she thought. She should have strapped Janet back in.

"It's going to be okay, baby," Maggie said, stroking the sweat from her daughter's forehead.

"Mag?"

Ned's croaking voice came faint through the hot air, not really coming from any direction. Maggie cleared five feet into the grass and looked around for him. She knelt, still holding Janet, thinking that being more level to the ground would help her find her husband.

"Ned? Where are you?"

"It's cold," he said. His voice was louder, almost leading to echo. Maggie's arms were near atrophy, becoming solid support beams that did their best to hold and not crush her daughter, but she refused to let Janet go. She studied the SUV, now perpendicular to the road, the gleaming front bumper smiling back at her. From there, she traced her eyes north, back to the 'L' shape on the road and took in the reality of her husband's dismembered leg. Suddenly, Ned's morbid phrase he would say on occasion to her popped into her mind like a dirty joke: '*I love every piece of you, my dear*'.

*Call someone now*, her mind demanded and then she remembered her cell phone was in her purse still in the blasted car. "Mag, I can see you," Ned said, and as if the sound of his voice had spiked into her eyes and pulled them down to show where he was, she found the rest of her husband sunken in long grass, nearly enveloped in green. He was easy to miss, as if he were being pulled into the ground. Beyond him, Maggie eyed the strange structure she had seen just before the hit-and-run, something like a wooden box, gnarled and dark.

"Ned!" she shouted and stood erect, keeping Janet intact.

"Don't come here," her husband said. "Don't let her…see me."

Maggie stopped and looked down at Janet. The young girl's eyes were still closed, but they moved behind her eyelids as if lost in nightmare. Maggie set Janet down as gently as possible onto the field, feeling replenishing blood course back into her arms. She stood up, giving Janet a reproachful look, and then ran toward Ned.

"It hurts, Mag. God, it hurts."

Maggie ran fast, her sandals flapping hard against her feet through the waves of grass. When she stopped short a few feet in front of Ned, she nearly slipped in a pool of his blood. She looked with disbelief at the amount of red that puddled before her and streamed slowly between the blades of grass like a swampy murk.

Ned shook with gasping breaths, his bulging eyes darting about. He lay there clutching something tight against his chest with both hands. Maggie opened her mouth in horror, seeing him splayed out on the ground with two legs extending from his drenched shorts, one of them made of pure, wet crimson.

"Janet?" Ned said. Maggie was silent for a moment and then blinked.

"She's fine, Ned. She's okay." *Tourniquet,* Maggie thought and wanted to cry. She needed help. Because she was no life-saver. She was no Girl Scout. She couldn't even begin to know how to tie a tourniquet knot or do something even more profound like cauterization or whatever the hell else trauma surgeons did. What could she possibly use? Her shirt? *No,* her mind objected, *his belt.* And, with that cosmic joke, Maggie looked above the fly of Ned's pants to see the belt loops empty. From far off, she heard Janet crying.

"I'm sorry," Ned cried. He shook harder, his entire body quaking, his head pitching back and forth on the ground. He said again, "I'm sorry," muttering it over and over. Again, from far off, Janet continued crying. Only, it really wasn't crying. It was laughing.

"Don't let her go there," Ned cried, his voice straining in between grunting breaths. Maggie had gone into action, putting her hands down – palms flat – below Ned's left hip, where his hipbone once resided. She pushed above the torn stump of him; ignoring the disdainful voice telling her it was pointless. Ned struggled, releasing the thing clutched to his chest, his cell phone falling away, greasy with his blood. He pushed Maggie's hands away.

"Keep him away from her," Ned said, and then went into full convulsions. Maggie cried back at Ned, wanting him to be still – *please just be still.* Then, in one final jerk, tensing for the last time, Ned Rollins did go still, staring with eyes that had finished crying under the vaporous sky above.

"Mommy, come here," Janet said.

Maggie leered behind her, still in shock. She wiped hard at tears, spilled more from relief than horror. Janet came into focus about twenty feet away. She was jumping up. Dancing. No. Not exactly dancing. Catching. Catching the air.

Bubbles.

They glistened in the sunlight like faint fireflies twisting around the little girl. Janet reached out into what seemed like random pockets in the air, ending the lives of these strange spheres with her small hands.

Maggie stood up slowly. She stared silently, first at her daughter and then simply at fuzzy light. The world wavered and the acute treble of sounds around Maggie was slipping off to muffled white noise. Maggie slapped herself until she could feel the sting on her cheek. She dispelled the urge to pass out and breathed in and out slowly.

"Janet, stay right there," Maggie said, her own voice a stratosphere away. She knelt back down, not looking at Ned's eyes, and grabbed his cell phone. She then walked, lurching at first and then striding slow and careful, toward Janet. The phone was a bloody mess in her hands, but there was electronic life in the glare of the screen. She dialed 9-1-1 and increased her pace toward Janet. Because those bubbles weren't really there. Maggie was in shock. So was Janet. So this was okay. Let them share imaginary bubbles together.

Maggie heard the unfeeling beep of a failed call and tried again, caking the phone screen with blood-spackled fingerprints. Little Janet continued running through the swarm of bubbles, heading closer to the box ahead. Maggie heard another call beep with failure, and then she dropped the cell phone to her side when she saw the person in the box.

From this close, the box was more like a dilapidated woodshed. The roof was rusted tin, ruffled with the edges curled down like dog-ears. Wooden boards, aged to grayness from long years past, lined together like gaping teeth for walls; they slanted the entire structure unevenly to the left, making the small house appear tired of being upright. There were no windows among the wooden walls, or any kind of thoughtful disruption to decorate the structure.

The person sat on the ground directly in front of the house; sitting on three boards laid unevenly to what Maggie could only guess was the vestige of a porch area. The person was shaded black under the shadow of the shed, but it was clear to see that the trail of bubbles spewing out, long and plentiful into the air came from where the person sat.

"Janet, get back here, now!" Maggie shouted. Janet, ignoring Maggie, leapt forward in the next fray of bubbles, twirling about and laughing, her urine-soiled shorts now nearly dry in the summer heat. Maggie double-timed it and caught up with her daughter. She grabbed at the little girl, gingerly at first, remembering the image of the unconscious child from before.

*Forget the phone*, Maggie thought. They were getting out of here. She had the car. She would take Janet and drive them far away from here. And if the car didn't work, she had her legs. Both legs. This made her think of Ned again, the feel of his spongy stump under the weight of her hands.

The person stood up slowly. Maggie couldn't make out any features in the shadow, but she saw the person's frame was short and frail, with drooping shoulders, clearly soft and unintimidating. Before she could think of why, she said, "Excuse me."

There was no reply. Maggie pulled Janet closer to her, considered picking her up, but then decided to pull them both back, away from the stranger.

"We had an accident," Maggie continued. No reply, but the person stepped forward into the sunlight and Maggie saw the oldest man she had ever seen in her life. His yellow-egg eyes were crossed. He was bald; his head blotched with red, flaky sores. His faded blue shirt and jeans were nearly colorless, almost blending with the dark boards behind him, stained only under the armpits and crotch from body sweat.

"I saw," he said slowly, his southern voice low and gravelly. He raised his hand, holding what Maggie could make out as some type of bottle. It was ceramic, mud-like, riddled with cracks. The top of the bottle narrowed into a long, gooseneck tip, where the man put his ancient lips around and blew. Through the middle of the bottle, a flap suddenly opened and a flurry of fresh bubbles shot forward. Janet giggled, reaching out for the next wave coming her way.

"You saw," Maggie repeated back. The old man removed the bottle from his cracked lips and watched the bubbles make their way to the woman and child. Maggie looked down at Janet and then back up at the old man. Just harmless old mountainfolk. "So then, you know my husband is hurt really bad."

The old man grinned, his toothless gums showing like a second row of lips. "Naw'm," he said. "He dead. Burnin' in Hades."

He started laughing in slow, soundless, heaving breaths. Maggie recoiled, pulling Janet closer to her. She yelled back, "You think that's funny? You stupid old hillbilly bastard, think that's funny?"

Bright pain suddenly burned into Maggie's eyes when a cluster of bubbles landed on her face, bursting whatever foul juice came from the old man's bottle into her eyes. She blinked rapidly, feeling the burning intensify. She cried out, rubbing at her face. She tasted her tears and detected the medicinal taste of the strange bubbles mixed in. She hit the ground, screaming on both knees, dropping the cell phone and letting go of Janet. *Dear God, I'm blind*, she thought. *Blinded by some backwoods moonshine.*

"Janet, don't touch the bubbles," she cried. "Stay right here and close your eyes.

"Come on, chile," the old man said. The music of Janet's laugh was soft and distant. Maggie forced her eyes open, but no light came to her sight. She screamed out again at Janet, reaching blindly through the bubble slime around her.

"Chile, come over," the old man cooed. At this, Maggie found direction and ran full-speed to where the old man's voice came from, feeling more obscene bubbles burst upon her bare skin. Through the unseen air, Maggie's groping hands found pigtails. Maggie grabbed and pulled hard, reeling Janet back into her arms. If the *chile* felt pain, she laughed through it. *She's gone*, Maggie thought. *Her mind is gone.* Maggie held on tight, falling onto her back with Janet on top of her, contained in her arms.

The old man said, "Ye shall judge angels, chile. All stillborn."

Maggie kicked out, hoping to break some fragile part of the old man. She tried desperately to see, feeling the hot wind around her eyes, but saw nothing. As she kicked away, she felt a bristled heat go down her bare thigh, the prickling sensation hardening to a grip and she understood the old man was holding her leg. Janet laughed as Maggie reeled away, nearly steamrolling her daughter as she moved from the old man's touch. One of Maggie's sandals flew off as her foot connected with something hard, cracking it. She heard something fall next to her with a dull thump.

"Angels be damned!" the old man cursed. Maggie heard him hawk back and spit. She felt warm liquid pelt her left cheek and she twisted her face away, her mouth gaped open in disgust and then mindfully shut.

"Stupid hillbilly!" she shrieked.

Maggie thrashed her legs farther out, but hit nothing. She kept at it, scissoring her legs out blindly until the fatigue from her hysterics started burning through her body. Panting hard, she heard the low sound of an approaching car.

"He's gone," she heard Janet say. Only it was her own voice that said it. Not Janet.

Maggie felt her eyes cooling, her vision returning. She could now see faint sunlight trickling through. She remained still on the ground for another minute, listening to the approaching footsteps crunch through the grass, the concerned but reassuring new voices of help on the way.

Maggie touched her face, wiping away her sweat. *The old man's spit,* she remembered. She smeared the sopping wetness onto the grass and then stood up, staggering for balance. A hand cupped her right shoulder, steadying her.

"Ma'am," said one of her rescuers. She looked at the young man's pale face, scrunched under a John Deere cap. He stared back at her with wide eyes.

"What happened?" he asked, his adolescent voice breaking. "Is she...?

He pointed down to something on the ground. From behind him, a child-faced woman stepped up next to him, a hand over her mouth.

"They're dead," the young woman said.

Maggie ignored them both, her rescuers. She kept looking around for the old man, looking for his strange bottle, now broken somewhere on the open field. Whatever she would do, she would not look down at the two bodies on the ground–one, a man, the other, a small child–her frayed, dark pigtails, buried in deep grass.

# THE NOX
## D.J. Schuette

No one knows exactly what they are or where they came from, but that doesn't really matter now. There were rumors and any number of crazy theories on the Internet—disease, genetic engineering, aliens, even reanimation. Odds are, if anyone ever knew the truth about their origin they're probably dead now. Or don't remember.

Everyone was focused on the Ebola scare. People were losing their fucking minds, convinced that it was the beginning of the hemorrhagic apocalypse. The Centers for Disease Control and the World Health Organization assured everyone that the situation was under control, but you'd never know it to watch the news. Pundits fueled a barely-contained panic, airports screened everyone that stepped onto and off of a plane, and nutjobs called for the immediate executions of anyone testing positive for the virus. People wore masks in public and steered well clear of anyone with a mild case of the shits, and anti-bacterial sanitizers flew from store shelves.

Meanwhile, the *real* contagion went completely unnoticed.

I call them the Nox, because like most monsters, they come for us in the night. The Latin word 'nox' can also mean darkness, obscurity, confusion, and death—all of which are extremely fitting. And *goddamn* it, their *eyes*. They're the color of a morning sunrise and they glow like burning flame. The nightmares are hard, because you really can't tell if they're nightmares at all, or if they've come for you at last.

I saw the first of them while working a lunch shift at Subway. Hanna slid a footlong tuna to me and kicked my foot under the counter. When I looked up to ask what kind of veggies my customer wanted, I sucked in a startled breath, and felt the blood rush from my head. I had to fight against a warm darkness that pressed in on me from all sides. When the vertigo passed, my first instinct was to run, but where the hell could I go?

To say the guy was pale wouldn't do him justice. His skin was almost gray, like that of a beluga whale. His eyes were the color of molten gold, and his short, spiky blond hair was almost the same shade. He looked *subhuman*, if that makes any sense, but there was something very intelligent behind those bizarre yellow eyes—and something very unsettling. Something *hungry*.

My voice shook as I asked him if he wanted the works. His only answer was a nod, and a curl of the lip that I can only describe as the scariest goddamn smile I've ever seen. I loaded up his sandwich, and ducked into the walk-in cooler for pickles that we didn't need. The sense of relief was immediate. I started to laugh, and had to bite the inside of my cheeks before it could bloom into full-blown hysterics. How stupid. He was probably just an albino wearing colored contact lenses. And it was October—maybe he was just testing out the creepiest fucking Halloween costume of all time. When I came out of the cooler, he was gone.

I should probably mention that I'm a scientist. Well, in school to be one, anyway. Biology major. I bring it up only because I'm probably the last person that you'd expect to spook so easily. Scientific method and all that. But that dude seriously freaked me out.

\*\*\*

Two days later, buried beneath news of yet another Ebola case, baseball playoff results, and the ongoing battle against ISIS, was a story about a family of three that woke without the ability to form new memories. Their condition was described as a rapid-onset and progressive dementia, similar to Alzheimer's. Each had inexplicable damage to their hippocampus—the area of the brain that sorts memory, along with a major deficiency of acetylcholine and dopamine. Doctors were perplexed. They'd never seen anything like it—a man and woman in their early thirties and an eight-year-old all with Alzheimer's? All occurring at the same time?

Initially, nobody thought very much of it—it was just one of those bizarre and inexplicable tragedies. The story hung around for a few days as doctors and neurologists tried to figure out whether there might be some sort of infection or poisoning involved, and then it must have just stopped being newsworthy. The articles vanished, much like that poor family's memories. I suppose liquefying organs and blood oozing from the eyes and anus make for more attention-grabbing headlines. But I couldn't get it out of my head. There weren't many things scarier to me than the thought of waking up with this new variant of Alzheimer's. I watched my grandfather deteriorate through the dementia—slowly forgetting everyone he loved and everything he knew. It was awful. For the next few days, I spent every waking moment between classes and sub sandwiches Googling every keyword I could come up with. I just couldn't let it go.

As it turned out, there *were* a handful of similar cases. One in Australia. Another in France. Still another in Brazil. A few decidedly imbalanced bloggers had gotten wind of the phenomena, posting sensationalist theories about a vengeful God's wrath for our immoral deviance, or another in a long list of improbable government conspiracies. Then I stumbled upon a news article from Indonesia. Thank God for Google Translate. I quickly scanned the article to see if the cases might be related when I saw the words that made my blood run cold: "yellow eyes."

*A twenty-seven-year-old man from Kendari province woke this morning with an acute case of spontaneous amnesia. He cannot recall anything that has occurred in the last two weeks, and is unable to create new memories, his ex-wife and doctors from Bahtera Mas hospital report. He is currently undergoing a battery of tests and MRI scans in an effort to ascertain the cause of the unusual memory loss.*

*Adding a chilling element to the case, the couple's five-year-old son told me repeatedly that 'the man with the yellow eyes came in the night.' At this time, police are not investigating the child's claims, believing them to be a product of nightmares or the boy's way of coping with his father's sudden illness.*

The article knocked the wind out of me. It couldn't be. But somehow I knew it was. These things—the Nox—were destroying people's brains, leaving them with varying levels of permanent memory loss.

Soon enough, everything came together.

A guy in Texas got one. He was one of those paranoids who always slept next to his gun. Apparently, he wasn't so paranoid after all. He woke up in the middle of the night with those glowing amber eyes hovering just a few feet in front of his face. He said the thing had its hand cupped beneath the base of his head, as if it were readying for an intimate kiss. Terrified, the Texan grabbed his gun from the nightstand and shot it point-blank. He alleged the scream it made was entirely inside his own head and he could feel its pain, like an explosion of rage and agony within his mind. The man claimed that he then blacked out, and when he came to—with the worst headache he'd ever had—the being was gone. At first he thought maybe he'd dreamt the whole thing until he found a dark, almost black, viscous fluid all over his bed sheets. It wasn't blood—at least not as we know it. Chemical analysis determined it was comprised mostly of dopamine and acetylcholine, the memory molecules in our brains.

Now I was in a full-blown panic. Scientific method be damned. If I was piecing this together right, these yellow-eyed creatures—the Nox—were entering people's homes in the middle of the night, and leaving everyone inside with Alzheimer's-like memory loss. And worse, you'd wake up with their hand on the back of your skull and their eerie, glowing eyes hovering in front of you? Fuck that, man. Fuck that.

I sent a dozen emails to any contacts I could find at the CDC, but they still had more than enough on their plate with the Ebola scare. And let's not forget, I'm just a bio student. Who's really going to listen to my crazy theories? Even my professor laughed at me. She said I would need more than half a dozen unrelated articles and some weirdos wearing yellow contact lenses to form a reasonable scientific hypothesis, let alone draw the wild conclusions I'd come to.

Meanwhile, under the cover of hemorrhagic fever and a heavy dose of denial, the Nox started to ravage us. After a few more days, the cases of what I'd started calling the Dark Dementia numbered in the dozens. The CDC and WHO finally took their heads out of their collective asses and started investigating the outbreak. They ignored my continuous barrage of emails, and wasted precious days following more logical hypotheses first—disease, infections, poisonings. They tried, with no success, to connect the victims. Foods they might have eaten, places they may have gone, could they have had contact with one another in some way? They poured over receipts and airline records looking for outings that the victims themselves could no longer remember. They followed every possible lead *other* than the Nox. No one wanted to believe that there were *things* out there that were leaving people helplessly trapped in a painfully slow disintegration of their own existence.

\*\*\*

Some of their victims died right away. Always of heart attacks. In addition to being a neurotransmitter that conducts memories along the proper synapses in the brain, acetylcholine, in particular, helps to regulate heart rate. But autopsies would invariably reveal the same damage to the hippocampus that I knew was indicative of a visit from the Nox. And without fail, everyone else in the household would present with the Dark Dementia.

As if it wasn't already bad enough, some woke saddled with Parkinson's-like tremors on top of the Dark Dementia. Severe dopamine deficiencies are attributed to the onset of Parkinson's. At least some muscle control could be restored by injections of L-DOPA, but whether or not the typically degenerative disease will continue to progress is still unknown.

Still others lost their spatial memory. They were entirely lost in the space that they occupied, unable to recall where things were around them, and were constantly disoriented. Imagine having to visually search for the same glass of water every single time you want a drink. Never knowing whether you should go right or left, and with no memory of visual reference points that were literally in your brain seconds before. Scary doesn't even begin to describe it. Sometimes I think those who never woke up were the lucky ones.

This was just the beginning. It started with households—often several in the same night—and spiraled outward into surrounding neighborhoods. It certainly spread like a disease, whirling out from its epicenters in ever-widening circles. But it happened too quickly for a typical contagion. No one knew what to think, or how to respond. Hospitals were inundated and quickly overwhelmed. Abandoned buildings were commandeered and hastily refurbished to serve as triage units for new patients, sanitariums for the fading, and hospices for the dying.

\*\*\*

The media, finally focused on the contagion, still failed to make the leap to the Nox. Sightings of the Nox increased, often in the vicinity of the outbreaks, but they were initially dismissed as a group caught up in a growing, if peculiar, trend in fashion eyewear. It didn't help that people then *did* go out in droves to buy a pair of the hot Halloween fad, and started smearing gray makeup on their skin. The Nox were suddenly the "in" craze, and inadvertently, the costumed masses provided perfect cover for the real monsters.

On Halloween night, I discovered how to tell them apart. My local news station was broadcasting live amid a small sea of costumed revelers dressed as the Nox. Most were engaged in an oddly intimate slow dance with their hands on the back of a partner's neck. They swayed in pairs and small groups to rhythms measured in ways I couldn't discern.

Standing among the undulating throng was the Nox from that afternoon in Subway. Seeing him for the second time had no less an impact on me, even through the camera lens. I freaked out, pointing at my television set with my mouth dry and hanging open. He had the same face, the same horrible smirk, and the same hair, but he had *changed*. His skin was much darker—it was now the leaden color of a dark storm cloud. If it weren't for his clothes and shimmering eyes, he might have been almost indistinguishable from the darkness behind him.

He took four of the crowd on camera before anyone even noticed. No one else had yet made the link between the Dark Dementia and the emergence of the Nox, so no one else was paying attention. But I was. I shouted futile warnings at the television like a damn fool. I watched in horror as the Nox placed his palm on the back of a young woman's head. The whole thing was surprisingly quick—no more than a minute. I fumbled for my phone as I watched, transfixed, but I had no idea who to call. The police? The TV station? The Army?

The Nox's eyes flashed and flickered like an oxygen-fueled inferno and his skin literally *dimmed* as I watched. I screamed and dropped my phone. When he stepped away from the girl, her eyes rolled in her head, and she staggered for a moment like she was drunk. Then she straightened and looked around, clearly bewildered. She shrieked. The crowd shrieked with her, taking it up as if it were the Nox's cry.

The reporter looked bemused and turned to a kid pumping his fist into the air while he shouted for the camera. I have no idea what she said to him, or if he responded. I was too busy watching the Nox take another girl a few rows back, then a man. Drowned out among the roar of the revelers, the second girl was crying and appeared to be saying: "I can't remember, I can't remember!" her face a mask of confusion and dread. No one heard her. It was only when the fourth, a boy of about fifteen, fell to the ground and cracked his head open on the street, that people scattered like startled birds and their screams became real.

As the imitators ran, the Nox walked calmly out of the shot, wearing his terrible grin.

\*\*\*

Panic went from zero to absolute. The news footage was the proof people needed to finally come to terms with what we were dealing with. Things that looked almost human but weren't. Things without a known origin, that fed on us like vampires, leaching away bits of our pasts and leaving only the promise of a miserable, undignified end.

\*\*\*

I tried to proceed from a biological perspective. Given the little I knew, I thought it could be safely assumed that the Nox drew sustenance—or possibly pleasure—from the chemical hormones that govern memory in humans. Without the benefit of a physical specimen to study, I hypothesized that there must be either a physical or osmotic extraction method involving the Nox's hands. By placing their hands on the base of a human's skull, they were able to "mine" dopamine from the substantia nigra and acetylcholine from the substantia innomata. Extractions of either type would almost certainly damage the hippocampus and other parts of the brain's limbic system in the process, leaving their prey with the Dark Dementia and potentially a host of other neurological impairments.

Both dopamine and acetylcholine are molecules essential to the arousal and reward systems of the brain. The fact that they are our "feel-good" neurotransmitters wasn't lost on me. As horrifying a thought as anything else, I realized that the chemicals themselves could act as a drug to the Nox, which might suggest humans as nothing more to them than a delivery method to be used and discarded—much like a biologically complex needle.

Also not lost on me, was the name substantia nigra, which translates to "black substance." Dopamine contains high levels of neuromelanin. In theory at least, it's feasible that as the Nox consume our dopamine, this dark melanin byproduct bonds with the melanin in their skin. If true, it might explain the darkening that I'd witnessed. Could their gray coloring be based on how much, or how recently they'd "fed?" And was the change permanent or temporary? I suspected the former: the more of us the Nox devoured, the more they would dim and better blend into the darkness. And of course, the more indistinct they became, the better predator they would become as well. Given enough time and sustenance, only their brilliant gold eyes and devastating touch would give them away in the night.

\*\*\*

By the end of the first week of November, there were an estimated fifteen thousand cases of the Dark Dementia and more than eight hundred deaths. Based on the geographic patterns of the spread, epidemiologists believed there were between six and eight hundred Nox in our midst. People were asked to be vigilant, especially at night and in the areas surrounding the various epicenters. Law enforcement and military personnel not already assigned to medical support were activated in coordinated overnight efforts to locate and capture (and to kill, if necessary) the Nox. If they had dens or hives, or lairs, or covens, they were exceptionally difficult to find.

\*\*\*

I had no idea what to do. It didn't seem possible that I was the only person to have figured this out. I mean, I'm no idiot, but I'm hardly a genius, either. I went to my professor again. This time, she didn't laugh.

Instead, she put me in touch with a few people she knew. They all politely thanked me for my input—the nicest way possible to dismiss my amateur sleuthing. But as the Nox became the *only* news story, I knew I had been right.

And then the impossible happened.

\*\*\*

It was caught in northern Colorado. The Nox surrendered to the police without a fight or a word and was taken into custody. It was decided his first stop would be the CDC Installation in Denver. From there it was anyone's guess.

The media frenzy was insane. They waited at the installation for the Nox to arrive, armed with cameras, lights, and microphones. Every major media outlet had teams camped there hoping for a glimpse, a shot, or a sound bite. No one could possibly have predicted what was about to happen.

A car pulled up and was immediately surrounded by a swarm of reporters and cameramen. They were instructed to clear a path, only doing so when they were physically maneuvered out of the way by security and police. The door opened and two men emerged, followed by the Nox, his hands cuffed in front of him.

A sobbing teenage girl broke through the line of reporters and stood in front of the three figures. Over the clamor of the crowd, she screamed: "What did you do to them? What did you do?" I recognized her from an earlier news report as the sixteen-year-old daughter and sister of a family that had been taken a few days prior in a Colorado hot zone. She'd been staying at a friend's house the night everyone she loved was stolen from her. I felt sick for her. It had been hard enough going through it with my grandpa but this young woman would have to endure the heartbreaking process with both of her parents and her three younger brothers—*simultaneously*. I couldn't even imagine.

The mob of reporters fell silent with anticipation. I doubt anyone breathed.

The Nox was the color of ash, and bigger than the others I'd seen. He looked at the girl with his preternatural blazing eyes and tilted his head slightly. Then he began to sing:

*Hush, little munchkin, it's too late for tears.*
*The bad things are gone and your Mommy is here.*
*Hush, little munchkin, there's no reason to cry.*

*Your tummy is full and your diaper is dry.*
*Hush, little munchkin, it's time to go to bed*
*With your favorite blankie and a pillow for your head.*
*Sleep, little munchkin, everything is all right.*
*Remember Mommy loves you. Goodnight, goodnight.*

The Nox's eyes flickered and his lips twisted into a cruel smile.

The girl stared at him, open-mouthed and silent, tears spilling down her cheeks. Then she fainted dead away.

Verbatim, she said later. The Nox had repeated the rhyme word for word. It was a lullaby that her mother had made up and sung to her when she was a baby. And her mother had been singing it to her baby brother when she left for her friend's house the night the Nox came.

Not only did the Nox know the song, but it also recognized the girl and her relation to it. Unbelievably, it had her mother's memories.

The precise processes by which a memory is encoded, transmitted and stored are still largely unknown. Though the hippocampus does not actually store information, it does sort it before it's ultimately encoded into a neural pathway. It is believed that much of this occurs during REM sleep. Somehow, when the Nox feed while we slumber, they not only interrupt the encoding process, but also intercept data from our hippocampi.

This latest twist gave me an idea of where the Nox might be. The houses of many of the taken families remained empty, their occupants learning to deal with their dementia in hospitals and makeshift convalescent homes. Authorities would not have looked at their residences since, if at all. And if the Nox really possessed the memories of those that they'd taken, maybe they would find comfort in familiar places.

In the relative safety of daylight, I took a drive to the home of one of the local families I knew to still be gone. The streets were eerily empty. I tried to tell myself that my scouting mission wasn't an idiotic idea. If I came across any evidence of the Nox, I would call in the cavalry. Besides, this wasn't much more than a wild shot in the dark. Even if my latest theory were true, what were the odds that I was heading to the right house?

I was peeking into the back window of the house when the bright reflections in the glass disappeared. My stomach fell and my heart smashed against my ribcage. I knew. I turned slowly and looked into the brilliant, blazing eyes of my old friend from Subway. He was now slate gray. His eyes burned like small suns and he wore his signature, contemptuous sneer. I planted my feet for a fight and fumbled for the phone in my pocket when I heard the door open behind me. I spun around, and was shocked to see a female Nox. She was lighter—if he was slate, she was steel. Her eyes shone, the color of butterscotch. They were the last things I saw. I sensed a movement behind me, and then there was darkness.

*** *** ***

It was dusk when I came to. I was tightly tied to a twin bed in a girl's room decorated in pinks and pompoms and One Direction posters. I struggled against my restraints and the dark depths of unconsciousness trying to reclaim me. I was scared, but not as much as you might expect— not nearly as much as I thought I would be.

I knew what the Nox were waiting for. They needed me to sleep—to enter REM—so that my hippocampus would be awake. They could already have mined my brain of dopamine and acetylcholine, but they *wanted* my memories. Tapping into them probably gave them a way to understand us, and for a time, to live as us—to *be* us. Maybe observing those small bits of our lives gave the Nox a purpose beyond feeding. Perhaps they even felt what we felt, amplified by the chemicals they mined from us.

He entered the room. It was disconcerting how much he blended with the darkfall. He was nearly formless and vague—only his eyes were visible as he moved.

"Just kill me when you're done," I said.

He grinned as if he knew what I was asking for and why. And perhaps he did, but I knew he wouldn't be granting my wish. It was in the nature of the Nox to take pleasure in our suffering. I supposed we wouldn't grant them any favors either. His counterpart in Denver was probably just now discovering how cruel we humans could be. He would be granted no quarter, and neither would I.

He forced two pills into my mouth. Probably a sleeping pill prescribed to the previous owners. I could have fought. Spit them out. But I didn't. I swallowed them. Eventually, sleep would come, anyway. One way or another, they would have what they wanted from me.

He left me alone in the girl's room again. The shadows darkened and crept along the walls with the waning light. I realized that when I woke up tomorrow—if I woke at all—I wouldn't remember any of this. I likely wouldn't remember anything about the past few weeks. But the Nox *would*. They'd have my memories, and perhaps they would feel compelled to act on them as they had with others—to finish what I'd started. Perhaps they would tell of my final hours and provide an ending to this horror. The thought brought me a glimmer of peace, so I chose to hang on to it. I envisioned it in my mind—the Nox writing about the end of me. I burned it into my memory. If you are reading these words now, it worked.

My eyes grew heavy. I tried to stay focused, but my thoughts were swimmy and broken. Fragmented. Nonsense. Then, something important. What was it? I grasped for it with my mind, but it was out of reach. What did it matter anyway? All would be gone soon. Something about the boy. Don't forget the boy. I wondered if I would wake up when they came. Darkness.

I did wake. Terrified. So dark. Pressure on the back of my neck. The boy. And her flickering gaze. Adrenaline. Heart racing. *Oh my God, the BOY.* No pain. Scared. Over soon. Her breath is cool on my face. The Indonesian boy. I'm not me. Remember the Indonesian boy. *They're* me. This is them. They didn't mine the Indonesian boy. Must remember. Finish. Write it. The boy. Remember. **He's the vaccine.** Remember. Remem...

# NIGHT SEASON

## Tom Breen

Even the most dedicated truffle-snuffler of the horror undergrowth, the most jaded and indefatigable seeker after stranger and rarer cinematic sensations, would have stopped in her tracks, as I did, and uttered a reverent "Whoa" upon seeing the flyer I spotted on campus the other day. There are not many opportunities to see "Night Season", after all, and certainly not on an actual movie screen.

You're lucky to find someone at a convention peddling a shitty eighth generation VHS dub that turns out to be, as you peer through the milky murk, not "Night Season" at all, but rather, "Slasher High", a hideously bad film often confused with its inscrutable cousin because of a few minutes of allegedly shared footage. You may have also seen legions of blurry, indistinct clips on YouTube purporting to be from "Night Season": again, "Slasher High". There are occasional clips of the real "Night Season" on YouTube, people claim, but they get yanked down almost immediately. Copyright claims, supposedly. I have my doubts.

A lot of lore surrounds the movie. Accurate information is not easy to come by, but a few details about the production of the film are accepted with something approaching unanimous agreement.

It was directed, and perhaps financed (but with that "perhaps" I'm already lapsing into disputed territory; unavoidable where "Night Season" is concerned) by an NYU dropout named Michael Stern. Curiously, Stern was not a film student, but a philosophy major. Joel Moscowitz claims, in his Online Dictionary of Horror Film Biography, that Stern is the same Michael Stern who emerged as a spokesman for the far-right Kahane Chai party in Israel in the 1990s before going underground after the party's proscription in 1994, but Moscowitz's source for this information is questionable.

At any rate, Stern shot the movie on what must have been a tiny budget (but there are reasons to doubt that "must have been," as we'll see) in 1983 and 1984, although subtly disorienting details pop up throughout the movie that complicate exact dating, like a wall pasted with "Dinkins for Mayor" signs in the background of one scene, and footage from what looks like the

Tompkins Square Park riot, even though that wouldn't happen until 1988.

It's possible the footage was spliced in later, but the first mention of "Night Season" pops up on May 2, 1986, with a brief item in the *Village Voice* giving vague details on an "art riot" at a grimy performance space on the Lower East Side during an event that included, the article said, "sideshow freak acts, a hardcore band that played with industrial tools instead of instruments, and an underground splatter film called 'Night Seasons,'" with the unnamed writer getting the title slightly wrong.

The description is also off; it's not really a splatter film at all, with most of the gore coming only in the final reel. For much of its run time, the film is a series of increasingly eerie set pieces strung across a strange and unfamiliar Manhattan. You recognize the landmarks and the neighborhoods, but the city looks half deserted, devoid of people, its walls covered with obscure graffiti whose messages never quite register.

The ostensible protagonist is a college dropout referred to as The Jew; he's never given any name, and no version of the film that's turned up seems to have a credit sequence. He's young, wiry, sweaty; he looks sick, with haunted, animal eyes. He suffers from insomnia, which is why he can't go to college anymore, and takes a series of nighttime jobs that we see pass by in a quick montage that ends with an incredibly aged woman of indeterminate ethnicity pressing her face against the window of the late-night bodega where he works and screaming, her skin leaving a gray smear on the glass as she lurches from side to side.

The Jew eventually gets a job as a Night Inspector, hired by the mysterious Department of City in a scene that would be funny for its youthful approximation of a parody of bureaucracy if it weren't for the leering, repulsive performance by the actor who plays The Jew's supervisor.

"We live on our bellies, we die in our dreams," he says to The Jew, apropos of nothing, in a line that will crop up again and again in the film.

As a Night Inspector, it's The Jew's job to make sure that New York's nocturnal aspects keep from penetrating its daylight ones, so that the commuters and tourists who pump economic life through the city's collapsing arteries will continue to come every day.

It's not clear how he's supposed to do this; The Jew's duties seem to consist of staggering through a collection of scenes ranging from derelict parking lots to bars where wrinkled people with scabs on their faces kneel in a circle around a dog skinned and gutted like a deer. These are the scenes that got lifted for "Slasher High," inserted in a dream sequence that, incidentally, makes no narrative sense in that film, but never mind.

At one point, The Jew finds a Chinese astrologer holding court in an empty, abandoned swimming pool with concrete walls that have almost turned black from years of graffiti. The astrologer tells The Jew he has to rescue a girl, Lex Credendi, from a foster home where the city has placed her in the South Bronx.

The Jew travels there, but first we see the inside of the little bungalow where an enormously obese woman with two puffs of black hair, Big Ada, has a group of wan, scrawny teenagers scrubbing floors and knitting puppets that look like squids. In one John Waters-esque touch, Big Ada takes a bunch of Oreo cookies and scrapes the filling off with her teeth, depositing a pile of the stuff between two moldy slices of bread, which she then gives to Lex Credendi, boyish figure and spiky black haircut, to eat.

By the time The Jew gets to the house, all the other kids seem to have gone, and as soon as he walks in the door, Big Ada is in his face, swinging at him with her meaty hands, while Lex Credendi stands mute and impassive in the kitchen doorway. The Jew takes a flower pot and caves in Big Ada's head, which discharges huge streams of colored sand instead of gore, a nice effect that encourages you to think of Stern as someone other than a grubby kid trying to make an "arty" film.

The Jew and Lex Credendi leave the house and go outside, but something's wrong. It's daytime, but the streets are full of junkies and homeless prophets, whores, and scabby skinheads brawling with Black Hebrew Israelites. The Jew and Lex Credendi run through vacant lots and potter's fields left in the yawning gaps between abandoned buildings, and soon, crops are sprouting up around them, black wheat and black corn and black soy, a great touch, and suddenly you're wondering how they pulled that off with what must have been a micro-budget.

The pair goes back to the empty swimming pool, where the Chinese astrologer tells The Jew that the night world is breaking into the daytime, and that this has been fated, it's in the stars, it comes around every couple of centuries, there's no point trying to change it. The Jew is furious and he takes Lex Credendi to the Department of City, but now everything there has changed; instead of the 1900s school building we saw earlier in the film, it's a derelict, Gilded Age mansion with no one inside. The Jew goes tearing from room to room, but all he finds are alabaster white mannequin parts, sometimes stacked knee-high, until he gets up to the attic, where he finds a pile of what initially look like squirming, fat, blue-gray moles with no hair.

As they start to vault into the air and attach themselves to The Jew, though, it becomes apparent that they're actually creatures with bodies like fish and heads like human babies, except for the suction cup mouths they're using to latch onto The Jew, who screams and tries to shake them loose. This is a great gore effect, and you have to really admire Stern, or his effects artist, because to pull off something like this on, what…maybe $30,000? Makes you wonder what he could have accomplished with a real budget.

The Jew runs back downstairs, pulling the baby-hagfish things from his puckered flesh, and he runs into his supervisor, who tells The Jew he's fucked up, he's blown it, he's let the night leak into the day. The Jew tries to protest, but the supervisor won't hear it.

"The only way to sanctify this calamity is with a foundation sacrifice," he says, and you understand then that The Jew is going to kill Lex Credendi, which makes you sigh a little because what's been an unpredictable surrealist horror movie up to this point is now about to become another "Wicker Man" derivative, albeit with an urban setting.

The Jew goes out into the street where Lex Credendi is waiting, and tells her they have to go to his apartment. Lex Credendi agrees; so passive, to this point in the film it's hard to remember if she's even had a single line of dialogue.

The two get in a dilapidated cab and you can see The Jew shaking and nervous and turning over in his head what he's about to do, and it really looks like the actor is thinking it over, too; it's a remarkable performance. Lex Credendi looks bored and inscrutable while the cab moves slowly through city streets that are now choked with crumbling people walking in a daze, not Romero-esque zombies, but human beings who look identifiably sick, instead of actors in makeup. Some of them bump into the cab and desultorily rap on the windows; the cabbie honks his horn and drives on.

Finally, they get to The Jew's apartment building, and it's tense as they walk up the three flights of stairs and into his grimy little room. He starts pacing, trying to get a sentence out, wishing he could explain what he's about to do, when all of a sudden, Lex Credendi swings a baseball bat and cracks him right across the face.

There's a crunching noise. It's a sick hit, and she immediately follows up with another swing, and then another, merciless, drawing blood, while The Jew can barely get more than a shocked, pained noise out. You're sitting there thinking what a well-composed stunt this is until The Jew finally manages to say something:

"Michael," he screams. "Jesus Christ, Michael, she's really hitting me!"

At this point, you freeze. Your first impulse – this is an arty way to break the fourth wall – is tempered by the sickening beating The Jew is getting; Lex Credendi is *fucking him up* in a way that doesn't look like other movie beatings you've seen, and as he starts to scream, "Please! It's a movie, oh God, please!" You really wonder how much of this is weird Lower East Side types pushing the envelope and whether, no way, *can't be*, but maybe it's real.

The camera pulls back, and the supervisor is in a chair, sobbing, trying to look away as The Jew finally stops staggering and goes down, first on one knee, and then laid flat out, while Lex Credendi relentlessly winds up and delivers hit after hit.

It takes nine minutes. It's excruciating. There are no cuts, no editing tricks, just one long shot of a woman beating a man to death with a baseball bat, finishing on a shot of her breathing hard and covered in gore. It's hard to watch; Gene Siskel walked out of "Maniac" when Tom Savini faked getting his head blown off, but this makes you want to call a cop.

Finally, though, after Lex Credendi catches her breath, she walks over to the supervisor, who's stopped sobbing, and takes his hand. She leads him outside, and here's where all your prior assumptions about this film and the talents of its creators go out the window, because outside, they're in Times Square and Jesus Christ, it looks exactly like the Times Square of today, with family-friendly neon and billboards everywhere, huge crowds of tourists milling around, the streets swept of peep show booths and vomiting winos and prostitutes and religious cults, and in the middle of this scene that would have cost *millions* to stage in the mid-1980s, Lex Credendi and the supervisor step out into the street and, as the cabs buzz by them, start dancing.

It's a nice conceit, but after what you've just witnessed, you start to feel queasy, and then suddenly, the camera zooms in on Lex Credendi's face so fast, it feels like someone just picked up a camera and threw it at her, and it pauses there, showing an expression that hovers between fear and triumph, and something you can't make out, and then the movie ends. Black screen, no credits, everyone go home.

"It's a snuff film," wrote Meredith Willis in 1986, an aspiring film critic living in a Brooklyn that then seemed as far from chic as it was from the Sahara, for a piece she intended to submit to *Film Threat*.

She never got the chance, because 10 days after she wrote the review, she was murdered by a burglar who came in through a fourth story window and didn't seem to steal anything beyond a photo album and a class ring.

Willis's unsent review was crucial, though, because it's the only description we have of what "Night Season" was actually like. She was one of the few people to see the movie during the summer of 1986; as far as anyone knows, there was only a single print, lost very early on, except for the two minutes or so that ended up in the dream sequence in "Slasher High." Stern left town that fall after he got a girl pregnant; he left behind a string of unpaid debts, bad checks, angry roommates, and soiled mattresses. He was a lowlife and no one was sad to see him go.

But he had been the sole source of the film's distribution, arranging for it to be shown on bills aimed at the city's outré art crowd, or at performance spaces in back rooms for sparsely attended showings on his own. He seemed to have no intention of getting professional backing for the film, but who knows. It was a long time ago, long before the film festival circuit infrastructure that's helped so many shitty independent filmmakers in the last 20 years.

So we wouldn't even know about "Night Season" if it weren't for Willis and her review, which later found its way into the hands of Spike Diamond, an aging punk rock scenester who had been hanging around the Lower East Side for 15 years and who had recently scored a $1,200 assignment from *Hustler* magazine to write the definitive debunking of the existence of snuff films, which *Hustler* publisher, Larry Flynt, considered an urban legend that anti-pornography crusaders deployed against his industry.

Spike was given Willis's manuscript by her roommate, and he quickly became fascinated with "Night Season," tracking down some of the people who had seen it, trying to get a copy for himself, writing a lengthy and Lester Bangs-ish response to Willis's review, although Diamond's article, like her piece, never saw print. Before he got around to mailing it to his editor, Spike was standing in a dirty bookstore when a robber jammed a .38 Special into his right eye socket and squeezed the trigger.

There was not exactly a major battle among scholars for control of Spike's papers, but after a while, in the summer of 1988, the bass player in a scabrous local punk band called Unsought Ideals got ahold of the "Night Season" material, thinking it was perfect for an article he wanted to submit to a forthcoming Feral House anthology on extremist culture.

Ten days after he completed his manuscript, though, was the night of the Tompkins Square Park riot, and the bass player was chased down an alley by a pack of what witnesses later described as skinheads with pockmarks all over their faces, who kicked him to death.

If you're starting to discern a pattern here, it's thanks to an artist named Salvatore "Dandy" DiDonato, who was a prominent gay activist in the 1980s. Dandy's preoccupation was the response of the U.S. government and the health care industry to the spread of AIDS, and as he burrowed deep into his research, the Expressionist-inspired paintings of his youth vanished in favor of vast canvases that looked like org charts for some incomprehensible and sinister corporation. Drawing on campaign contributions, research awards, public statements, foundation memberships, board vacancies, and other arcane but public data, Dandy showed the links between pharmaceutical companies pushing AZT, government health agencies, ostensibly progressive congressmen, and even the various gay and AIDS-related activist groups he scorned as sellouts and patsies. His paintings were less aesthetic depictions of reality than some giant brief for a cosmic prosecution, a germ map of the plague's enablers.

Somehow Dandy got interested in the increasingly grim reputation enjoyed by "Night Season" in underground circles which, by 1990, had all kinds of people whispering that everyone in the cast had died, that Stern was the head of a satanic cult, that anyone who watched the movie died, and so on. All of which was preposterous.

But what Dandy the indefatigable researcher, the identifier of unlikely connections, was able to piece together was in some ways even stranger. The people associated with "Night Season" who had died violent deaths all had two things in common: they had somehow come into contact with the review of the film originally penned by Willis but since added to by a slew of subsequent writers, and they had failed to pass on that review to anyone else within nine days.

Dandy had no idea how many copies of the review existed, but he was able to track its distribution within a relatively small circle of cineastes, gorehounds, junkie poets, punk rockers, and porno bookstore owners in New York City. And as far as he knew, everyone who had read the papers and failed to meet that nine-day deadline had died by violent means.

The deadline seemed to be important. Julio Maron, for example, a freelance journalist, well known locally for his scabies and fondness for homemade gin, wrote some garbled piece about "Night Season" based on the earlier work and sent it to Bret McCrea, an editor at ArtSEEN, within about a week. Maron lived until 1998, when his liver exploded. But McCrea didn't do anything with the piece, and 10 days after he got it, he died in a carjacking while trying to buy drugs in the Bronx.

Dandy was a man who believed in the scientific method, though, so he devised a test. He gave his lover, Brody Mayer, a condensed copy of the "Night Season" papers and explained that he had to pass it on to someone within nine days; Mayer dutifully sent it on to a friend, with explanation that the friend was to do the same, and so on. Dandy gave a second copy of the condensed work to Ian Tennay, a rival artist who painted "consciousness raising" works about HIV that Dandy thought were naïve and shameless copouts to the pharmaceutical-industrial complex. Dandy explained the paper was going to be the inspiration for a future series of paintings, and asked Tennay for his thoughts. Tennay, who despised

Dandy, ignored the request, and 10 days after he got the package in the mail, he was beaten to death in the laundry room of his apartment complex, his hands nailed to a board, crucifix-style.

Maybe it was a coincidence; New York was a violent city in 1990. Maybe Dandy would have gotten different results with a larger sample size, but we'll never know; wracked with guilt over Tennay's death, Dandy stepped in front of the F train one morning about a month after his rival was murdered.

And so, Dandy's hypothesis – read and pass on the description of "Night Season" within nine days, or else – hardened into dogma, and from Brody Mayer, it went to the "landscape disruptionist" Mikyell Argentina, who passed it along to the filmmaker, Ivy Pearse, who passed it along to the poetry night organizer, Wardell Coleman, and so on, for nearly a quarter century. Meredith Willis's original piece was warped and redacted and expanded beyond recognition, nervously passed from reader to reader, eventually finding its way through some hopelessly occult chain of communication, to a 21-year-old named Chris Ackerman, president of the Underground Film Club at the university here, who organized the supposed screening of "Night Season" I attended nine days ago.

As you've guessed by now, I didn't see "Night Season"; I doubt anyone's seen it since 1986. Instead, I saw "Slasher High", a witless stabfest with only the eerie dream sequence to make it stand out from all the other "Friday the 13th" clones spewed out in that awful decade. I sat in the dark, polite and bored, with about two-dozen other people, wondering what on earth we had sacrificed a Thursday night for, and when the movie was over I got up to leave.

On my way out the door, I was stopped by Ackerman, whom I had never seen before in my life, but who appeared to be a nice, well-adjusted young person, the kind of undergrad – they seem to be endemic these days – who is at peace with the world and himself.

"Pretty interesting film, huh?" he asked.

"Not really," I said. "Have you seen 'Combat Shock'? That's a much better version of what this was going for."

"I haven't seen that!" he said, and he typed the title into his iPhone. "But take a look at this and see whether you still think the same thing about 'Night Season, '" and he handed me a sheaf of photocopied papers.

Within those papers, I found, as I'm sure you realize by now, this text, or a version of this text, and I laughed out loud while reading it. I put it aside, thinking I had to write a blog post about this, because it ticked off so many of my boxes: horror movies, urban blight, obscure cultural curiosities, urban legends. A good joke, a 21st century chain letter, something worth telling the Internet about, but nothing important. I have a lot of stuff on my mind these days, and I tossed the photocopies to one side of my standing desk and mostly forgot about them.

This morning I woke up and one of the suction-mouthed baby-fish was attached to my chest.

I screamed and thrashed in bed, rolled out and fell onto the fucking floor, and crawled on my belly into the bathroom, kicking and flailing the whole time. After maybe a minute of blind panic, I realized there was no blue-gray creature with a toothy suction cup attached to my flesh, that I was alone in my apartment, and that I had clearly endured some kind of panic attack brought on by stress and overwork.

I lay on the cool, bathroom floor until my breathing returned to normal, and then I stood up and looked in the mirror. On my chest was a red, puckered wound about seven inches in diameter, which instantly began burning and itching.

I called my doctor, who told me to calm down, and then I called in sick to work. Trying to rationalize the wound to myself didn't work, so I drove to the liquor store up the street, in hopes of buying enough bourbon to drink myself calm. On my way in, I was brushed aside and nearly knocked over by a gray-faced, scabby woman who threw a shoulder check like a linebacker and hissed something about dying dreams as she passed me by.

And so, now I'm here, standing at my computer desk, my hands shaking as I type as fast as I can, looking at the clock as it marches without pause toward midnight and the 10th day. I don't know how much of this is true, if any of it's true; some of it is stuff I added, some of it is from those papers that fucking kid, Ackerman, gave me, but I know a lot of it is a lie; Joel Moscowitz and his Online Dictionary of Horror Fiction Biography don't exist, and as far as I know, "Night Season" doesn't exist either. Who knows? Who knows what Meredith Willis actually wrote in some squalid walkup back in 1986, but she was murdered by a burglar, that's for sure, you can look that up, friend, and Spike Diamond is dead, and Ian Tennay is dead, and Bret McCrea is dead, even though there may not be a "Night Season" at all, or maybe there is, maybe it's "Slasher High". After all, if you look at IMDB you'll see the director of that is credited as "David Tenafly" which IMDB says is a pseudonym for someone named Michael Stern, who went on to direct undistinguished teen comedies but THAT'S NOT THE FUCKING POINT, it doesn't matter if "Night Season" was a different movie or if it's "Slasher High", the movie isn't the point, the movie isn't the point, THE MOVIE WAS NEVER THE POINT. The point is this review this is how "Night Season" lives and perpetuates itself through the things we write about it, the words we write, the scenes we create for it, the very words you're reading right now, like this one, and this one, and that one. This is how it lives and you're part of it now, you're known to it now and you're going to die like all the rest if you don't let it keep living. It will find you through these words these words you're reading right now and you're sitting there scoffing and FUCKING LAUGHING at me because you think I've lost it over some goddamn horror movie but it's not the movie it's the words, it's these words that are alive and kill us and you can laugh and laugh but I have this wound on my chest and now I'm passing it on to you.

What you do with it is your decision. You have nine days.

# UNSAFE

## Ryan Neil Falcone

Missy was five years old when her father broke her arm. Pretending to lead an imaginary parade around the coffee table in front of where her irritated father slouched watching a car race on television, she accidentally lost her balance and sent the contents of the rickety table tumbling to the floor.

She watched in horror as a dark stain of chewing tobacco spread outward from the overturned plastic cup he'd been spitting into. Nearby, the bottle of Jack Daniels he'd been consuming emptied out onto the dingy carpet with a series of slurping glugs. Her father leapt to his feet, snarling as he painfully seized the little girl's arm. "You idiot—look at the mess you made!"

"I'm sorry, daddy," she apologized, her voice scarcely a peep.

"Do you know how much that bottle cost?"

When he tightened his grip, a shockwave of pain rippled through her when the bone in her slender arm cracked with an audible *pop* they both heard. Eyes wide with shock, Missy saw her father's face grow pale as her body began to go numb.

The next few hours seemed to pass in a blur. Missy sat on the couch trying not to cry while her too-drunk-to-drive father begged his girlfriend to take them to the hospital. That he offered a bogus explanation over the phone about how the injury occurred didn't matter to her; despite what he'd done, she still loved him.

Lori escorted her into the emergency room (while her father remained outside, smoking cigarettes in the cold winter air to sober up), accompanying Missy as the admitting nurse led them down a long, sterile hallway to an examining room. Once they were alone, Lori knelt in front of the injured child, her face awash with sympathy as she lifted Missy's chin. "Oh, honey—I'm so sorry this happened. Your father...he didn't mean to do it. But I'm here now—I'll take care of you."

Missy dropped her gaze but didn't respond. While she didn't doubt Lori's sincerity, she had no reason to believe the kindly woman's reassurances, either. Lori was the latest in a long list of her father's revolving door girlfriends who came and went before she got to know them. There'd been a Tammy, an Ann, a Lizzy, a Darlene, a Hope, a Charity (whom Missy hadn't particularly cared for), to say nothing of Angel, Pam, Darcy, and Kim, as well as several others whose names Missy hadn't bothered to learn. So as much as the young girl wanted to believe Lori's words, she knew better than to get her hopes up; there was no reason to believe Lori would be around longer than any of the others.

She tried not to cry when the kindly doctor painfully set her broken arm. His smile disappeared when the nurse put Missy's arm in a cast. When he turned to confront Lori, Missy overheard him threatening to call the police, since this was the girl's fifth emergency room visit in the last year. She began to feel uncomfortable when he banished Lori from the room so he could question the young girl alone.

After closing the door, the doctor sat down in front of the mistrustful girl, his smile belying the concern evident upon his neatly shaven face.

"Does your arm feel all right?"

She nodded, despite the throbs of pain flaring beneath her cast.

"I need to ask you some questions—is that okay?" When she didn't respond, he prompted: "How did you hurt your arm? Did you really fall down the stairs, or did someone do this to you?"

Understanding that telling the truth would get her father in trouble, she looked down and said nothing. The doctor paused to give the girl time to answer, but when she remained silent, he added: "Missy, I can't help you unless you tell me what happened."

Missy popped her thumb into her mouth, preventing her from having to answer.

Back home, Lori helped the girl clumsily undress and get into her pajamas before tucking her into bed. Her father, reeking of cigarettes, paused in her bedroom doorway as if embarrassed to enter. He sat down on Missy's bed, looking ashamed. "I'm... I'm sorry, Missy."

This time, she couldn't hold back her tears because she believed him, despite the perpetual physical and verbal abuse. Deep down, she suspected the reason he mistreated her was because he'd never forgiven her for killing her mom during childbirth.

"I'll make it up to you," he promised, grasping her in an awkward side hug as though she were a stranger.

Lori shook her head with disappointment when he hurriedly left the room, sighing as she turned her attention back to the little girl. "Try to get some sleep, Missy—everything will be all right in the morning."

Again, Missy didn't reply as Lori flicked off her overhead light. How could she possibly explain that this wasn't true—that being alone in her room at night was when she was most frightened of all?

# Unsafe

She couldn't remember when the shadow man first began emerging from her closet. At first, the apparition seemed harmless, tossing toys across her room with arms made of indistinct, billowy mist that reminded her of smoke, but the visitations had become progressively more frightening over time. Whenever it appeared now, she pulled the covers tightly over her head to shield herself from the chilling cold that filled her room whenever it was there. Sometimes, she could feel it clawing at the blanket with raking talons that didn't feel like hands, while it whispered terrible things to her. Somehow, she knew she'd be safe as long as she stayed under the covers. Eventually, it would return to her closet, slamming the door shut when it departed. But even after it was gone, Missy would sleep with her head under the covers for the rest of the night.

Worst of all, the shadow man's unwelcome intrusions seemed to coincide with her father's mood swings. She had little doubt that today's incident would trigger a visit. When her closet door inevitably creaked open later that night, flooding the room with a frosty chill that made the winter cold outside seem balmy in comparison, she buried herself under the covers and tried not to scream when she felt its foul fingers tracing down her back from the opposite side of the blanket.

When her father got home from work the following day, he presented an unexpected surprise. Missy squealed with delight when she saw the puppy, falling in love with it instantly. She was surprised when her father let the new puppy, which she named, "Muffin," sleep in her room. She drifted off to sleep with Muffin nestled against her legs, feeling happier than she could ever remember. That night, her closet door remained shut.

Her father seemed less volatile over the next few weeks, as if injuring his daughter had been a wakeup call. That changed the night he gambled away his paycheck in a poker game, precipitating an enormous argument with Lori. Missy listened to their heated argument take place in the kitchen, while pretending to watch TV in the other room, her heart sinking when Lori stormed out at the end of the fight.

She put herself to bed to avoid disturbing her father, who drank alone in the darkened living room. Later that night, she wasn't remotely surprised when her closet door noisily creaked open. The freezing cold seeping into her room caused her to stir in her sleep, and when she sat up, she was startled to see the shadow man's glowing red eyes staring at her from the foot of the bed. She quickly pulled the covers over her head as Muffin began barking.

Before she could throw the covers aside to go to her puppy's rescue, the bedroom light flicked on and her sleepy father's perturbed voice rose above the racket that the dog was making. "What the hell's going on in here?"

Missy sat up, following her father's disgusted gaze toward the middle of the room, where Muffin had urinated on the rug. Before she could say anything, he strode across the room and seized the puppy by the collar, roughly dragging the cowering dog from the room. She cried herself to sleep, listening to the chained up puppy howl in the backyard.

Muffin became skittish after the encounter with the shadow man, refusing to go back in Missy's room, no matter how hard she tried to coax the dog to enter. Even worse, Muffin's housetraining regressed. Missy cleaned up these messes as quickly as she could, in hopes that her father wouldn't notice, but his temper flared when he inadvertently stepped in a pile of feces she'd somehow missed at the bottom of the stairs. Missy followed him into the kitchen, begging him not to punish her dog, but froze in her tracks when he recoiled sharply; clutching a hand pocked with visible teeth marks. A lump formed in her throat as she watched her enraged father's anger predictably overflow.

Missy's eyes overflowed with tears as she watched her irate father drag the puppy outside to his truck and drive away down the dirt road leading toward the woods behind their house. Something inside her died when the sound of the gunshot echoed throughout the woods somewhere nearby.

Lori was horrified to discover what he'd done later that evening, and the grieving girl excused herself from the dinner table so that she wouldn't have to listen to them argue about it. When the shouts downstairs finally died down, Lori appeared in her doorway. Missy sat rigid when her father's girlfriend embraced her, too numb to return the affection. "Honey, I'm so sorry," Lori began. "What your father did was so unfair. He—"

"Quit babying her," her father growled from the hallway, glaring at them both with disdain. That night, he didn't tuck her into bed. She lay there feeling helpless, and when the shadow man appeared, she curled into a ball under the covers, sobbing as it whispered frightening things to her in the darkened room.

The tension inside the household worsened when her father lost his job a few days later. Even Lori's presence did little to console the girl as her father's drunken disposition worsened considerably. He spent long evenings at the bar, sometimes coming home after Missy had already put herself to bed. Every night, she lay in her quiet bedroom alone, dreading the unwelcome visitation from the shadow man that awaited her.

The next Saturday, her father left her alone in the house all day, staggering back home that evening, reeking of alcohol when he leaned down to kiss her on the cheek. They ate dinner in silence, her father taking frequent swigs directly from his bottle of booze while she munched the TV dinner he'd prepared for her. When she reached for her glass of milk to wash down a mouthful of the tasteless meal, she accidentally knocked it over and doused the food on his tinfoil tray. Missy didn't see the backhand slap coming. The unexpected blow knocked her sprawling, and her eye had already begun swelling by the time she hit the ground.

When her father ordered her to go to her room, the sobbing girl scampered up the stairs. By the time she reached the top of the stairwell, she'd made up her mind what to do.

When her father pushed open her bedroom door a few hours later, he was surprised to see Missy seated on the floor, facing her closet.

"Missy?"

When she didn't react, he angrily strode into the room, his breath drawing short when he felt how unnaturally cold the room was. "Is there a window open or something?" When she didn't respond, he strode forward, toward his unresponsive daughter and gruffly shook her shoulder. "Hey— I'm talking to you!"

Missy jumped, as if startled by his presence. She looked up at him, her face expressionless.

"I have a *surprise* for you, Daddy."

"A surprise?" the confused, drunken man repeated. "What is it?"

"You'll see," she replied. "It's in the closet."

Curious, he staggered toward the closet, fumbling inside for the string that would turn on the overhead light. But before he could locate it, he let out a startled cry when something wrapped around his wrist. Unable to comprehend what was happening, his gaze shifted to his daughter, who awkwardly clambered to her feet and scrambled across the room, toward her bed. As her unsuspecting father gaped, Missy pulled the blanket over her head, blocking her view, as multiple, spidery tendrils slithered out of the closet, wrapping themselves around her shocked father's body.

A terrifying, unearthly roar that shook her bed enveloped his cries for help. Missy covered her ears when her father's voice rose several octaves, into a high-pitched scream as the entity that lived in her closet pulled him inside. When the closet door slammed shut, the room was bathed in merciful silence.

When Lori arrived the next morning, ready to break things off with Missy's father, she was surprised to see that the front door was unlocked. Even stranger, she found the young girl sleeping on the downstairs couch. Sitting down next to the girl, Lori gently shook her awake. Missy awakened with a start, burying her face against Lori's shoulder when she saw who it was. Frightened by the girl's behavior, Lori asked, "Missy, where's your father?"

The girl pulled back from the comforting embrace, staring at Lori with frightened eyes. After several, long moments, she popped her thumb into her mouth to prevent herself from having to answer.

When her father failed to turn up after several days, Missy was remanded to the county home for children. Two weeks into her stay, Lori visited with exciting news: since Missy didn't have any relatives, the court had agreed to grant Lori temporary custody. Missy ran into her arms even before Lori could finish asking whether the girl wanted to live with her.

The last time Missy set foot in her house was when Lori brought her to pack her things. She felt uneasy when she noticed that her closet door was slightly open, and couldn't help fidgeting while Lori boxed her meager belongings. Lori seemed to notice that something was amiss, too, as she bent to pick up the box; her arms rippled with gooseflesh over how cold the bedroom had suddenly become.

"Let's get out of here, honey," she suggested, offering her hand to the grateful little girl.

Missy paused at her bedroom doorway, looking back across the room toward the closet, where she could almost see the shadow man's ominous red eyes glaring back at her from the narrow crack in the open closet door—but for the first time, she wasn't afraid. Somehow, she knew that once she left this place, the shadow man would never bother her again. She turned when Lori pulled on her hand, coaxing her away from the room for good.

"Everything's going to be okay, Missy—I promise."

For the first time in her life, Missy allowed herself to believe that this was true.

# THE JUJU
## Jim Cort

You could hear them from a long way off.

I passed down the gritty streets and heard them before I ever saw them. They were a ragtag collection of hippies (or am I showing my age?), senior citizens, professor types with the patched-elbow tweeds, slim, graceful male ingénues that had to be fags, sturdy pitbulls in woolens and slacks that had to be dykes, here and there a smattering of housewives in cloth coats and sensible shoes. They were all so intent, so serious, so dedicated. I just wanted to give them all a big hug and sing "Kumbaya."

There were a couple dozen of them, crowded around the entrance to the Rochester hotel, standing wherever the cops would let them stand, chanting, "Murderers must go." The Rochester wasn't the best hotel in the city, but it certainly wasn't the worst. It was the oldest, and still projected an air of elegance and refinement. It had been ground zero for the latest round of urban renewal that had pushed westward from its doors. On the east side of Bellevue Avenue, facing the grand old dame, was some urban the renewal hadn't reached yet. It was tired and seedy, and looked like it needed help standing up. Of course, this was where I was headed, to a bar called Mulligan's.

I paused at the door and regarded the crowd marching around, singing their tuneless song. I pumped my fist in the air. "That's right," I yelled. "Down with the system. Whatever." They didn't give any sign they heard me. I opened the door and stepped into Mulligan's.

It was a dim, down on its heels sort of place, longer than it was wide. Near the front window was the bar, a venerable expanse of wood that had seen countless baptisms of spilled beers. Behind the bar was a floor-to-ceiling mirror that I don't think had ever seen a rag or a squirt of Windex. At the far end of the room was an ancient jukebox, and in between that and the bar were five or six wooden tables. Mulligan was behind the bar like he always was. He had the TV on. There was a young newscaster standing in front of the Rochester with a mic in her hand. The protesters were putting on their own show in the background. She looked like she'd been carefully coiffed and made up and then dipped in plastic to keep her that way.

The newswoman said, *"This is Blair Holland, Channel 12 Action News, reporting live from the Hotel Rochester. Demonstrators began arriving as early as 6 O'clock this morning at the Rochester to protest the continued presence of deposed dictator, General Immamu M'Buotu. The impetus for this latest wave of demonstrations is surely the official request by the Provisional Government of the troubled African nation of Shambra that the General be returned to stand trial for, as they put it, 'Crimes against the people.'"*

Mulligan looked at me like I'd caught him watching kiddie porn. "I was tryin' to get the game," he said.

*"The State Department has promised a response to this extradition request some time today, and Action News will report it as it happens. In the meantime, these demonstrators from the Coalition for International Justice are leaving no doubt about where they stand on the matter."*

I didn't bother telling Mulligan what I wanted. Mulligan didn't bother to ask. He just drew a beer and slid it down to me.

"Big shot at the Rochester?"

Mulligan said, "Yeah, some African guy. I seen him goin' in one time. Bodyguards all over the place. You could spot 'em right away. They were in suits and ties, but you could tell they were all packin'. The big shot had on this fancy uniform, all drippin' with medals. We had a name for guys like that in the Army."

"Probably the same name we had," I said. "Some things never change. So, how's business?"

"Terrible," he said. "Those screwballs out there are driving everybody away.

*"I'm* here."

"You're always here. I'm surprised you're not out there with those guys, trying to change the world."

I took a sip of beer. "I don't want to change anything."

"Sure you do," he said. "You're one of them young guys with all the answers, ain't you?"

Sometimes Mulligan could be a real pain, as opposed to what he was most of the time, which was annoying. "I don't have any answers," I said, "and I'm not all that young."

"You're younger than me."

"Who isn't? Look, Mulligan, you've got me all wrong. I'm a solid citizen. It's true, I am temporarily between jobs, but—"

Mulligan snorted. "Temporarily!"

"I'm just waiting for the right position to come along," I told him. "The point is: I'm just a regular guy. I'm a veteran, just like you."

As soon as the words were out of my mouth, I knew I had said the wrong thing. Mulligan shot me the steely eye and said, "Just like me? Wait a minute, Jack. I was in the Nam, the real thing: Khe Sanh, the Mekong, up to my hips in sword grass and VC. I didn't spend my hitch flying over the desert mowing down camel jockeys from a helicopter."

That was all it took. All at once, I was back there, hanging out the door of the Huey, strapped into my monkey harness, the hot wind from the rotors in my face, the mini-gun stuttering in my hands, shitting hot brass, tearing up the countryside and the people below. They didn't look like people. They looked like cartoons in a video game. Sometimes one of them would give a jump before he fell. We all thought that was funny. *Run, you suckers!*

"You've got quite a way with words, Mulligan," I said. "May I have another beer?"

"Oh, what's with the face?" Mulligan said. "What, I hurt your feelings or something?"

"Just give me the beer." I was seeing, again, everything that had happened after that. My tour was up and I went Stateside and promptly disappeared. There was nothing left of me. I even tried becoming a priest, looking for what? Redemption? Remission? Reformation? I couldn't make the cut. They told me I had lost my faith. If only that's all I had lost.

"You're pretty touchy all of a sudden," Mulligan said, drawing another one.

Mulligan is like a three-year-old. He can't keep his fingers off a scab. "I can see you're not going to let this go," I told him. "All right, I'm not outside there with the Junior Woodchucks because I don't give a damn what happens. You know what happens if you mow enough camel jockeys down? They don't seem like the enemy anymore. They were just poor, frightened SOB's, running for their lives, running from *me*, like I was the freaking Angel of Death or something."

Mulligan stared at his shoes. "Hey, look Jack, I didn't mean—"

But I was wound up. It was like I had to punish him. Or myself. "You should have seen them run, Mulligan. You should have seen them fall. I did see them, and finally, I had to tuck them away in a little back corner of my brain and decide I didn't give a damn about them. After a while *that* wasn't enough, and pretty soon, I didn't give a damn about anything.

"That's why I come to this genteel establishment every day: because I don't give a damn about finding a job or making the world a better place or making myself a better person or anything else. I am contentedly and categorically *uninvolved*. I do care about you, though, Mulligan. I love you, because you're the only human being on the face of the earth with an attitude that's worse than mine."

There was a silence like a cancer ward, and then Mulligan said, "Here's your beer," and set it on the bar.

I took a long swallow and glanced up at the TV. "The game's on."

Mulligan turned the sound back up and we watched in silence for a while. Both teams played like they'd been partying all last night. There were intermittent displays of uninspired action separated by long stretches where nothing happened at all.

The thing about Mulligan was, he really *was* like a three-year-old. You couldn't stay mad at him for long. "Listen, Mulligan," I said, "why don't you drum up some business with the 'do-gooders' brigade out there? That yelling must be awful thirsty work."

Mulligan shook his head. "Nah, look at 'em. They're all granola-heads. College kids. They don't drink nothin' but bottled water and fruit juice. They're not gonna come in here. I figure today, it's just me and you..." he whispered the last part, "and that crazy guy at the last table."

"There's somebody crazy in here besides you?"

"Shhhh!" he said, like we were passing gossip in the schoolyard. "Back there."

"What, that black guy? *He's* crazy?" The guy in the last booth was maybe forty, well groomed, and dressed in a three-piece suit, obviously expensive. He was sitting quietly, staring into his drink. The man did not look like a lunatic. Mulligan said, "He don't look it, right? All dressed up like a Harvard p'fessa." He leaned even closer. "He plays with dolls."

"What?"

"He's been here since five O'clock, drinking Bermuda highballs and playing with this doll. You don't believe me, right? You think I'm making it up? Go look for yourself. G'wan, it's right there on the table. I'll bet you a beer it's like I said. I'll bet you *two* beers."

See what I mean? Three-year-old. All you can do is humor him. I strolled towards the back of the room, hoping I was doing a convincing imitation of someone going to check out the jukebox. Sure enough, sitting on the table, by the ashtray, was a *doll*. It was about five inches tall and made of straw or something. I shifted my gaze slightly and found myself looking straight into the black man's eyes. He was staring right at me. I should have just walked back to the bar. I'm sorry I didn't. What stopped me were his eyes. I had never seen eyes like that before. It was like something was *smoldering* behind them.

"I was just noticing your doll," I said. "I was wondering where you'd gotten it. I'd like to get my kid one like that." Lying like a rug here.

He stared a little longer and then said, "It is not a toy; it is a juju." His voice was smooth and cultured, very quiet. He sounded British.

"A juju. Okay," I said, and started back to the bar.

"Wait," he said, "sit down." Those eyes again. "Sit down."

I sat, throwing Mulligan a helpless look. He was engrossed in the game. Some pal. The black man took a cigarette from a pack lying on the table and lit it with a gunmetal Zippo lighter. He said, "Would you like a cigarette?"

"I don't smoke."

"You have no child," he went on. "You wanted to find out about me. I shall tell you. All these years I have never told anyone, but I shall tell you, because I need to tell someone now. Perhaps it will help me decide."

"Decide what?"

"What is to be done with him," he said, motioning towards the doll.

"Oh, I see."

"No, you do not. But you will. Do you know what a juju is? It is a man. A man's soul. And his body."

"Who's this?" I asked.

His face never changed. "General Immamu M'Buotu."

"That's the guy all this fuss is about," I said. "Over at the Rochester. Some kind of dictator or something."

"Not *some* kind," said the black man, "the **worst** kind. A murderer, countless times over." He took another puff on his cigarette, and a nimbus of smoke began to form about his head.

"I remember seeing on TV," I said, "after the revolution that kicked this General out, there was a concentration camp out in the jungle—"

"Mogandu."

"Yeah, that's the place," I said. "I remember there was this ditch all filled with skulls."

He paused, took another drag. "Some of them were of children. He has spilt much blood. My country has been drowned in it. He took most of the treasury with him when he fled and went from country to country looking for a haven. And now he is here, right across the street. I am afraid your government may let him stay."

"What's all this got to do with you?"

"I owe him a debt that only the juju can repay," the black man went on. "Sit quietly and I shall tell you a story."

I considered making a break for it, but I didn't think I needed to. If things started to get too strange, I knew that Mulligan kept a Louisville Slugger behind the bar that was very effective at calming people down. It seemed more prudent to stay. And there were those eyes.

"Many years ago," he said, "when I was a boy, I lived in a small village with my father and mother and sisters. The name is not important; it is not there now. Life was good then. My clan was respected. My father's brother was *nganga* to the village.

"You would say 'witch doctor', but you would be wrong. That is not what *nganga* is. My uncle was a healer. He could set a man at peace with the *vadzimu*—the ancestors. He knew the herbal lore and the spirit talk, and he could break spells. These things are true. I have seen them. My uncle was a good man, but that does not matter now.

"One night, hours before dawn, the soldiers came. M'Buotu was not yet a general, but even then he was a powerful man. He owned copper mines and he needed workers. My village was small. No one would miss it when it was gone. The soldiers turned us out of our homes and began to herd us into the trucks.

"We had heard about the mines. No one ever came back from them. My father tried to resist, and the captain in charge took out his pistol and shot him dead. He forced my uncle and me into one of the trucks. My mother and sisters were put in another; I never saw them again. As the trucks pulled away, I saw my uncle staring at the captain. I heard him say in a voice that chilled me, '*Ti cha sangana.*'—We will meet again.

"The trucks drove on through most of the night. When they finally slowed down to ford a stream, my uncle leaped from the back, dragging me with him. We ran and hid in the tall grass. We could hear the soldiers searching for us, and then, after a long time, the trucks pulled away and there was silence.

"I was frightened, exhausted, but my uncle forced me to stay awake with him. He took some of the grass and fashioned two jujus. Then he took something from the *zango* 'round his arm and showed it to me. It was a button from the captain's tunic that he had torn off in the confusion. He tied it to one of the jujus. Then he gathered several long thorns. What happened after that, I have seen many times since in my worst nightmares."

Now he seemed to be someplace else. I wondered if he could feel the hot wind of the savanna on his face, hear the rustling of the long grass, smell the animal smells.

"My uncle took two of the thorns and placed them on the head where the eyes would be. Then he slowly pushed them in. A while later, he pushed in another, just below the head. After that: another, in the middle of the body. Then another: between the legs, where they joined the body. Each time, he told me what was happening to the captain.

"Finally, just before dawn, he built a fire and hung the juju over it. It was a mad thing to do. I watched it scorch and blacken and burst into flame. And I watched my uncle's face as he stared at the fire, saw it change. I realized he was no longer a *nganga*. He was a *muroyi*—a witch.

"Then we heard the shouts, and we knew that all of the soldiers had not left with the trucks. They had seen our fire. My uncle thrust the second juju into my hands and made me swear that I would do for General M'Buotu what he had done for the captain. He called down the wrath of the *vadzimu* upon me, should I ever break my oath. Then he left me, to go draw the soldiers away. I sat there, too terrified to move. Shortly afterwards, I heard the shots.

"I do not know how long I sat there. Someone found me at last and brought me to the missionary clinic. I was almost dead from exposure, but I still clutched the juju so tightly that they could not prise my fingers from it."

He lit another smoke, snapped the lighter shut and stared at me. "You're very quiet."

"None of this explains how you wound up here," I said, "or what you're intending to do."

"When I finally told my story, they realized at the clinic that I must be got away. They disguised me as a servant and brought me to England. The missionary's brother was a bishop. He adopted me and sent me to public school, and later to university. Everywhere I went, the juju went with me.

"Through the bishop's influence, I obtained a position at the university. I saved every penny I could. Throughout all those years I kept hearing of the General—his seizing of power in the capital and the bloodbath that followed—all those years of anguish and degradation in my homeland. I was the one man who could stop him, but I had to obtain something that belonged to him first, to set the juju's spell.

"I was ready to go, last year, when the coup came that toppled him from power. The General was expelled from the country and all my plans had come to nothing. I followed him in the press to Italy and Brazil. I flew to Mexico to intercept him there, but I could not get near him. Then Colombia, then Ecuador. My money was almost gone. At last, he came here. This afternoon, the last of my money went for a bribe that got me into his room at the Rochester. I took one of his handkerchiefs and walked across the street to this place to keep my oath, to pay my debt, to have my vengeance."

And then he stopped. His eyes had that faraway look again. I waited a few seconds and then said, "Well, what happened?"

He gestured with his cigarette. "There is the juju, you see, with the

85

handkerchief 'round it, just as it was when I came in. I have done nothing, nothing at all."

"I don't understand."

"Nor do I, sir." He shook his head ruefully. He stabbed out his smoke and lit another. "When I first came in, I went up to the barman to order a drink. I saw my face in the mirror behind him. But it was not my face; it was my uncle's face, flickering in the firelight. It was the face that has terrified me in my nightmares ever since that night. I took my drink and walked over to this table. I sat down and started to think about what I had become, what I might yet become."

"Listen, Mister—"

He looked at me suddenly. "Have you ever killed a man?"

*Run, you suckers!*

"Yeah," I said after a moment, "One or two."

"I have never done. I can't imagine what it would be like."

"Nobody can," I told him. "When you're doing it, you feel like the wrath of God."

"The wrath of God—"

"Then afterwards, you feel like crap. It's the second feeling that lasts."

I'm not sure he heard me.

"I do not know if I can do it," he said. "To take a man's life, even a man like the General, is a terrible thing. I think this, and then in my mind, I see the ditch at Mogandu: all those skulls. And I think: Who can allow such a creature to live? I have no answer."

He stopped for a moment, as though he had emptied himself. I just looked at him, failed priest of a sort. I noticed there was more than anger in his eyes. There was despair as well. I felt we had something in common.

"Thirty years I have waited for this moment," he went on, "and now I do not know what to do. Not so long ago, in my homeland, that was a man's whole lifetime…a man's whole life."

His drink was mostly water now, but he drank it down as if the answer were there. "They said on the television that the General might be extradited. There will be a decision today. He would have to return to Shambra and be punished for his crimes. If this is so, *they* will take my vengeance. I would not have to make this awful choice, the choice I have sworn to make.

"So, I sit here and wait, hoping to take the coward's way out."

"Listen," I told him, "I don't think you're a coward. I think you're showing a lot of sense. If I were in your shoes, I'd be doing the same thing. Let somebody else handle it. I'm telling you, if you do manage to take this guy out, you'll have to carry the weight of it for the rest of your life. I know what I'm talking about."

"So, you do believe me?" His face had the expression of someone plucked from the ocean after being adrift for weeks.

"I don't know," I said. "I feel like I'm about to make Pascal's Wager. Do you know about that?"

"About the existence of Hell."

"Pascal said if you don't know for sure that Hell exists, all you can do is bet your life against the afterlife. Try to live as if there were a Hell, and when you die, if it turns out you're wrong, you haven't really lost anything, except maybe a couple of cheap thrills. But, if you were right, and there really is a Hell, then you've managed to avoid it by living a good life.

"Well, I figure the prudent thing to do is to act as if your story were true. If it turns out it's not, nobody gets hurt. If it is true—well, I don't know what the hell that means."

"I am in no uncertainty about the existence of Hell," said the black man. "I have been there."

"That's what I mean." I grabbed his shoulder; I tried not to fall into those black, terrifying eyes. "You're all tangled up in this mess; you're not thinking clearly. Walk away from it now, before you're in something you can't walk away from."

I think I startled him.

"Why do you care about this?" he said.

"Why did you start talking to me?" I asked him.

"I told you," he said, "I had to talk to someone. No, that is not entirely true. When I saw you, I felt…"

"Some kind of connection."

"Yes." He just looked at me, the smoldering cigarette forgotten in the ashtray.

"I felt it, too. I don't know what it is, but you and I have more in common than we realize."

"What could the two of us possibly have in common?" he asked, as if he were asking the Universe.

"I don't know. Maybe because we're both…unfinished. You feel it, too. Maybe when you sat down here, you weren't really waiting for what the State Department had to say."

"What do you mean?"

I scarcely knew what I meant, myself.

"Maybe you were waiting for *me*. So I could talk you out of this. Call it Fate; call it whatever you want. I think I was supposed to meet you here to stop you."

Saying it out loud made it seem like the truest, most self-evident statement in the world.

"And that's why I'm telling you to give this up. All right, so he's a horrible guy and he should have been shot in the cradle. I'm not trying to make light of what happened to you, but what real difference does it make if the General is stopped or not? It's not going to change anything. In the end, it won't matter at all. It's not worth destroying your life for."

"You don't believe in good and evil?"

That hit home.

"I used to, a long time ago. I believed in a lot of things a long time ago, but it never did me any good. I wound up like that old joke of the guy out on a limb with a handsaw, just sawing away between him and the tree. That's my life in a nutshell."

"And what do you believe in now?"

"I believe in self-preservation."

"No, you are wrong." He shook his head violently. "Evil does exist, and it must be resisted. It is worth something to stop it: a man's whole life, perhaps."

Behind me, I heard Mulligan say, "Oh, Jeez, what now?"

I could just make out the TV screen. The reporter was back.

"There's a bulletin coming on the TV," I said.

The black man and I both stood up and hurried to the front of the room.

Mulligan said, "Carpenter was just gonna hit into a double play."

"Shut up, Mulligan," I said.

There she was again, the plastic news lady. *"This is Blair Holland, Channel 12 Action News, reporting live from the Hotel Rochester. The State Department has just announced that deposed African dictator, General Immamu M'Buotu, will not be returned to Shambra to stand trial. This owing to the absence of any valid extradition treaty between the two countries, according to a State Department spokesman."*

The black man looked like someone had just handed him a cobra. His eyes were wide, his face twisted in a look of horror. He kept repeating, "Oh, no, no."

"Take it easy," I told him, but I don't think he heard me.

*"Police have cordoned off the demonstrators here outside the Rochester, and we have word that General M'Buotu will be leaving the hotel momentarily on his way to a meeting with State Department officials. We're going to try to get some kind of statement when he comes out."*

He started pounding on the bar. "No, this cannot be."

I didn't know what to say. "Calm down, now. Maybe there's something—"

But all at once, he was staring at the mirror behind the bar. His face had such a look of terror, as I have never seen before. He pointed with a trembling hand, "Look!"

Mulligan and I both gave him a blank stare.

"In the mirror; don't you see?" His voice was *all wrong*. He was getting hysterical.

"What are you talking about?" I said.

"It's my uncle," he said.

"Mister," I told him, "there's nobody in that mirror but the two of us and Mulligan."

"He's watching me." He was almost shrieking. "He knows what I have tried to do!"

"I'm telling you, there's nobody there."

But he was beyond listening. He began to babble, "I must get the juju. I must get the juju." He nearly fell, scrambling back to his table. He grabbed the little doll and headed for the front door.

I grabbed him. "Get a hold of yourself!" I yelled. "Stop and think. Do you know what you're doing?" I'm a big guy, and I'm in pretty good shape, but he had the strength of a maniac.

"Let me go!" he shouted. "I know what I must do. Let me go!" He broke free and was out the door before I could stop him. I ran after him, but he was gone, lost in the crowd.

I came back inside and looked at Mulligan.

"Didn't I tell you that guy was screwy?" he said.

"Mulligan, don't you ever make a bet with me again."

"What did I do?"

On the TV, the newswoman said, *"And I see the General's limousine has just pulled up here, so we should be seeing — yes here comes the General, flanked, as always, by his many bodyguards.*

*"General! Do you have any comment on the State Department—"*

"Give me another beer, Mulligan," I said. "This one's gone flat."

He drew another and I sat sipping it with the jabber of the news in the background, trying to make sense of what had just happened.

"Hey," he said, "I heard a swell joke the other day. There's this rabbi, a steamfitter and a topless dancer, and they're all up in this hot air balloon, see? So anyway, the rabbi says—"

But something on the screen had caught my attention.

"Wait a minute."

What," said Mulligan, "you heard it?"

"Pipe down."

The cameras had pulled back to show a commotion in the crowd. It was the black man and he was yelling, **"Murderer! Monster! You cannot escape!"**

The newswoman said, *"There's some sort of disturbance in the crowd. Someone has apparently slipped through the police line."*

Mulligan said, "Hey, it's that guy with the doll."

I was just staring at the screen.

"Oh, no," I said. "Get away."

*"A man there in the open, you can see him. He's calling something to the General. I see some police officers coming now to round him up—and he has gotten past the police. He's running this way."*

On the TV, the man was yelling, **"You cannot escape, you murderer!"**

I was yelling, too.

"Get out of there, you idiot, go back!"

The TV screen was filled with swirling movement. *"The man has something in his hand, I can't quite make it out, like straw or something, wrapped in a white cloth. Wait, there's something in his other hand, something metallic. It's a gun!"*

I shouted louder. I pounded on the bar.

"No, no. It's not a gun! No!"

We heard three gunshots in rapid succession. The camera swirled and bounced as if it were on a roller coaster.

*"And the General's bodyguards have shot the man. He's down. You can see him there on the pavement."*

Mulligan said, "Jeez."

For the first time in I can't remember when, I started *weeping*. I put my head on the bar and just sobbed.

"No, no, it wasn't a gun; it was his damn cigarette lighter."

*"He's not moving. The man is down and I can't see any movement. Police are coming from every direction now. I guess they've disarmed him."*

Before I quite knew what I was doing, I was out the door and into the crowd. I heard Mulligan calling behind me. I was jostled and shoved, and pushed back. The cops were having a hard time riding herd on the gawkers. I finally found what I was looking for and went back into Mulligan's.

Mulligan said, "Where'd you go?"

*"I don't see that other object the assailant was holding, that thing that looked like a clump of straw or dried grass, perhaps, or possibly—"*

"Hey," said Mulligan, "you got that doll."

"Turn that off," I said.

He switched off the TV. "What do you want that thing for?"

"I *was* meant to meet him here, Mulligan, but not to stop him."

"Huh?"

"Have you ever heard of Pascal's Wager?"

"What's that, like a Trifecta?"

"Never mind. Let me have that ashtray."

He slid the heavy glass along the bar. "Jack, what's got into you? What's with the doll in the ashtray?"

"Do you have any matches?"

"What are you gonna do?"

"Just give me the matches, Mulligan."

He tossed a box of kitchen matches my way. I struck one and touched the flame to the juju. A fire blossomed at once with a crackling sound.

Mulligan reached for it, "Hey, I don't want no fires in here!"

I grabbed his arm, more tightly than I meant to. "Don't touch it! Let it burn."

Mulligan looked at me with something like fear in his eyes. "What's this all about, Jack?" he said in a low voice. "What do you think you're doin'?"

"We'll see, Mulligan," I told him. "We'll see."

# THE TRAP
## Dale W. Glaser

"Hey, demon!" an eager voice called out.

Corin Garry stopped in his tracks, turned around, and crossed his arms over his chest, a slow and deliberate performance that also took care not to snag any of his black, press-on talons.

"What?" he snarled, compensating with guttural ferocity for having removed his plastic fangs.

They pulled up short within a few feet of him, two boys no more than eleven years old, in semi-disheveled costumes; the light-haired boy in the black *gi* had been wearing a ninja mask earlier, as Corin recalled. His dark-haired friend still wore his bone-embossed gloves and polyester reaper's robe, but the hood had fallen back to reveal his unadorned face.

"That haunted house was so boss!" Reaper said. He let his plastic scythe fall to the crook of his arm, reached his free hand into his bag, and pulled out a Tootsie Pop.

"Thank you so much," Ninja said, with the earnestness reserved for heartfelt gratitude, absent from mumbled thanks prompted by parents. "Nobody around here ever does anything that awesome."

Corin couldn't help but grin at that, despite the expression tugging at the spirit gum holding his demonic half-mask in place. "You're welcome, little dudes," he said, in his normal voice.

"You gonna do it next year?" Reaper asked, Tootsie Pop bulging in one cheek.

"Probably," Corin said. "If we all still live here."

Someone coming up from behind bumped Corin's shoulder. "Nice hair," Alyssa said.

Corin shook his head, tossing the mask's cascade of black nylon strands. "This old thing?" he asked. "My real hair was longer, in high school."

"Yeah?" Alyssa asked.

"By graduation," Corin confirmed. "Cut most of it off after I got to college. Too much hassle."

"Because you stopped showering before classes?" she teased.

Ninja and Reaper had been staring at Alyssa since she approached. Finally, Reaper recognized her. "No way, it's the girl in the TV!"

The boys had to be younger than Corin had thought, ten years old, maybe nine. Alyssa was a gorgeous fairyland vision: hair swept up off her long, slender neck and piled in a dirty blonde flounce atop her head, shimmering blue eye makeup rendering her green eyes more come-hither than usual, lips glossed iridescent pink, clear straps of diaphanous wings clinging to bare shoulders, mini dress showing off cleavage and curves, glittery tights sheathing shapely legs. But Ninja and Reaper's matching expressions conveyed no lust, only the curiosity and awe of boys beholden to cooties, not beauties.

Alyssa gave Reaper a quick glance and polite, yet confused, smile. Her eyes flicked to Corin as if seeking a proper introduction. Then her brow knitted as a haunted, faraway look fell across her face. She looked back at the boys, stricken, back at Corin again, and started shaking her head, rhythmically, relentlessly. "No, no," she chanted, closing her eyes. "No, no, no," she repeated. "No!" Her eyes flew open, pleading and drilling into Corin's. "You promised! You promised I would never have to think about that place again! Never! No! Noooo!" The last was the keening of a forsaken soul.

"Yo, let's get out of here!" Reaper said, smacking Ninja's shoulder as he spun on his heel. Ninja was already in parallel flight. They whooped as they sprinted across the common green, children pretending to be in mortal danger, but Corin heard an undercurrent of genuine fear as he watched them go.

He looked at Alyssa, who was smiling, kittenishly pleased with herself. "Yes?" she asked innocently.

"I ...was not expecting that."

"And...?"

"And, I am impressed."

"And...?"

"I think I'm in love," he half-sighed, half-laughed.

"Idiot," she grinned, pushing him away. "I take it the haunted house was a hit?"

"Big time, and obviously in large part thanks to you," Corin said.

"Well, I'm glad you guys had fun."

"That's why I moved down here," he said. "You theater kids know how to have a good time."

"So why aren't you at the after party?" Alyssa asked.

"Dave made, like, six hours of mixed CD's, but Becky asked if we'd put on the Donnas. Who are not in the mix," he explained.

"But they're in your car?"

"Well, a copy of their CD is," he admitted. "If the four ladies are actually in my car, I might not be back for a while."

"Shame," Alyssa cooed. "So, I have to walk the rest of the way by myself?"

"Unless you come with me real quick …"

"I wouldn't want the Donnas to think you were taken," she said with mock solemnity. "Besides, these heels are cute but killing my feet. I gotta get inside in the fewest number of steps possible."

"I'll buy you a drink once I get back," he promised.

She threw a scoffing "ha" back over her shoulder. Corin continued in the opposite direction. Streetlights glowed as the twilight shadows deepened. He leaned across the driver's seat, ejected the CD and didn't bother to locate the jewel case. Holding the disc on one finger like an ill-fitting silver ring, he jogged back, taking the steep front steps two at a time.

In just a few minutes, he had missed a small wave of arrivals. Mitch's cousin, Lisa, dressed as a slasher surgeon, hospital-green scrubs and cap liberally splattered with fake blood; her boyfriend, Steve, kitted out in an ironically ill-fitting sexy nurse costume with matching bloodstains; two of Blake's co-workers, who either hadn't heard or hadn't believed that it was a costume party.

Blake was working the bar, his face still painted like a demented jack-o-lantern, although he had shed the heavy black leather biker jacket. Corin held the CD out to him. "One sec," Blake said, cracking open a can of soda and finishing a cocktail. "Seven and seven for you," Blake said, passing the drink to the co-worker to his left, whom Corin was gratified to see had at least worn an orange t-shirt with GENERIC HALLOWEEN COSTUME block-lettered across the chest. "And you wanted...?" Blake pivoted to his other colleague.

"G and T?"

"Right, right," Blake nodded, taking the CD without looking. He swapped bottles, whiskey for gin, with one hand, and fed the disc into the stereo with the other. Corin, Blake and Mitch had thrown enough house parties to know that the stereo belonged behind the bar, where only authorized persons could operate it. A moment later, the opening riff kicked in. From a corner of the couch, Becky shouted, "Woo!" Corin was already injecting himself back into the party, crossing the room to Lisa and Steve.

"Hey," he yelled above the music, shaking Steve's hand. "Long time!"

Steve nodded. "How ya been, man?"

"Good, good." Corin looked around restlessly, scanning the faces in the gathering. "You guys good? Drinks?" Steve and Lisa both held up full beverages. "Cool. Be right back!" He headed for the back door.

The townhouse's deck was so small it felt overcrowded by the half dozen assembled partygoers, including Mitch, in torn clothes and werewolf makeup. Cigarette smoldering in the corner of his mouth, he was giving a light to a girl dressed as a go-go dancer, standing next to another smoking girl in a nearly identical costume. Corin didn't recognize either of the go-go girls. Alyssa stood by herself, in the far corner, leaning against the railing. Corin moved to join her.

The deck shook as heavy footfalls bounded up the stairs, and Paul appeared, dressed in jeans and a white tank top with a red cape tied around his neck and a beer in each hand. "Cor-blimey!" Paul boomed as he spied Corin; he never tired of making that play on Corin's name. Paul handed one bottle to Alyssa and offered the other to Corin. "Beer?"

"What about you?" Corin asked.

"I'll get myself another. Take it, take it!" Corin accepted the bottle and Paul thundered down the stairs, cape flying out behind him.

"I didn't know he was coming," Corin said, twisting off the bottle cap.

"Captain Wife beater? No, me neither," Alyssa sighed. "That get-up of his is so stupid." She attempted to open her beer barehanded, gave up, and then plucked at her skimpy costume to gather enough material to palm the cap. Corin silently held his hand out, took her beer, opened it, and passed it back. She tipped it toward him appreciatively and they clinked longnecks.

She was lying about Paul. Neither Blake nor Mitch would have invited him. Corin couldn't understand why Alyssa wouldn't simply admit having mentioned the party to Paul, unless their perpetual cycle of reuniting and splitting again was nearing another reconciliation phase. Paul reappeared and Alyssa's shifting body language gave Corin the confirmation he hadn't really needed. "Be right back," Corin excused himself, retreating inside.

Already, more costumed revelers had joined the scene, none of whom Corin knew well, if at all. He looked around the room and saw nothing but conversations, already deep underway, circles already formed by Mitch and Blake's friends, and friends-of-their-friends. Blake was constructing a complicated, layered drink, for an audience surrounding the bar. The consummate theater techie, always happiest building something, like the bar itself, a stage prop he'd kept after a summer production, or like the deceptively simple structures that had transformed their garage into a hall of horrors.

A flush of envy and isolation roared through Corin, propelling him through the crowd, toward the door to the basement. He descended the staircase and passed through the garage door at the bottom, entering the now empty haunted house.

Blake had framed out two rough, freestanding walls, a long one and a short one, at right angles to each other, all in one day's vacation from work. With the evening hours of children trick-or-treating past, the pine two-by-fours, draped in slashed black garbage bags and decorated with cobwebs, had been pulled all the way into the garage, the door rolled down. Earlier in the afternoon, the structure had jutted out into the empty driveway. A child walking up the driveway would see the left side of the garage blocked off and the right side open. Younger or fainter-hearted children could collect candy from a bowl at the bottom of the front steps, near the open side of the garage. The brave ones could enter the garage, proceed all the way to the back, walk a 180 hairpin around the temporary center wall, and follow it out to the dogleg exit. The horseshoe path took the trick-or-treaters past a cinderblock utility alcove, converted into a cage with spray-painted plywood and dowels, also Blake's handiwork. Corin had played the demon in the cage, slavering and growling and trying to grab children through the bars. In the back right corner, Mitch had hunched and lunged as a chained werewolf; in the opposite corner, a jumbled pile of televisions and electronic junk were stacked on a table. Down the other side of the garage, the trick-or-treaters proceeded to Blake, the punk-pumpkinhead handing out candy and ushering the children back into the night.

Corin approached the televisions; his major creative contribution to what was otherwise a borrowed idea. The annual Halloween haunted house garage was a Donnelly family tradition from Mitch's childhood, one which Alyssa had taken part in many times, growing up right around the corner.

Corin and Mitch had gone to Mitch's parents to raid their basement for haunted house props and supplies: old chains, rubber bats and rats and spiders, strobe light and smoke machine. In the back of the basement, Corin noticed multiple television sets gathering dust, several of them with built-in VCRs. He asked if they still worked, and Mitch explained they had been replaced by newer models, not damaged, with enough interrogation in his voice to prompt Corin to explain what he was thinking.

"The garage has four corners, but there's only three of us, since Alyssa wants to come to the party in something cute and doesn't want to change out of a monster get-up, right?" he began. "So, we set these up where Alyssa should be. We put in some videos of horror movies and just let them play. Not really graphic ones; the classics. Your dad collects *Universal Monsters* movies, right?"

"They aren't going to work perfectly," Mitch warned. "This one, for sure, had squiggles down one side of the picture."

"That's OK," Corin said. "Don't you think? If the TVs are a little bit off, kinda broken, that just adds to the ambience. Neglect and disrepair, man. It's the video equivalent of cobwebs in the windows or moss on a tombstone."

"Maybe. But then, this one is older than VCRs," Mitch kicked a set with a faux-wood case. "I don't think you could even hook one up."

"We can work with that," Corin said. "We just have it on, showing snow. It'll be super-creepy, like Poltergeist."

Back at the townhouse, unloading the televisions, along with the rest of the gear, Mitch mused aloud, "We could make a movie, too, with my camcorder."

"Totally," Corin agreed, inwardly cursing for not thinking of it. "You think Alyssa would be in it?"

"Our little diva? She'll do it, if it's good material."

"Like what?"

"You tell me, hoss, you're the writer," Mitch had delegated.

In the main set's inert screen, Corin could see his own spectral reflection. He didn't see a writer, he saw a temp who did clerical work for slightly more than minimum wage, dressed in too tight Lycra and wearing a prosthetic hooknose and horns. He pulled the mask off, spirit gum stinging as it tore away from his cheeks, and felt profoundly foolish. What had he thought? That Alyssa would want him if he proved he was just like them, that he could join their garage troupe, wear a costume and get into character and put on a show? Had he honestly, for one moment, expected that near the end of the party, sitting on the couch, Alyssa would lean over and start kissing him deeply, with yearning, while stroking his fright wig? Or that she would sit on the edge of his bed and wait patiently while he ditched the costume and took a jar of Noxzema to the red greasepaint on his face? Stupid moron.

Corin reached behind the televisions, felt for the surge protector, toggled its power switch. The screens came to life, slowly, long-neglected cathode tubes warming up. The central monitor, the largest in the group of four, became a slightly brighter shade of dark gray, with yellow-green letters reading A/V in its upper corner. The TV to the right, cocked at a 45-degree angle against the central set, was somewhere in the middle of the *Creature from the Black Lagoon*. The TV to the left, flat on its side, was the antiquated static-only set, and the small TV surmounting the sideways set and the central one, in a crooked straddle, showed the end of *Frankenstein*.

The central television was connected directly to a camcorder wedged into the angular space beneath the *Black Lagoon* set. Corin pressed 'Play' on the camera. Alyssa's crying face appeared in close-up on the big screen, her makeup in ruins, bloody welts at her right temple and on the left side of her neck.

"Let me out! Let me out! Hello? Anyone? I don't belong in here! Please let me out! Please!" She banged her fists on the screen, sobbing. "Somebody get me out of here!" she wailed.

Alyssa had, of course, thrown herself into the role, once Corin had suggested the basic concept he'd come up with; not a narrative movie, but a character – another prisoner in the hall of horrors, like the demon and the werewolf. Alyssa insisted on improvising for several minutes without the camera running, brainstorming with Corin, then managed a single, uninterrupted fifteen minute take. Alyssa was born to perform and could turn it on at will. Given the slightest time to compose herself and get into the zone, she was devastating.

She still looked beautiful, magnetic, even with multiple fake wounds and runny mascara streaming down her cheeks. It wasn't that the thought of her being terrified or in pain turned Corin on, but the power of her performance. Alyssa was insanely talented and possessed of so much passion that she could evoke exactly what he had envisioned and make it real. That passion made her incandescent to him, regardless of the subject matter. He wanted to incorporate himself into it somehow, any way that he could, and always had. From the day they had met years ago on campus, an English major seeking actors to put on a one-act play he was writing for class, and a drama major trying out for extra credit, Corin had wanted to give Alyssa the perfect words to speak, the quintessential character to play. Anything that involved mingling her passion with his, on stage, or in private.

Corin drank some more beer, barely tasting it. It was too late for him and Alyssa; even in college it had already been too late. He cast her in his play, but the parts had already been written before he met her and the deadline for the assignment left no time to re-write for her. They never collaborated again. And she had already been on-again, off-again with Paul by the time she met Corin, too. She had no reason to look twice at Corin, with someone taller and fit, and with a real career in IT consulting locked in her personal orbit, and her locked in his. Which left only this: a slapdash home movie to liven up a Halloween lark; the closest Corin could ever get.

His beer was emptied. He briefly considered heading out back for another one, but watching Alyssa's inspired and virtuosa freakout, he had no desire to be interrupted. Instead, he turned off the overhead lights, leaving only the irregular glow of the four TV screens. He could still hear a steady murmur from overhead, so he turned up the televisions showing actual movies. If this was the only way he could be alone with Alyssa, he wanted the illusion of perfect solitude.

On screen, Alyssa threw her head back and screamed. The recording was close to the end, and Corin told himself that when it ran out he would rejoin the party, salvage what he could of the night. He could claim he had turned on the televisions on impulse and been drawn into watching Alyssa against his will, but restarting the recording of her from the beginning would be a conscious choice to wallow in pathetic misery. And although a very large part of him wanted to, he had enough pride to stop himself from giving in to it. He hoped.

Alyssa continued calling for help that would never come. For the haunted house, they had balanced the volume of all the televisions so that Alyssa was audible, but just barely; her voice bound up in the mix of hissing snow and dialogue and music, just as her image was imprisoned in the confines of the screen. With *Frankenstein* and *Black Lagoon* turned up even louder now, Alyssa was drowned out. She almost seemed to realize it, as she stopped calling for help, only crying and slapping her open palms against the screen in abject frustration. The screen effect was a nice touch, courtesy of Blake, who had obliged Corin with a large, clear sheet of Lucite from his set-building stockpile. Corin had filmed Alyssa through it, removing the need for her to mime the front surface of her cage. Now, in the playback of her recorded gestures, fatigue was setting in, as the blows of her hands came slower, weaker. Her forehead thudded against the screen in defeat.

Corin didn't remember her doing that when he had filmed her.

How could he *not* remember? He had been just as riveted by the live performance as he was by the recording. He might have been a little distracted, since they were in her bedroom, and the backdrop was one of her black silk bed sheets, which Alyssa claimed was for special occasions. Certain thoughts, neither unpleasant nor entirely unbidden, had entered his mind, and might have distracted him. But he would have remembered a gesture as dramatic as her forehead hitting the screen. Wouldn't he?

Corin tried to remember what came next, how close the recording was to hitting the end. He had no idea. He stared at Alyssa's larger-than-life face on the screen. She stared back at him, her breath hitching, as if all her tears were spent, exhaustion overtaking primal terror. *Imaginary primal terror*, Corin reminded himself. He had given her the idea of being trapped inside a television, a tiny, isolated, solitary confinement, and she had run with it, but it *wasn't* real. No matter how distraught, how destroyed, Alyssa looked on the screen, it **wasn't real**. It wasn't her, it wasn't even an image of her, it was an image of a fictional character they had co-created and hadn't even bothered to give a backstory or name. Corin felt a twinge of retrograde guilt.

Alyssa's lips were moving, and some of the hopelessness had faded from her eyes, replaced by something compelling. Corin was inexplicably curious about what she was saying; the same word over and over again. Alyssa swallowed hard and spoke again; if the television had not been muted, Corin knew, her voice would have been louder, more insistent. She had a strong voice. He wanted to hear it.

The set filled with static had a silver knob the size of a pushpin, which he turned to the left until it clicked and the screen went dead; the snow condensing to a fading dot of light. The sets showing the monster movies had square power buttons, inset flush along their front frames, but Corin found himself reaching for the volume controls and turning them all the way down. He didn't necessarily want to be alone with the recording of Alyssa, he just wanted to hear what she was saying. When Richard Carlson and Colin Clive had been silenced, Corin found the buttons on the central set and turned the sound up.

"Corin?" Alyssa asked, her voice raw from screaming. "Corin?"

It was a different version of the recording; that was the only explanation. His mind might have wandered in Alyssa's bedroom, he might have drifted in and out of a daydream or two, but he could have been visualizing her naked and writhing in graphic detail and he still would have noticed if she had begun calling *his* name. Corin didn't know when Alyssa had recorded the additional footage, or why; most likely, Mitch had put her up to it, as a joke.

He reached over and behind the television to grab the camcorder and turn it off. He disconnected the coaxials and pulled out the camcorder, half-tempted to smash it on the garage floor, which would serve Mitch right. He stepped back, and the sight of Alyssa peering out at him froze him in place.

Alyssa onscreen.

The disconnected camcorder, in his hand.

No feed to the television.

Alyssa *onscreen*.

"Corin? Can you hear me?"

The amplified terror in her voice was painfully real, an icicle plunging into the base of his skull, making him blink, as cold pooled behind his eyes. Corin dropped the camcorder, not in anger, but because his limbs had gone numb, as if he were having some kind of waking dream, the kind where a monster was charging up behind him and he couldn't run, couldn't even move.

"Corin," Alyssa pleaded. "I don't know where I am, how I got here, I'm so freaked out right now. I think I see you out there. Is it you? Corin, please answer me!" Hysteria crept back into her voice, climbing through the upper registers, over the last few words.

He had to stop the video. He could hit the power button on the television, or flip the switch on the surge protector, but either of those would require getting close to the screen where Alyssa was trapped; a prospect that made his stomach pitch like the thought of wading into a river full of piranhas. Then he remembered the circuit breakers, behind a panel near the garage door. Corin edged along the fake wall, ignoring the cotton cobwebs tickling the back of his neck and the way the polyethylene clung to his clammy palms.

He reached the panel, opened it, and looked back at the television. Alyssa was staring at him, *directly* at him, and even when he turned away, he could feel her eyes on him like frozen barbwire scraping the back of his neck. Corin returned his attention to the decal affixed to the inside of the panel. In the distant, phosphorescent glow from the television screens, he found the grid square labeled GARAGE. His finger counted off circuit switches and pushed the twenty-third one.

*Frankenstein* went dead instantly, as did *Creature from the Black Lagoon*. The central screen remained bright, the only illumination in the garage, which had become a mausoleum, dark and silent, except for Alyssa's ragged breathing, and Corin's, mimicking her. No more noise drifted down from the party. Corin knew, with bone-deep certainty, that if he were to try the garage door, or the door back into the townhouse, neither one would open. Or, if they did, what he would see on the other side would be anything but the driveway or the Berber carpet of the basement hall.

He was already trapped – trapped in a miniature, haunted house – trapped with a television that had trapped Alyssa. Some alternate version of Alyssa, terrified of the inescapable, willing to be with Corin as a final, viable option. Maybe that was the Alyssa he deserved. Maybe he should embrace being trapped, so that he could finally embrace her.

Corin bent over and picked up the camcorder. His momentary fears that the short drop to the concrete had damaged it were allayed as soon as he thumbed the power button and the green diode appeared, floating in the darkness like an unmated firefly. He approached the televisions, reached over them, and felt for the coaxial cables attached to the main set.

"Hold on, Alyssa," he muttered shakily. "I'm coming."

He re-plugged the cables into the camcorder. The large screen went dark, not because it had finally turned off but because it was now showing exactly what the camera in Corin's hands could see; the featureless floor of a dark garage. He rotated the camcorder, aimed it at his face, which appeared on the television screen; sweaty hair matted, cheeks and chin and eye sockets smeared with crimson. He stared into the lens as if it were the black barrel of a shotgun. And when he pressed the record button, it was not unlike pulling a trigger.

# CARRYING THE APOCALYPSE TO TERM

## Fredrick Obermeyer

"You're pregnant with the end of the world," Dr. Farrows said.

Gillian Youngwood blinked several times, wondering if she had heard the old obstetrician correctly. She was sitting on a paper-covered table in the hospital exam room when he delivered the bad news.

"I'm sorry?" Gillian said.

Farrows sighed, walked over to a plastic chair near the exam room door and sat. His liver-spotted hands shook as he reached into his coat pocket and took out an orange pill container. "We did a couple of tests on you and, uh..." He shook out one pill and dry-swallowed it, then closed the container and put it back in the pocket. "There's, uh, no doubt about it. In less than nine months, you'll give birth to the Apocalypse."

"But...but...how? Why?"

"I was hoping to ask you the same thing." He tapped his right knee with his right hand three times. "Because I have no idea. I mean, in the past few years, women have been birthing some weird shit – pardon my French. But I've never seen anything like this in my life."

"Neither have I." Gillian scratched her left arm stump.

She had seen the tabloid articles of women around the world birthing two-headed calves, ghosts, demons, the devil's son and even one woman who supposedly birthed a small, black dragon. But she never thought that she'd be one of those women.

*Christ, I'm only seventeen*, Gillian thought. *I'm supposed to be going to Vassar in the fall.*

"This is a delicate question, but I have to ask. Do you know who the father is?" Farrows tapped his knee three more times. "Is it the devil?"

"No," Gillian said. "I'm a virgin. I never even tried doing it. I...I thought I had a stomach bug." Her voice trailed off. She blinked back tears. "How can you be sure it's the Apocalypse?"

"It told us through the ultrasound we took..." His voice wavered. "I heard the most horrible voice in my life. It said, 'I am the Apocalypse. Prepare for the end.'"

Farrows reached over to a nearby table, grabbed a manila folder, took out a small ultrasound sheet and held it up. Gillian took it with her remaining hand and looked at it in horror. A dark, whitish-black ball lay inside her womb. For a moment, she thought that it might have been a baby. But no, looking closer, she saw a tiny human skull staring back at her.

Fear slammed into Gillian's nerves. Her left arm stump burst into pain. She dropped the picture and burst into tears. Farrows stood, walked over and held her.

"What am I going to do, Doc?" Gillian said. "I can't give birth to this...to this **thing**."

"I understand your fear. Frankly, I'm scared shitless myself – pardon my French." He let go of her. "If you wish, we could try to abort it – actually I'm not even sure it can be. But if it can, we'll try."

"But I can't abort it, Doc. I'm pro-life."

Farrows blinked. "You may be pro-life, but what you're carrying isn't." He swallowed hard. "I believe it's in your best interests—not to mention the world's—if we get rid of this thing at the soonest possible opportunity."

"I don't know what to do." Gillian sniffed and wiped her tears away. A terrible thought occurred to her. "You won't tell anybody about this, will you?"

"Of course not. We're legally bound by patient confidentiality not to reveal your condition to anyone, except in the case of a subpoena." Farrows shifted. "However, even with such legal obligations, secrets do have a way of slipping out and..." His voice trailed off, and he tapped his right leg. "Well, I think it would be in your best interests to go someplace quiet for a while. Do you have a place to stay?"

"Yes, my—"

Farrows put his hands up. "Better you don't tell me. When you're ready, we'll talk more about the situation and explore our options."

"I'm not going to abort it, Doctor," Gillian said. "If it's God's will for me to give birth to the end of the world, then that's what I must do."

Yet, even as she said the words, doubt crept into her mind.

*How can I give birth to everybody's death, including my own? My parents, all those other people on Earth. But it was put in me. Christ, what do I do?*

"I'm glad you feel that way, but I'd suggest giving the matter a bit more time and thought," Farrows said. "For all our sakes."

"All right, Doc, I will."

"Here's my card." Farrows reached into his coat pocket, took it out and gave it to her. She dropped it into her purse.

"Thank you, Dr. Farrows."

"No problem, Gillian. Just...be careful."

"I will."

Shaken, she left the doctor's office.

\*\*\*

Gillian's parents owned a cedar cabin around ten miles north of Watertown, New York. That day she took off work and drove up to the place.

When she arrived, she parked her jeep in the back and got out. She hadn't been to the place in five years and was dismayed to see that part of the roof was starting to cave in.

She got the key from under the front eave, unlocked the door and walked inside. A musty smell assaulted her nose. Dust motes danced in the sunlight pouring through the windows.

She returned the key to its spot, then walked back inside and found a few logs near the fireplace. Deftly, she slid them into the hearth with her lone hand and started a fire. As it crackled to life, she walked over to one of the lamp tables, opened its single drawer and took out a copy of the King James Bible.

Unnerved, she sat in the rocking chair by the fire and opened up the book to Revelations 6:8.

\*\*\*

**"And I looked, and behold a pale horse: and his name that sat on him was Death, and Hell followed with him. And power was given unto them over the fourth part of the earth, to kill with sword, and with hunger, and with death, and with the beasts of the earth."**

\*\*\*

As Gillian read the words, she shivered. She stopped reading, laid the book on the table and touched her belly. Although it had not swollen yet, she could feel the Apocalypse slowly growing inside of her.

Curious, she took off the gold crucifix that she always wore and laid it up against her abdomen. Slicing blades of pain shredded her uterus; she cried out and dropped the crucifix.

Slowly, the pain subsided.

*What do I do, God? Please, tell me. Do I really have to bear the end of the world? Can't it just go away?*

The idea of abortion was becoming more desirable with each passing moment, but she couldn't see herself killing something inside her. Even if it wasn't human. As a staunch Christian, it went against everything she believed in.

Yet, at the same time, she feared the idea of dying and destroying the world. Deep in her soul, she worried that she had done something wrong in the past and now her punishment would be to give birth to the End Times.

*Why would God do this to me? Or maybe it's the devil. Maybe I am his vessel. Could I be his means to victory? No, it can't be. There must be some other reason for this. Perhaps God is testing my faith as he did Job.*

She lay back and closed her eyes, hoping for a sign.

\*\*\*

In the midst of a dream, she recalled the day that she had lost her arm. Gillian's older brother, Aaron, and his girlfriend, Terry, had taken her down to the Brewster's Ice Cream Shoppe to get a chilidog and a vanilla swirl. They were laughing at a joke he had just told about stealing one of his fellow football players' jockstraps.

As they drove up the mountain, a blue van came around a corner and suddenly swerved into their lane. Aaron pulled out of the way, just in time, but the sudden turn made them crash through the guardrail. The world suddenly went upside down and that was the last thing Gillian remembered.

Until the pain woke her up.

Gillian screamed and found herself hanging upside down. Her left arm had been crushed under the wrecked door frame. She had suffered several compound fractures and the bones lay jutting out, the flesh purplish-black. Only a small bit of flesh kept her arm attached.

Terry's head had cracked the passenger side window and her neck was twisted at an unnatural angle. Blood stained the spider-web cracks.

"Aaron?" Gillian said, her voice weak.

Aaron's face stared back at her through the broken, slanted rearview mirror. His face was a mask of blood and his eyes were dead.

Gillian moaned and tried to pull free. The movement sent more pain through her arm.

"Aaron?!"

Aaron blinked.

Gillian's heart stopped. He hadn't blinked in the accident. His body had remained completely still until the rescue team had found them minutes later.

Her older brother leaned back to her and opened his mouth. A river of blood spilled out from his dead lips.

"Don't let it happen," he said.

\*\*\*

Gillian gasped and shot up. Sweat dripped off her and she lay shaking in the chair. Had Aaron spoken to her from beyond the grave?

It couldn't be. Then again, she was carrying the Apocalypse. Anything was possible.

She leaned over to pick up the phone and screamed.

Her left arm was back. Stigmata in the shape of upside down crosses lay on the new flesh. Blood spilled down from them and coated the regrown appendage.

Weeping, she touched the flesh. It was real. It hurt.

*Dear Christ! How did this happen?*

She rushed over to the phone, picked it up and dialed Dr. Farrows' number. Once his secretary put Gillian through, she said, "Dr. Farrows, I need you. Something's really wrong."

\*\*\*

Back at the hospital, they did a CT scan on the arm. When Farrows came back to the exam room, he held up an image. His brow was furrowed and his face was slack with puzzlement.

"I can't explain this," Farrows said. "Your arm did seem to grow back. I don't know how, but–"

"Doctor, Aaron came to me in a dream and told me to get rid of the Apocalypse," Gillian said.

He placed the scan on the table. "So, you do want the abortion now?"

"Yes, please. Get this thing out of me."

"We'll fit you in as soon as possible."

\*\*\*

Gillian lay on a surgical bed in one of the abortion clinic's operating rooms. Despite wearing a blue surgical gown, she still shivered from the cold. Harsh, white light shone down from the ceiling lamp and the air held the scents of lemon cleaner. A female nurse and two orderlies stood by to assist in the procedure.

Gillian's legs had been placed in stirrups. Her lower body felt numb and exposed.

Dr. Farrows stood nearby with the attending surgeon. He held Gillian's hand with his own rubber-gloved hand.

"Now, just relax, Gillian," Farrows said. "The anesthesiologist has just administered a local and Dr. Mekedahl is ready to begin the procedure. It will all be over soon."

"I'm scared," Gillian said. She started to rise. "Maybe I shouldn't–"

"Shhh." Farrows pushed her down gently and patted her head. "It's all right. You have nothing to worry about. The vacuum aspiration is a simple procedure."

"What will you do with it?"

"We're going to send it to the NIH for study after this."

"Suppose it doesn't want to come out?"

"It will. Now, relax. Take several deep breaths. It's all right."

Gillian did so. Still, her heart raced. This didn't seem like such a good idea. But if they could get it out of her and into a safe place, then maybe it would be all right.

"Okay, here we go," Dr. Mekedahl said. "Are you ready, Gillian?"

"Yes."

"Just breathe easy."

Gillian felt something pushed into her cervix. She shuddered and tightened her grip on Farrows' hand.

As Mekedahl worked, something stirred deep within her womb. If it were a baby, she would have said that it was kicking. But it wasn't a baby and Gillian felt certain it was doing **more** than kicking.

It was fighting back.

Despite the anesthetic, a burning pain stabbed her womb. She gasped and bucked in the stirrups.

"Stop!" Gillian said.

The surgeon grunted.

"What's wrong?" Farrows said.

"The cannula is stuck," Mekedahl said. "It's like it hit a brick wall."

"Can you re-insert it?"

"I'm trying." He groaned as he yanked the cannula out of her.

Another wave of agony struck her womb and abdomen. Gillian screamed and gritted her teeth. Her belly began swelling. Deep inside her, the Apocalypse roiled and thrashed. Gillian twisted her head back and forth in agony, flinging drops of sweat all over the place.

Farrows and the attending nurses and orderlies held her down as the surgeon tried to push the cannula back inside.

Overhead, the lights flickered.

As Mekedahl attempted to push the cannula in again, the Apocalypse pushed back with its own energy. The surgeon screamed as he and the cannula flew across the room and crashed into the opposite wall. He struck his head and his skull shattered. Blood and brains splattered the wall, and he left a slick red trail as he slid to the floor, dead.

The lights flickered faster.

Gillian screamed as her vagina sprayed a thick stream of blood-tinged black ichor. Some of the spray struck one of the orderlies. He screamed and collapsed as the awful liquid melted the skin and flesh off his face, neck and hands.

"Stop!" Gillian said. "Please, stop!"

The nurse cried out. Boils and sores appeared on her face and began leaking pus. She dropped to the floor and lay shrieking in a puddle of pus and blood. Seconds later, she let out one last gasp and then disintegrated into dust.

The other male orderly stumbled back from Gillian. He cried out, doubled over and clutched his gut. A reddish-brown stain appeared on his backside. He jerked his pants down and a thick spray of blood mixed with liquid shit burst out of his anus; it splattered all over the floor, walls and ceiling, filling the operating room with a terrible smell. He dropped to the floor and lay there dying as he shat the rest of his body's blood out of his anus in a thick geyser, further drenching the walls.

Screaming, Farrows pulled away and tried to run. He only made it a few inches, though, before he stopped and shuddered. Bloody cracks appeared across his head like fractures in an eggshell. He tried to clutch his head, but when he did so, his fingers rotted and fell off. His body floated up a few inches and Gillian stared in horror as the doctor's skull imploded.

Just as it seemed it could not collapse any further, the crushed remains of his head exploded and splattered Gillian and the walls with bits of brain, skull and flesh. His headless body fell to the floor and burst into flames. A field of locusts swarmed out of his bleeding neck stump and filled the room.

Gillian screamed and batted the insects off. As she fought them, she reached down, tore off the stirrups and fell to the floor.

"Stop it!" Gillian said.

As the locusts hit the walls, they burst into flames. Quickly, the fire spread across the entire operating room.

Trembling, Gillian crawled out of the OR on her belly. Acrid smoke filled the air and Gillian coughed as she emerged from the burning room and staggered down a hallway. She stumbled out through a fire exit near the back of the building, putting her hand over her vagina.

*No more, please. Please, stop.*

When she staggered out of the clinic, she looked back. The whole building was engulfed in flames.

*Did anyone make it out?* Gillian wondered.

Fire sirens wailed in the distance.

She ran around the back of the building to the parking lot. Several people had abandoned their cars and rushed over to check out the fire. While they were distracted, she hopped in the nearest available car and drove away.

***

By the time Gillian returned to the cabin, the Apocalypse had calmed down.

She parked the stolen car in the back, stumbled inside the cabin, collapsed in her chair and burst into tears.

Her mind struggled to process the fact that Farrows was dead along with Dr. Mekedahl, the nurse and the orderlies. She realized then that she couldn't risk bringing anyone else close to her, lest the Apocalypse kill them as horribly as it had the others.

Grief gave way to rage as Gillian looked down at her belly.

"What do you want from me?" Gillian said.

She balled her right hand into a fist and punched her belly. The blow sent waves of piercing anguish through her whole body. She fell to the floor and seized. The pain became so great that she lost control of her bladder and bit her tongue. Blood spilled down her throat, and she coughed as she started choking.

Slowly, the seizure stopped. She coughed and spat out blood.

*I can't give birth to this thing. I have to stop it before this goes any further.*

Yet, there **was** a way, she realized.

She staggered to her feet and limped up the stairs. In the family bedroom, she went to the closet, yanked on the light cord and reached up into the top shelf. A wooden box lay near the back. She took it out and opened it.

The box held her grandfather's Colt Official Police revolver along with another smaller box full of .38 special bullets. Gillian cleaned and oiled the gun, then took one round out and loaded it into the chamber.

*Suicide is a mortal sin,* Gillian reminded herself as she closed the cylinder into the revolver.

*If the world has to face what happened in that operating room, then I'd rather burn in hell.*

She stuck the revolver against her forehead, squeezed her eyes shut and took a deep breath. Her lips quivered and her mouth grew dry as she cocked the hammer.

*Just do it*, she told herself. *Don't hesitate.*

She squeezed the trigger.

A dry click echoed through the room.

Irritated, she looked down the barrel. There was a bullet in the chamber.

Frustrated, she dumped out the useless round and loaded six more. Yet, each one failed to fire.

"Goddamn it!" Gillian said, and flung the revolver away.

Distraught, she covered her face and sobbed.

*There has to be a way.*

Different methods of killing herself filled her mind. Hanging, drowning, jumping off a tall building, drinking poison. Yet, as she contemplated them, the Apocalypse flashed visions into her mind, showing her that it would stop her every time.

Distraught, she nearly gave up the idea of suicide. Until another thought came to her.

*I'll starve myself. The Apocalypse can't make me eat, and it needs me to live.*

Determined to beat it, she went downstairs. Her belly gurgled as she grabbed all of the food, carried it out to the woods and left it there to rot.

Once it was gone, she sat in the cabin and waited to die of starvation.

\*\*\*

Over the next two days, Gillian grew more ill. Her teeth and hair began falling out, her gums bled, and her skin festered with sores and rashes. She could feel the Apocalypse growing inside her like a cancer, consuming her flesh and soul.

Yet, she refused to move and go for food and water; she lay in her own waste and continued to wait. But she would not die.

One night, as she was sleeping in bed, the sound of creaking wood woke her. Before she knew what was happening, someone yanked her to the floor and tied her up. She screamed and thrashed.

Figures in black robes and masks stood before her. One of them forced open her mouth, another shoved a funnel into it, and a third poured bottles full of water and jars of baby food down her throat. Gillian tried to buck and thrash, but they held her fast.

Once she was filled, they took the funnel out and stuck her in the side with something sharp.

Before she could resist any further, she passed out.

\*\*\*

When she awoke the next morning, her stomach ached. Several jars of baby food and cans of creamed corn, soup and other vegetables had been left near her, along with several papers and plastic water bottles.

A card was placed amongst the food and water.

**Eat and don't vomit it up**, the card read. **Or else we'll come back and force-feed you.**

She tore the card up.

*Who are these people? And how did they find me?*

The Apocalypse summoned them, Gillian realized. *They're its servants, and they won't let me die.*

Defiantly, she stuck her fingers down her throat and forced herself to vomit up the food that they had given her.

\*\*\*

The following night, the figures in black returned. Gillian waited for them with a shotgun, but the lack of food and sleep had worn her out. Eventually, she passed out.

When she awakened, she found herself tied to a bed. The figures in black had set up an IV.

"Don't," Gillian said.

She tried to escape, but she couldn't move.

Out of sheer despair, she tried to bite her tongue off and choke on it. But one of the figures caught her. They forced her mouth open and stuck in restraints to prevent her from doing it again.

Imprisoned, she lay back against the bed.

\*\*\*

Months passed and Gillian lost the rest of her hair and teeth. Sores appeared on her body and she shrank down to a skeleton, even as her belly swelled. Each day the figures in black would feed her, but they never took off their hoods or said a word. Occasionally, they took her for supervised walks to help ease the bedsores that she suffered.

With every day that passed, Gillian longed more for death. She prayed to miscarry the Apocalypse, yet it remained strong, feeding off her body like a parasite.

When Gillian requested the newspaper, they obliged her. One of the papers said that she had perished in the fire along with Dr. Farrows and the rest of the surgical staff. Nobody knew she was alive. Nobody cared. If anybody knew, they probably thought that the end of the world had died with her.

But it was still growing strong.

As time passed, she devised ways to escape and die. Some outlandish, some not. Yet, all were doomed to failure. The figures in black watched her constantly and kept her restrained nearly all of the time.

She was about to give up all hope when she read some more newspapers. Seeing them began to change her perspective on the situation.

Terrible headlines and news articles filled the papers.

A man in Denver had set his dog on fire. Thirty people died in a bus bombing in Saudi Arabia. Government fat cats swindled veterans and retirees on social security out of billions. Some maniac in London poisoned bottles of baby food with cyanide. Countries always seemed to be on the brink of war with each other.

The more Gillian read, the more it seemed like the world was going mad and people were taking the insanity for granted. How much more evil could the world take before it destroyed itself?

*Could the Apocalypse be a good thing? Maybe we have become so rotten to the core as human beings that wiping everything out would be for the best.*

Yet, occasionally, she saw good articles about people, too. Deep down, she wanted to believe that humanity was ultimately good.

But the daily headlines said the opposite. Sooner or later, the world would collapse under the combined weight of all human evil.

*If not now, then when?*

Still, the memories of Dr. Farrows' death and the others tortured her mind. Would they all die as horribly as the others? Probably. Would their souls be saved? Some would. Others wouldn't.

As her time drew near, Gillian found herself torn. Her body was so weak that she could hardly think straight anymore. The world became like a dream and her dreams became reality.

In her mind, she saw Farrows and Aaron telling her to resist. Yet, she found that she hadn't the strength any longer.

The Apocalypse would win.

It was inevitable.

***

Seven months into Gillian's pregnancy, the Apocalypse came early.

Excruciating pain tore into her vagina and she howled. Two of her keepers rushed to her side and held her down. But the energy of the Apocalypse knocked them away.

One pulled off his hood, revealing a man. His mouth and ears had been sewn shut. Blood leaked out of his facial pores. He crashed backwards into the wall and began clawing the skin off his bleeding face.

An invisible force ripped the clothes off the other keeper, revealing a woman. Burning milk leaked out of her breasts and liquid fire leaked out of her vagina. The flames instantly consumed her and spread across the bedroom.

The restraints snapped off and Gillian floated out of the burning bedroom and through the cabin. As she departed, she saw the other charred and bloody corpses of her keepers lying in the living room.

The Apocalypse floated her out of the burning cabin and deposited her a few hundred feet away, near a pine tree.

Another spasm struck Gillian and her water broke. The dark liquid ate through her panties and blackened the ground near her.

*Figures it would be premature.* Gillian uttered a bitter laugh.

Contractions wracked her body in quick succession, each one worse than the last.

***

She tried to resist pushing the Apocalypse out into the world, but it would not stop. Menstrual blood mixed with ichor gushed forth from her body and her muscles forced the dark thing through her birth canal.

Yet, as it neared the opening, it got stuck.

Gillian wailed and violently shook her head.

It was too much. She had to get it out now, even if it meant the end of everything.

She pushed once more and the Apocalypse exploded from her vagina in a spray of blood and flesh.

Spent, Gillian collapsed and looked at the dark sphere of black foulness that lay steaming before her.

It pulsed and whined. Amidst the blackness, she could see the Four Horsemen of the Apocalypse straining to burst free.

She waited.

The Horsemen faded and the black orb grew silent. Bits of slime dripped down from it, and then it stopped and lay there.

It was stillborn.

Gillian stared in shock. All that pain, death and destruction had been for nothing.

In the back of her mind, a deep and abiding feminine instinct took over. Despite hating the Apocalypse with all her heart, she was its mother. Right or wrong, she had brought it into the world and she did not want to see it die, even if it meant her own death.

She crawled over to the Apocalypse. Its smell of carrion and death was so strong that it took every ounce of willpower not to vomit. Hesitantly, she placed her lips against the foul black sphere and blew into it, giving it all of the life she had left.

Once, twice, three times.

On the fourth try, her gag reflex cut in. She pulled away and vomited out of her nose and mouth.

Then she collapsed on the ground.

It was hopeless.

The Apocalypse had died.

Despite herself, she started weeping. She had lost her "child." And she would die now, too.

As she lay there, the black sphere quivered.

Then again.

And again.

She stopped crying and blinked.

It had come back to life.

The top of the orb burst like an overripe fruit and darkness spilled out across the land, blotting out the sun and the sky, killing the surrounding trees and grass, instantly. Gillian flew through the air and landed in a heap a few hundred feet away.

Dazed, she blinked and looked up. A tiny orange light appeared in the sky, which quickly burst into Apocalyptic Hellfire. Flaming pillars lit up the sky and rained down across the world, burning everything in sight.

Gillian laughed as the Four Horsemen of the Apocalypse emerged from deep within the orb. The skeleton of Death was at the head of the pack, riding a white horse and holding a scythe in its bony right hand. It galloped right towards Gillian and she couldn't stop laughing, caught in the throes of religious ecstasy.

She felt herself lifted into the air once more. As Death reached Gillian, it offered its left hand to her.

In the last moment of her life, Gillian accepted its hand and placed it lovingly against her cheek as the world ended.

\*\*\*

# APPROVED BY THE COMICS CODE AUTHORITY

### Ambrose Stolliker

The auctioneer gestured at a small display to his left. Behind the glass was a single, thin comic book, its front and back covers an opaque, lusterless black. "Lot 1408, the one and only existing edition of the notorious 1954 comic book entitled *The Darkness Within*. For those unfamiliar with the legend associated with this devilish little item, it falls upon me to provide you with a brief history. *The Darkness Within*, the supposed 'haunted comic book' that destroys whoever dares read it, was written, drawn and inked by Anatoly Grigg, a Romanian immigrant and one of the most revered and accomplished comic book artists of the so-called Golden Age of Comics. Known almost exclusively for his work on horror titles such as *Ghost in the Graveyard*, *Bloody Mary Came Home* and *Midnight Tales,* Grigg's talent was so in demand that he was able to eschew that most desired goal of those in his profession – a staff position at one of the big comic book houses – in favor of a lucrative freelance career. Now then, in late 1953–"

A loud voice interrupted the auctioneer. "Hey! We didn't come here for a history lesson! Can we just get on with it, please?"

The interruption had come from a man wearing jeans with holes at both knees. He had on a black T-shirt with the words "I'm Down with Cthulu" printed in garish red on the front.

The auctioneer's voice was all politeness, but the ice in his eyes made it clear he did not appreciate being cut off midsentence. "Ah, yes, one of our regular bidders, Mr. Thomas Sully, owner of Premature Burial Books. Good to see you again, Mr. Sully. May I remind you all that Merton's Auction House has strict rules regarding decorum on the auction floor?"

The man named Sully scowled and started to protest when another man, this one wearing dark sunglasses, stood up and glared at him. The man resembled a Bulldog dressed in a dark suit. Sully hissed something under his breath and sat back down.

The auctioneer continued. "Where was I? Yes, that's right. In late 1953, Grigg was commissioned by the After Dark Comics Co. to write 'the scariest comic book' of all time – a mere marketing gimmick to After Dark, but one that Grigg took quite seriously. He worked laboriously on the book for more than a year, missing deadline after deadline, much to the chagrin of After Dark founder and publisher Harry Kremmler. By the time he'd completed work on it, the Comics Code Authority had already begun its sweeping regulation of the industry, and horror comics all but disappeared from the stands in favor of more wholesome entertainment. Not only did After Dark refuse to publish the work, it refused to pay Grigg, and, so the legend goes, he flew into a rage and put what some describe as a gypsy curse on the book. How exactly he accomplished this is not known. Through the years, many have speculated that Grigg called upon the expertise of his maternal grandmother, a Roma woman native to Romania who accompanied his family when it immigrated to the United States at the close of World War II. Others say Grigg made a deal with the Devil, selling his soul in return for the ability to create a comic with the power to cause the death of anyone who read it. A few days after terminating Grigg's contract, Mr. Kremmler received a package at his New York office. The package contained *The Darkness Within* and an invitation signed by Grigg to read it.

"Within an hour of receiving the package, Mr. Kremmler called his secretary, Leslie Tooks, into his office. He instructed her to send Grigg's comic on to the office of U.S. Sen. Douglas Northman of Indiana, who, at the time, was head of the Subcommittee on Juvenile Delinquency and a driving force behind the formation of the Comics Code Authority. As Miss Tooks prepared the comic for shipment, Mr. Kremmler opened his office window, which happened to be on the twenty-third floor. He told her he needed some air, and proceeded to plunge more than six hundred feet to the south corner of Madison Avenue. Tragically, Mr. Kremmler was not the only casualty. He landed on a twelve-year-old paperboy who had just completed his morning route selling copies of *The Daily News*, killing the child instantly. As for the comic, it was eventually sent on to the famously pious Senator Northman's office. Upon seeing it had been sent from the offices of After Dark, Sen. Northman ordered it kept in storage so he could present it as evidence at a new series of public hearings he intended to hold on the moral decay of America's youth the following year."

The man called Sully stood up then, sighed heavily, and began to pace the back of the room and mutter under his breath.

"Mr. Sully?" the auctioneer began. "Please remain seated, sir. We're almost through with the preliminaries, I assure you."

"I can stand if I want. I'm not bothering anyone," Sully said combatively.

The man in the dark suit stood and shot Sully another harsh look from behind his sunglasses, but this time, Sully wasn't so easily cowed.

"Do you have a problem?" he all but shouted at him.

"Yes. You're being rude."

"Maybe we should take this outside then, mister," Sully said, approaching the man.

"Gentlemen, *please*, remember where you are!" the auctioneer pleaded. "This is Merton's Auction House! Mr. Sully, I beg of you, don't make me call security."

He took his seat again. "Whatever. Let's get this show on the road already."

The auctioneer nodded. "Indeed. Now, back to the comic's history. What was it I was saying? Yes, that's right. Senator Northman. Well, as fate would have it, the distinguished senator from Indiana was voted out of office a few months later, and Grigg's comic was packed up along with the rest of his papers and sent on to his law offices in Cleveland. There, the comic remained in storage until Northman's death in 1960, when it was discovered by one of Northman's law partners, Raymond Sandler. Sandler, a much less religious man than Northman, and a somewhat indulgent father, gave the book to his seventeen-year-old son, Adrian, an aspiring illustrator and a voracious comic book collector. As an avid reader of comics, Adrian knew well the story behind Grigg's *The Darkness Within*. As soon as he finished eating dinner with his parents and younger sister, Adrian disappeared upstairs and read the comic from cover to cover. An hour or so later, he emerged from his room, went downstairs into the basement and loaded his father's shotgun, which the elder Sandler used for duck hunting. He then proceeded to walk upstairs and shoot his entire family in cold blood before sitting down in his father's study and turning the gun on himself.

"Within days of the Sandler family tragedy, the comic was sold for thirty-five cents as part of the Sandler's estate sale to a woman named Martha Henderson, who then gave it to her son, Theodore, on his tenth birthday. Theodore, however, was an athletic boy with little interest in such things, though he did have an abiding passion for the acquisition and collection of vintage baseball cards. Six months after receiving Grigg's comic, Theodore attended a collectibles convention in downtown Cleveland where he found a dealer who had in his possession Bob Feller's rookie baseball card from Topps, autographed by Rapid Robert himself. When the dealer, a man by the name of Albert Hill, realized the boy had the only existing edition of *The Darkness Within*, he offered Theodore the Feller card in exchange, which Theodore readily accepted.

"After concluding his business for the day at the collectibles convention, Mr. Hill got in his car, crossed the Cuyahoga River and returned to his wife in the Cleveland suburb of Lakewood. In addition to his passion for collectibles, Mr. Hill was also an avid dog breeder with a proclivity for German Shepherds. As it happened, Mr. Hill was the owner of three of these powerful animals, which he kept in a large pen in his backyard. After arriving home that evening, Mr. Hill settled down in his basement to read the comic he had sought for so long, *The Darkness Within*. When he was finished, he went back upstairs, told his wife, Bernadette 'Netty' Hill, it was time for him to feed the dogs and went outside. Netty, who happened to be deaf in one ear, had the volume on the television turned all the way up so she could hear the band play on 'The Lawrence Welk Show'. When the show ended, Netty realized she had not seen or heard her husband in nearly an hour, an odd occurrence given it was near dinnertime and he usually asked her what she planned to prepare. Remembering then that he had told her he intended to feed the dogs, Mrs. Hill ventured out into the backyard where she found the largest of the Shepherds, Princey, gnawing on the remains of Albert Hill's right femur. At some point during their feeding, the dogs had turned on their master and –"

Red-faced and fuming, Sully was up out of his seat again, ready to unleash another verbal assault, but the auctioneer cut him off before he had uttered a syllable.

"Mr. Sully, this is your final warning. If you don't take your seat, I'll have you removed, is that clear? What's more, I intend to notify the board of directors of your outbursts."

Sully fell back into his seat and folded his arms across his chest.

"Now, then," the auctioneer continued. "A few weeks after her husband's funeral, Mrs. Hill had all three Shepherds put down and then held an estate sale at which every last item in Mr. Hill's vast collection of toys, baseball cards and, yes, comic books, was sold, including Grigg's comic. At this point, events surrounding *The Darkness Within* become murky. It's not clear who purchased the comic at Mr. Hill's estate sale, and Mrs. Hill would die from coronary disease just two years later. Over the years, there would be reports, nearly all of them false, of Grigg's comic being seen in large metropolitan areas from Montreal to Seattle and obscure towns such as Bull's Head, Oklahoma and Oxnut, Mississippi.

Then, just a few months back, it was discovered in the cellar of one Ernest J. Salinger of Crooked Falls, Connecticut. Mr. Salinger, a 54-year-old widower and father of three, showed the item to his son, 26-year-old Benjamin Salinger, a passionate comic book aficionado. Benjamin informed his father that his mother, who had passed away years before, had purchased the comic book at a rummage sale. She had given it to him as a reward after he'd achieved straight A's at the end of junior high school.

"Some may wonder how the comic could have remained in Benjamin's possession for so many years without causing him terrible harm. The explanation is simple. As a boy, he had never liked horror comics because they had given him nightmares, and *The Darkness Within's* dull black cover readily identified it as just the type of story that would induce said bad dreams. As it was, his preference had always been for popular superhero characters such as *Superman*, *Batman* and *The Fantastic Four,* and, in point of fact, he had never even bothered to take Grigg's comic out of its plastic sheath. Still not really knowing just what he had in his possession, Benjamin took *The Darkness Within* to a local comic book shop where the owner readily identified it for what it was and, in the same breath, attempted to purchase it from young Mr. Salinger. Realizing the comic might very well be priceless, Benjamin returned home to decide what to do. Eventually, he attempted to sell Grigg's comic on eBay, only to run into widespread skepticism that it was, in actuality, *The Darkness Within*. In an effort to convince prospective buyers that the comic was, indeed, the genuine article, Benjamin allowed it to be viewed in person.

"Only one prospective buyer would see it before Benjamin parted ways with Grigg's comic. Jonathan J. Hewitt of New London, Connecticut, came to Mr. Salinger's residence, read the comic and offered Benjamin ten thousand dollars in cash there on the spot. At this point, Benjamin decided that if someone was willing to pay such a sum for Grigg's comic, then they might be willing to pay a great deal more. He declined Mr. Hewitt's offer. On the way back to his New London home, Mr. Hewitt was killed in a seventeen-car pileup on Interstate 95, his Mini Cooper crushed under an eighteen-wheeler whose driver had fallen asleep at the wheel after too many hours of driving without rest. Two days ago, Benjamin contacted this auction house.

"And so, having informed all those in attendance of the legend associated with Grigg's supposed accursed creation, I present to you Lot 1408, the one and only existing edition of the notorious 1954 comic book entitled *The Darkness Within*. I will start the bidding, at Mr. Salinger's request, at twenty-five thousand dollars. Do I have a bid for twenty-five thousand?"

"Finally!" Sully said, returning from the back of the auction floor to his seat in the front row. He raised his white paddle and called out, "I've got your twenty-five!"

"Very well, thank you, Mr. Sully! Do we have another bid?"

The man in the dark suit held up a white auction paddle. "Thirty thousand."

The auctioneer pointed at him and called out, "The gentleman in front, thank you. We have a bid for thirty thousand. Do we have another bid, ladies and gentlemen?"

A middle-aged man dressed in a sweater vest and derby hat raised his paddle. "Thirty-five thousand!"

The auctioneer acknowledged him with a nod. "We now have a bid for thirty-five thousand. Do we have another bid? Another bid, anyone?"

The man in the dark suit raised his paddle again. "Forty-five!"

"Forty-five, ladies and gentlemen! Forty-five for the notorious final work of Anatoly Grigg!"

"Fifty thousand!" Sully called.

"Fifty thousand from Mr. Sully! Do I have another bid? Another bid, ladies and gentlemen?"

The man in the dark suit raised his paddle again. "Sixty thousand."

Sitting a few feet away, the man in the sweater vest and derby hat shook his head and placed his paddle between his knees.

"We have sixty-thousand! Sixty thousand! Is there another bid?"

"Eighty!" called out Sully.

Before the auctioneer even had the chance to repeat the bid, the man in the dark suit raised his paddle again. "A hundred thousand."

Sully shot the man a dirty look. "One-twenty!"

"One-fifty."

"Two hundred!"

"Three hundred thousand."

Sully stood up then and yelled at the man in the dark suit. "Seriously, dude? Three hundred grand? It's a goddam *comic* book! It probably isn't even legit!"

The look on the auctioneer's face soured. Evidently, he'd had just about enough of Mr. Sully. He nodded at two burly security men who immediately converged on Sully and escorted him out of the hall. Without missing a beat, the auctioneer called out, "The bidding for Lot 1408 now stands at three hundred thousand dollars, ladies and gentlemen. Three hundred thousand. Do I have another bid? Another bid? Going once!

Going twice! Sold!" He cracked a wooden gavel against a sound block and then pointed at the man in the dark suit. "Lot 1408, the only existing edition of *The Darkness Within* is sold! Thank you, ladies and gentlemen. Thank you." He put the mallet down. "Our next item is Lot 1409…"

\*\*\*

The man in the dark suit strolled out of Merton's Auction House and walked straight across the street to a black Lincoln Continental with tinted windows. The left rear passenger door opened for him. He got in and sat down next to an old man with thick, white hair. The olive-skinned, old man's eyes were a ghostly white from thick cataracts. In his left hand was a cane crowned with the fearsome-looking head of a mythological reptile.

"Did you get it?" the old man asked, his voice giving off the faintest traces of an Eastern European accent.

The man in the dark suit handed him the comic book. "How do we know it's genuine?"

The old man pulled the comic out of its glossy plastic bag, tracing his fingers gently along the edges, then, almost lovingly, across its opaque cover. He opened it to the first page, careful not to smudge its dark cover with fingerprints, held it up to his nose and took in a deep breath. The acrid scent of the yellowing pages wafted up into his nostrils.

"Ahhhh," he said like a man consuming water after a long day of hard labor. Next, he brushed his fingers as lightly as baby's breath across the pages, savoring the rough texture of the aging pulp paper before closing it once again and carefully replacing it in the glossy plastic bag. "This is it." Then, he cocked his head toward the man in the dark suit. "Did you open it?"

"No."

"Good. That's good." He put the comic book on the leather seat next to him and tapped the driver's shoulder. "237 Madison Avenue, please."

"Yes, sir."

The man in the dark suit turned to the old man. "Premature Burial Books?"

"Yes, of course. I want to see just how far Mr. Sully is prepared to go to obtain the only existing edition of *The Darkness Within*."

\*\*\*

Andrew Sully was still angry at being outbid by the man in the dark suit when he got back to his offices.

"No calls, Candace," he growled at the petite twentysomething sitting at a desk just outside his office.

"All right, Mr. Sully," she said, doing her best to avoid his dark eyes as he brushed by. She jumped when his office doors slammed closed.

An hour later, Sully was still stewing when his desk phone's intercom beeped. He tried to ignore it, but it continued to harass him. He jammed his finger on the phone's intercom button. "Goddamit, Candace, I said no calls."

"I'm sorry, Mr. Sully," the girl replied in her mousy voice. "But there's a man here to see you."

"What's wrong with you? If I said no calls, do you think I want any visitors? Send them away."

"He says he has something you'll want to see."

Sully shook his head, supremely irritated now. "What the hell is it?"

"It's a comic book. A black comic book."

Sully froze. "Send him in."

He stood when the doors opened and Candace appeared with an old man holding on to the crook of her arm. He held a cane in one hand and a black leather satchel in the other. She helped him into a chair opposite Sully and asked him whether he wanted a glass of water or a cup of coffee. He shook his head and thanked her. She left.

"Good afternoon, Mr. Sully," the old man said.

"You have something to show me?"

The old man's cloudy eyes had focused on the sound of Sully's voice. "Indeed, I do."

"Well, let's see it."

"You want it very badly, don't you?"

"Don't screw around with me, old man. Either show me what you've got there or get out."

"You *are* a prickly sort, aren't you?"

"I don't like to lose."

The old man nodded. "Yes, I am sorry about what happened at Merton's this morning. My man told me you were rather upset. But I had to know how badly you wanted the comic."

"You going to show it to me or what?"

The old man opened the satchel, reached inside and pulled out the comic book.

"Is that—"

He placed it on Sully's desk. "Mr. Sully, I present to you the only existing edition of *The Darkness Within.*"

Sully reached over and gingerly picked up the comic. He started to open its glossy plastic bag. "May I?"

"Of course, but I urge you not to read it."

He gave the old man a skeptical look. "Then how will I know it really is *The Darkness Within*?"

The old man laughed. It was an ugly little laugh, more a croak than anything else. "Why, simply have someone read it and wait for them to die."

Sully sat down, still holding the comic. "You're him, aren't you? Anatoly Grigg."

"Who I am, does not matter. What matters – perhaps the *only* thing that matters – is what you have there in your hands. My man tells me you were willing to pay two hundred thousand dollars for it. I'm curious. What else are you prepared to do?"

"I could read it myself."

"I would urge you in the strongest terms possible *not* to do that. Not if you wish to live to benefit from the sales associated with the mass distribution of my little creation."

"What makes you think I care about sales?"

"That's *all* your kind cares about."

"*My* kind?"

"Yes, *your* kind," the old man said, his voice taking on a nasty quality. "The kind of men who reap obscene amounts of money off the backs of those born with the talent to create. The kind of men who toss aside true art when it's no longer convenient or profitable to produce it."

"How do you know that's me?"

The old man scoffed. "Tell me, Mr. Sully. What have *you* ever created?"

Sully didn't answer. He chewed on his lower lip for several minutes before reaching for the intercom button on his phone. "Candace, get in here."

The girl appeared a moment later. "Yes, Mr. Sully?"

He held the comic book out to her. "Take this into the conference room and read it."

Candace made a look like he was holding a small, dead animal out to her. "I'm not really into comic books, Mr. Sully. Wouldn't you rather have someone who knows something about them read it?"

"No. I want *you* to read it. You've got half an hour."

She reached for it, still hesitant, then let out a little gasp when Sully drew it away again.

"Be careful with it. It may be priceless."

125

"*May* be priceless?"

"Just *read* the damn thing, Candace! *Jesus*!"

She took the comic book and fled his office.

Sully watched the old man from behind his desk. Even though he was obviously blind and infirm, Sully was glad the desk was there between them. Something about the way the man's cloudy eyes remained intently fixed on him made him uneasy. "Now we wait?"

"Now, we wait."

\*\*\*

Half an hour passed, then an hour.

"How the hell long does it take to read a comic book?" Sully complained, jamming his finger on his phone's intercom. "Candace, where are you? Get in here!"

A woman's voice echoed over the intercom. It was another one of the temps. "Sorry, Mr. Sully. Candace went into the conference room a while ago. Do you want me to get her?"

"Yeah."

Sully looked at the old man, who playfully arched his thin, white eyebrows. A few moments passed. Then there was a scream.

"Oh, Christ," Sully muttered, all but vaulting out of his chair.

He ran to the conference room down the hall. The temp, a middle-aged woman whose name he did not remember, stood at the door, a hand over her mouth.

"Out of the way, damn you," Sully said, pushing past her into the room.

Candace sat slumped over at the head of the conference table where he had negotiated countless publishing deals with illustrators and writers. Blood ran from a dark gash at her neck and down her white blouse, appearing almost black where it had pooled on the mahogany table and at her feet on the beige carpet.

"Oh, Jesus Christ," he whispered.

Next to Candace were the remains of a glass water pitcher, and in her hand, a jagged shard. Sitting in the middle of the table was Grigg's comic. She had even replaced it in its glossy plastic bag.

The temp was sobbing now.

"Call the cops," Sully said, moving inside. His eyes never left the dead girl as he picked up *The Darkness Within* and retreated back to his office. The old man was still waiting for him.

"She's…She's dead."

"Of course she is. She read my comic." He rested his hands on the top of his cane. "Are you convinced now that the item you hold in your hand is the genuine article?"

"It...It can't be...It's impossible...I never thought..."

"The girl is dead, what more proof do you need?"

Sully started to pace behind the desk. "This can't be happening...*Can't* be happening."

"I assure you, it *is* happening. The question is, are you going to take advantage of this opportunity or not?"

Sully stopped in his tracks. "A girl is dead! I have to call someone..."

"Who? Who are you going to call, Mr. Sully?"

He opened his Rolodex. "I'll call everyone I know in this business," he said, flipping through one business card after the other. "IDW. Image. Marvel. I'll call DC. I'll call..." He fumbled through the Rolodex, business cards spilling onto the floor. "I'll call...I'll call...I'll..." His eyes lit up. "I'll call the Comics Code Authority! Yeah! *That's* who I'll call!"

The old man laughed the same malignant chortle from before. "The Comics Code Authority, will you? Why, my dear Mr. Sully, you of all people should know how little regard this sordid industry has for that sorry group these days. When was the last time you printed a comic book with that august body's seal of approval stamped on the cover? Tell me, just how many of your gruesome titles have been approved by the Comics Code Authority?"

Sully fell quiet and did not move for several minutes. Finally, he answered, "None. None of them."

The old man pushed himself up out of the seat, his arms shaking as he used the cane for purchase. "Think of it, Mr. Sully. 'The killer comic book.' 'The haunted comic book.' 'The comic that scares you to death.' The marketing possibilities are endless! The advertising practically writes itself!"

Sully's eyes fell on *The Darkness Within*. His reflection stared back at him in the comic's glossy plastic bag.

"If you don't publish it, my friend, someone else will."

Sully shook his head, and then started to laugh. It was a small laugh at first, but soon escalated to a drawn-out, maniacal howl. Wiping the tears from his eyes and doing his best to ignore the sound of approaching sirens, he sniffed once and said, "I get fifty percent of the sales. Deal?"

"Twenty-five," the old man countered, with a note of finality in his voice that made it clear he would brook no argument. "However, I'm willing to split the digital sales on the Kindle and iPad down the middle."

"That's very generous of you."

"My magnum opus is about to be published, at long last, sir. I can afford to be generous."

Sully picked up the comic book. "You realize what's going to happen as soon as people start reading this thing in large numbers, right?"

"A small price to pay for the privilege of reading the scariest comic book of all time. What was it the great French poet, Alfred de Musset, once said? Ah, yes. *'Art does not apologize.'*"

"You're a sick old man, Grigg."

"No, my friend. You are wrong. I am an **artist**."

Sully watched the old man slowly trudge out of his office, leaning heavily to one side on his cane.

Three days later, as night fell across the city, the first of one hundred thousand copies of Anatoly Grigg's *The Darkness Within* ran off the presses, deep in the basement of Premature Burial Books.

# HAMMER EXORCIST

## Jeffrey Todd

The demon was up to its old tricks again. I could tell from the hellish knockin' at my door. But it ain't show itself right then—no, they connivin' little thangs. There was jest a man standin' there. Said he come from the bank over in Crenshaw. Had on a nice suit, gold-rim glasses an' a fancy tie. A real city fella if I ever seen one. He kept wavin' around a yella paper, tellin' me I had to git out.

"You have no legal right to be livin' here—you're trespassin', son. That can carry five years as a felony charge," he told me. I looked inta his eyes real hard, but the demon won't there right then. The man kept lookin' over at the Sheriff's patrol car that come out with 'im, parked right aside his silver Cadillac.

"But, sir, I been livin' here since I was a young'un," I tried ta tell him. But it won't no use. I thought Mama had made the rest of the payments on our little log cabin after Pawpaw died, but I reckon not. The Sheriff seemed to be waitin' on the fella, an' both of 'em looked like they meant business. So then I said:

"All right, gentlemen, if y'all say so. I jest need to get together a few thangs."

Then I went out to the shed an' got the old frame backpack Pawpaw use'ta use 'fore he got emphysema. The Sheriff got out an' walked on over an' both of 'em stood there, watchin' me real close. Then, the city fella said:

"Just make sure you're clear outta town by tomorrow and we'll let this whole business slide, son."

"Yes, sir," I said. I didn't want no trouble. I ain't even know what they was gonna 'let slide'.

"**This is the perfect idiot bumpkin to take the rap,**" I heard the Sheriff say ta the banker—but his lips won't movin' at'all, see. That's how I knew the demon had come back 'round.

"Where's the still, boy?" the Sheriff asked. *Still?* I ain't have a clue what he meant!

129

"The *what?*" I said. I thought they was jest jokin' 'round, judgin' from their grins. Then I decided to speak up.

"If y'all would jest let me get my Bible an' tarp an' a few other thangs, I'll gladly be on my way."

"Make it quick, son," the Sheriff said. There was a real familiar look in his eyes—one I'd hoped ta never see again. Well, I reckon they figgered I'd do like I said, 'cause they both got back in the car an' left. I went back in, tryin' ta hold back tears when I seen Mama's picture on the mantelpiece. If I'da had a little money saved up, I woulda tried to get a lawyer or somethin' so's I could stay. I stuffed a bag o' rice an' my other flannel shirt into my sack, rememberin' my Bible, too. Then I seen Pawpaw's pocketwatch on the milk crate an' slipped it into my coveralls. I stood there, feelin' sad, sorta takin' one last look 'round. I'd grown up here— it was a cryin' shame to be up'n leavin' so sudden. I rolled up my sleepin' bag an' tied it ta the backpack with balin' twine. Jest as I was leavin', I 'membert the hammer in the shed, reckonin' I'd be needin' it to drive tent stakes into the ground an' such.

***

I was glad when I seen a sign after 'bout two hours o' walkin' the highway. It was brown wood an' had a yella' arrow pointin' ta the forest. *Appalachian Trailhead,* it said. Well, I ain't have no money fer motels an' all that other fancy city stuff, so I figgered what the hell. It was steep, rough climbin' at first, but I managed. My heart was beatin' somethin' fierce an' I was breathin' real hard once I got ta the top. Even though it was summertime, I felt a little more chill in the air the higher I got. I started walkin' the ridgeline, jest enjoyin' the scenery. There was somethin' new 'round each corner—even more critters an' thangs than on Mama's property up past Shaw creek. That was my Grandmama, bless her soul.

Soon, I come to a nice spot where a buncha pine needles had fell real thick. I slipped out the backpack, glad to be rid o' the heavy load for a while. The part o' the trail I could still see, wrapped 'round a clump of maple an' cedar trees with a buncha ferns an' rocks goin' down a real steep, moist cliff, an' I heard water a-tricklin' from somewhere. I was right thirsty. I heard some voices from up yonder an' I stayed real still, knowin' it was sure to be huntin' season fer some kinda game or other.

Then I seen it was jest a coupla college kids. They had on fancy boots, walkin' with fancy, plastic ski poles an' all. They was wearin' these zippered, shiny sport-logo jackets that rustled real loud when they went by.

"Hey, how y'all doin'?" I said, jes tryin' to be friendly.

"Hello," they said together. I could tell they ain't like me though. The girl—I ain't reckon she had it in fer me at first, but then I seen that same look on her face the Sheriff had. Then the boy she was with said: "**I don't think he'll ever have money, or any kind of life. Stupid bum.**" Or somethin' like that, anyhow. Now I ain't know this fella from Adam, but Pawpaw use'ta say it takes all kinds, so I decided let it slide. After all, they coulda been talkin' 'bout someone else, but I ain't think so.

*** 

The day wore on. By the time the sun was gettin' low in the west, I was lookin' fer another good spot ta roll out my sleepin' bag fer the night an' boil some water fer rice. Jest rice won't gonna fill me real good, though—not after a hike like that. I sure wished I'd had enough room in my backpack for a coupla chickens from the pen. I cursed myself fer not pickin' up that possum I seen kilt back on county road 31 jest afore I fount the trail. Soon as I start gatherin' twigs, an older man come up outta nowhere.

"How ya doin', sonny?" he said. He had on farmer's britches an' a flannel shirt. Had a walkin' cane an' a can o' dip in his chest pocket. Bandana was tucked in his back pocket, too, just like Pawpaw use'ta do.

"Jest fine, sir, thank you," I answered.

"Why don't you come up to my place and have yourself some of my wife's home-cookin'? Rest your feet for a spell? You look like you could use it, son," he said. My stomach growled. It sount too good to be true. He let fly a brown plume o' juice an' shifted the lump under his lip to th'other side.

"Yes, sir!" I said. I was real grateful. My stomach was a-burnin' somethin' fierce as I rolled up my sleepin' bag real quick.

"My pickup truck's just past this here ridge," he said, once we started walkin'. "What's your name?" he asked.

"Melvin, sir. Melvin Smith," I told him.

"Well, Melvin, I'm what they call a trail angel. Ever heard of 'em?"

"No, sir. What're they?"

"Well, we see hikers comin' through, you know—most on their way up to Moose Junction up yonder in Yankee country—and offer to put 'em up for the night. Sometimes we come out and set up a table with food for 'em at the crossroads every now and then."

"That's a real nice thang ta do, mister," I said.

"Yeah, I done a good chunk o' this trail myself, back in the day. Food's heavy to carry, you know. We let 'em use our shower and get a good night's sleep afore they get on their way. If they ain't killers, that is. You ain't one, are ya?" I could tell he was a-foolin'.

"Naw, not really," I said. We both laughed hard.

Now I ain't ever heard o' much kind-hearted folks doin' stuff like that—not in this day an' age. But he looked old an' weak, an' I could tell he was jes' tryin' ta help. "So, how about it?" he asked me.

"'Bout what, sir?" I said.

"You wanna bed down in our spare bedroom for the night?" I thought real hard 'bout it. Didn't want ta put this nice old feller an' his wife out none, ya know? Jest the home-cookin' woulda been all right by me. I reckon he saw me thinkin' too hard, cause then he said:

"Okay, it's a deal. And by the way, my name's Henry, and my wife—you'll meet her—she's Henrietta."

"Well, thanks a bunch, Henry," I said. I was glad he offered, 'cause it looked like it was gettin' ready ta pour down real soon. I ain't have a real tent, neither—just that old, moldy green tarp from before.

***

Not 'fore long, we got to his little brown Toyota pickup in a parkin' lot. I reckon it was part o' the National Forest, 'cause of all the picnic tables, trashcans, an' brown signs with history an' other stuff I cain't read too good. I got in an' we were off. I guess he seen I was tired an' ain't feel like talkin' much, which was good. I seen his CB radio an' the .16 gauge across his back window. Then, I reckon I musta nodded off a coupla times afore we pulled into a steep gravel driveway. The grindin' an' bumpin' sound woke me up. Boy, was I hungry! We come up on a little frame bungalow with all kinds of shade trees an' other stuff growin' real close to it. There was cane rockin' chairs an' a swing on the porch, along with a buncha hangin' plants I ain't never seen before. Smoke rose up out the chimney.

"Henrietta! Got another one! Is the soup on?" he yelt out. A little ol' lady with glasses come ta the door, all but five foot tall. "Bring 'im on in," she said. "I got some coffee on, too!" I followed him up the porch steps an' caught a whiff o' somethin' meaty that made my mouth start a-waterin'. An old, shaggy dog barked. Soon as we stepped in, I felt right at home.

"You can put your bag in that little room down yonder the end of the hallway," she said. "Oh, and if you wanna wash up it's got its own little bathroom."

"Thank you much, ma'am," I said. I walked on back. The floorboards creaked under me an' I seen a mouse dart 'round the corner, but how could I complain? I thought I'd be swattin' at skeeters an' gettin' soaked right 'bout then. It was a neat little room. There was some stitched sheep an' farm designs on the walls in circle frames an' a nice thick quilt on the bed. Even had a little basket o' Southern Living sittin' by the commode an' checker hand towels with roosters on 'em. I run some water over my face an' looked in the mirror. I reckon I looked good enough to eat— 'specially if they was cannibals. Haw-haw.

***

I went back ta their little livin' area. The side part served as a kitchen. It had a wood stove in the middle. Everythang was real cozy. Dark wood wall panelin' an' a mounted deer head over the fireplace an' all.

"Have a seat, Melvin," Henry said. I coulda sworn I heard somethin' diff'rent in his voice, though. Like he was only bein' friendly as a kinda act. I sat down in one o' the armchairs an' Henrietta come shufflin' over with a steamin' cup'a coffee.

"Now you just make yourself right at home, now, Mr. Melvin" she told me. I took the cup outta her wrinkly, cool an' spotted hand. Well, I done come this far—I may as well play along an' try ta' enjoy thangs a little.

"Yeah, we get lots of hikers this time of year come through these parts," Henry said.

"Yes, sir, summer's a real fine time to be livin' like this," I said.

"Well, don't fool yourself, son—**sooner or later we're gonna put you where you belong**," he said. I couldn't believe my ears, lemme tell ya. I looked 'round real careful-like, tryin' ta make sure he won't on the phone or jest talkin' ta one o' his cats. I thought I seen Henrietta flash him a little smirk (**"It's gonna get to him sooner or later—he'll snap."**) while he kept on starin' at me. There it was again—she ain't move her lips none at'all, but that's what I heard—God's honest truth. I couldn't think o' much ta say after *that*, so I jes' kept quiet.

Then Henrietta, bless 'er heart, she come over with a steamin' bowl o' chili an' a big old square chunk o' hot, buttered cornbread. Right then I thought maybe she won't conspirin' with Henry after all. I was glad fer the food—at least I ain't hafta talk ta no one with my mouth full. When I got the spoon close ta my mouth, I thought I smelt somethin' like the ammonia Mama use'ta use on the commode every coupla months. But I felt like I had ta be polite—I was a guest, after all—so I dug in. It was real good home cookin'—jest like Henry said it'd be. Spiced up jest the way I like it, with lotsa meat an' kidney beans. I put spoon after spoon in my mouth, every now an' then lookin' over at Henry.

\*\*\*

I'm surprised I ain't figger everythang out sooner. The demon had come back—he was just a-waitin' fer me ta let my guard down. Somehow it done fount me again, an' it was right there 'hind Henry's eyes. I'd recognize that hateful look an' evil grin anywhere. Use'ta be, when somebody started talkin' without movin' their lips, I figgered they was takin' the demon's side. But Henry kept sittin' there, lookin' at Hee-Haw with the sound on low. The demon hidin' inside him kept lookin', whisperin' sayin' thangs to me, while I was eatin'.

**"Didn't think I'd find you out on the trail, did ya?"**

**All these sinners are gonna frame you. I'll see to that."**

It was real sly an' narrow–eyed. I kept thinkin' Henrietta shoulda heard it, but she ain't seem to. I reckon since I was in them folk's house, the demon thought it could do whatever it wanted to me. Henrietta, she kept on putterin' 'round in the kitchen, washin' dishes an' what not. Won't no doubt, though—Henry ain't look *nothin'* like the nice fella who invited me over. Once I got done, I set the bowl aside, tryin' ta think of somethin' nice ta say. I woulda up'n left right then, but my feet an' back was so dang sore an' I was gettin' real sleepy. I was nervous, too—musta been why I kept feelin' the beginnings of heartburn.

"I got more if you want it," Henrietta offered.

"Oh, no ma'am; I can't handle no more. Thank you, though," I said.

**"So, *Melvin*...where did you say you're from?"** Henry asked me. Ain't even sount like him no more.

"Gorman's Pass. Jest this side o' Calumet County," I said. He looked at me real suspicious, jest like the Sheriff done. But there won't no doubt 'bout it: I'da known that same demon from anyplace. I jest couldn't figure out how it fount me. I thought I done got rid of the pesky little varmint for good when I seen it in Mama. Then, a big ol' clap of lightnin' flashed outside. Made me cringe. The rain got real loud against the tin roof.

"Well, I'm awful tired," I said ta them. I had ta play real dumb-like—I ain't think it knew I was onta it right then, see. "I thank ya for invitin' me, Henry. I don't wanna take advantage of yer hospitality any more'n I hafta, so I'll jest go get some shut-eye now."

**"Well, it's too late for that—you already have, you dumb friggin' mooch,"** Henry said. That time, I coulda sworn I seen his lips move! Then he flashed me a real angry look. Now, see here—there ain't no way any *real* person woulda invited me, bein' all nice at first, then up'n try'n make me feel like I done wrong. There was some dark forces at work in that place. But I jest played along, bidin' my time.

"Yes, sir. Well, goodnight," I said, turnin' ta leave. Then Henrietta's bony little hand suddenly gripped my wrist somethin' fierce. I couldn't believe what I seen in her eyes. I looked over at Henry, who seemed back to bein' all down-home friendly again. I reckon the demon musta jumped clear outta him an' inta her. I seen it happen afore. I could also tell from the way she was clutchin' my wrist that the demon was in 'er. Can't no woman have a grip like that, not less'n she's possessed! Then she said:

**"Yeah, you just go lay down, you freeloadin' bum! Think about how it'll be when we finally put you away for good."** Yeah, she said it for real! I ain't have no right answer fer that one, neither, so I stood there like a fool, hopin' Henry would stick up fer me—after all, he's the one who invited me. But he jest kept a-watchin' Hee-Haw like everythang was just fine. After a spell, Henrietta's eyes got normal again an' she looked all country-folk-friendly, jest like at first, same as Henry. Even the rain died down.

"You sleep good now, Melvin," he called over from his chair. Then Henrietta said:

"Yeah, you got lots of miles ahead of you. Good Night."

"Good night, folks," I told 'em. I think my voice was shakin' a little, but what do ya expect when one minute, yer up against Satan an' his 'fernal Legions, then they jest up'n disappear? I turnt 'round an' walked back down the creakin' hallway to the guest room.

*** 

When I shut the door, I seen a John Deere calendar from 1984 was tacked on the back. I flipped through, lookin' at the pictures of tractors in wheat fields an' then started tryin' ta read some of the little squares:

*Marcus Witherby—Lake Harris, PA 22*
*Jonas Frampton— Altavista, VA 19*
*Sally Rutherford— Stone Mountain, GA 28*

Ain't no tellin' who them people was. I was too tired, anyway. I flipped back the quilt, shucked off ma' boots, an' my head sunk right inta the pillow. This was way better'n how I woulda been sleepin'. I said my prayers like always. Trouble was, after a good long while, I couldn't get no peaceful rest 'cause o' the stuff they done said to me. I knew it was only the demon talkin', but still…it's hard ta know *what* to think sometimes. People out there, some of em's good folk, I reckon. Most try ta live right—

go ta church an' all. But that still don't mean ya should stop bein' careful an' watchin' yer back…not in this day an' age.

I kept a-layin' there, jest thinkin' 'bout stuff. After a good while, I heard them hallway floorboards start creakin' an' I lay *real* still. Maybe Henry was jest goin' to the bathroom. It was dark outside by then, but the moon come through the window onta my backpack. I lifted up the flap an' seen the gleam on my hammer. Real quiet, I moved my extra flannel off the handle an' stuck it out so's I could grab it quick. Jest in case. Ya never know. Crazies.

\*\*\*

Well, I woke real early the next mornin'. All the stars was still out. I ain't hear no snorin' comin' from their bedroom. Maybe they was jest quiet sleepers. I thought 'bout findin' some paper an' leavin' a thank-you note, then I 'membert what they said ta me afore I hit the hay last night, so I decided to jest go.

I headed north up the Sycamore Rock trailhead. The heat o' the day started gettin' to me long 'fore the sun was halfway up the sky. A couple miles on, I come to a nice, cool stream an' took me a long drink. It hit the spot—tasted jest like the mineral spring Pawpaw use'ta take me to. There was a big ol', steep wall o' rough rock with all kinds o' moss an' fungus on it. I climbed on up an' looked out over a big valley. I seen a buncha puffy green tree-clumps, every one of 'em look alike, but some poked through mist that was down aways. Then I heard an eagle screech, I think. With all that fog off in the distance, I won't real sure. It was still a real nice view, though. Then, I heard a helicopter from somewhere due south. It jest ain't seem quite right, out here 'round all these quiet trees an' all.

After awhile, I headed on. I seemed ta be makin' good time that day. The sun was nice an' gold on everythang, 'cept for the cool shadows under the trees. I went 'bout four miles or so afore I seen a lady hikin' alone, comin' from th'other way. She won't no more'n twenty-five years old, I'd say. She won't even wearin' a backpack or nothin'.

"How ya doin', miss—nice day, ain' it?" I said. The closer she come, I seen she looked sorta worried or sad.

"Have you seen a girl with blonde hair come your way?" she asked me.

(I ain't seen no one since I started hikin' that mornin'). "I don't believe I have, miss," I told her. When I looked up at the helicopter, everythang 'bout her changed real quick.

**"Well, they're still gonna get you—you can't run but so long,"** she said. That same feelin' come over me right then, jest like when Henry an' his wife turnt like they done. I wanted ta' ask her what on earth she was talkin' 'bout, but then I seen that dark glare in her eyes an' I jest knew— the demon. But I won't gonna let it git away *this* time. If I did, it would jest keep on followin' me, hauntin', tauntin', an' a-tryin' to make life rough fer me. No, I known what I had ta do. The girl went up a hill an' turnt left on the Cumberland Pass trailhead. The brown wood sign said **2.3 mi. loop.** She'd *have* ta come back this here way once she got to the top. I just lay low, off in the brush, makin' sure the hammer was ready. Pawpaw told me I'd know how ta use it when the time come. I reckon this was it.

\*\*\*

Them demons are real sneaky. It kept tryin' ta' act like it won't there no more when she come back down the trail, but I known better. Pawpaw was a Preacher, see—told me all 'bout them evil spirits. Once I jumped out, the demon tried to make like *I* had *it* inside of *me.* I ain't bother listenin' that time, though. Won't nothin' but a buncha *lies.* That's who them demons serve, ya know—the Father of Lies. I could tell the hammer had the powers Pawpaw said it did soon as it done its work. I yanked it from the purdy mask the demon was wearin', seein' a black cloud come seepin' out the mouth. It swirled up in the air like a tornado with a buncha flies in it.

"**Oh, you done screwed yerself this time**," they buzzed at me. Then, other voices start comin' out the thang like a buncha people talkin' all at once.

"**Let's see how psychic you are now, you dumb fucking country prayboy**," they said. Well, I couldn'ta said nothin' back, noways—the dark cloud done up an' took off inta the trees 'fore I could.

I come down the service road after I rinsed the hammer off in a stream. It was good ta be back 'round the critters. Won't never no bad voices 'round them. I seen a red-headed woodpecker and an armadillo less'n two minutes apart. On both sides of the road, the grass started getting' real high, lookin' lighter, softer, an' all the weeds had purdy yellow flowers on 'em. I was real careful not ta turn my ankle on the big, loose chunks o' gravel.

Purdy soon, I seen a buncha them grey boxes the 'lectric company put up, sure I'd be comin' up on a road real soon. I was glad, tired an' hungry as I was. Maybe I could find somethin' more than jest rice to eat by checkin' in one o' the dumpsters wherever I got to next. Or, there mighta been 'nother 'possum or coon just a-layin' there, fresh-kilt. I could git back on the trail once I stocked up on supplies. A real tent would be good, too. With one'a dem, all's I had ta do was zip up the flap—no more swattin' at them dang skeeters! Rain or shine, I'd be *ready*. Never have ta be 'round people like old Henry an' his wife ever again, neither. I couldn't believe how nice they *seemed* at first, 'fore they turned on me. I'd hoped I finally got rid of that demon, 'cause everything I'd tried afore the girl jes' won't cuttin' it.

Well, jest as I come to the road, I seen a Sheriff's patrol car a-sittin' there. The lights on top start spinnin' real bright an' he stepped out. An' would ya believe it was the same one that done run me off from Mama's cabin? He sount a lot less friendly than ol' Henry *ever* did, that's fer sure. I kept a-waitin' fer him to say he remembert me an' all, but he never did.

"Let me see your ID, son," he said.

"Okay, sir," I took out my billfold an' gave 'im the plastic card.

"Wait here," he said. I jest stood there, watchin' as he got back in an' started pushin' buttons. He got on his radio fer a spell, but I ain't ever hear no one else talkin' on it. Then, he come out with a pair o' handcuffs an' pointin' somethin' at me like a gun with no barrel.

"Hands behind your back!" he yelled, real stern-like.

"But, officer," I started ta say, jest 'afore I got a real bad jolt. It was like a flash o' white punchin' me clean in the mouth. Next thang, I was a-layin' on the road an' he was hog–tyin' me with them dang cuffs while his knee pressed hard on the back o' my neck. My face was gettin' scraped up an' I got grit in my mouth.

***

"**Yeah, them voices *told* you this was gonna happen. Didn't they, boy?**" he asked me. I ain't want ta say much, 'cause I 'membert somethin' from a TV show 'bout that kind o' stuff bein' used 'gainst you. But he ain't seem ta care if I answered or not, jes' went over an' opened my pack an' took out the hammer. Kept turnin' it over an' over, lookin' at it real close afore he got a big Ziploc bag from the trunk an' put it inside. I coulda sworn I seen a girl a-layin' real still down in there with gray tape 'round her hands an' mouth. After that, I pretty much jes' 'member the demon grinnin' at me in the mirror every now an' again, while we rode along. I kept noddin' off, see. I ain't never really feel right since eatin' that chili, the more I think 'bout it. But there was a thick, wire cage 'tween me an' the demon in the cop, so's I knew he couldn't do nothin' else ta hurt me.

***

Purdy soon, I fount myself sittin' in this here room. Ain't no pictures or nothin'. No windows, neither. The walls are soft an' grey, though. They give a little bit if you hit 'em real hard, but it still hurts. Scraped the skin clean off my knuckles first few hours in here. The commode's real diff'rent from most. Jest metal bars over a deep hole in the floor. I can't get no clothes or toilet paper from these folks, neither. They said I might try an' stuff it in ma mouth so's I can choke ta death. Why on earth would I do that? But I knew I done got lucky when this here pencil stub come a-rollin' under the door th'other day, right along with a paperback New Testament. I been writin' this in them blank pages at the end ever since, but it's real slow-goin'. Anyway, I reckon this place is still better'n half-starvin' to death an' gettin' rained on out on the trail. Ain't no skeeters in here, neither. The light is always on, so's I kin read my Bible an' write whenever. I ain't known if it's day or night outside ever since they put me up.

\*\*\*

After a few days in here, I got a little down. Started thinkin' 'bout how I was really enjoyin' nature an' all a few weeks ago. A person'd never think that out in all them purdy natural wonders, somethin' like a demon would come along ruin it all. I thought once I got clear of the wrong folks, everything'd be all right. But I guess it's jest the way thangs are.

\*\*\*

They won't let me have no toothbrush or comb or nothin', but I'm readin' a lot in this here Bible, jes' like I use'ta.
*"And he shall rule them with a rod of iron..."*

Yeah, I use'ta think that was me when I used Pawpaw's hammer. Doin' God's will. I still gotta do it. Few minutes ago, they slid my food tray in through the metal slot. The boy was wearin' some plastic gloves with bright orange coveralls that had shiny snaps. Wish I could get me one. Yeah, he bent down, lookin' through the slot so's I could see his eyes. I'd know that unholy glare from anywhere.

**"Let's see you do God's work in there, you backwoods, hillbilly loon,"** he said. He even had the nerve to spit at me, jest like they done to Jesus.

But that was all jest the demon talkin'.

Sometimes, at night, I'll be a-layin' here an' get ta thinkin' 'bout them times when my gut told me that the demon won't in them folks no more. Well, it had ta be *somewheres*, right? I think I done figgered out where. I think I seen it somewheres in them little black, sleepy spells I had, when it was hard ta 'member much o' anythang—'cept for Pawpaw teachin' me 'bout demons up yonder at them mineral springs.

# HELL OF A DAY
## Nick Nafpliotis

*Tires squealing. Metal crunching. Glass shattering.*

Brian Carl awoke with a start; his heart beating like it was trying to escape from his chest. It was the same car accident nightmare he always had, but a little more of it stuck to his waking mind. This time, he'd been texting something to a friend when the familiar headlights rushed to meet him. The extra detail didn't help the dream feel any less horrifying, though. It also failed to provide any context for the talking snake, which always preceded it.

Brian rolled over, looked at the clock, and instantly forgot about the bizarre and terrifying images that had haunted his sleep. He'd overslept once again. His boss already warned him that if he were late again, it would cost him his job. After unleashing a stream of profanities, Brian scrambled out of bed toward a pile on the floor containing yesterday's work clothes.

"Don't you have to be at work?" his girlfriend, Jennifer, croaked from under the covers.

He didn't answer. His mind was completely focused on getting to the call center. He was supposed to be there by 9:00, but his boss didn't start logging calls until 9:30. If he could sneak past her and start dialing before then, she might not realize he was late.

Unfortunately, the traffic that day was doing everything possible to delay him. Constant red lights, left lane slow pokes, school buses making stops—all the usual suspects decided to show up on his morning commute en masse. Brian's road rage (which was bad even on a good day) came to the fore, making his already sour mood infinitely worse.

After screaming himself hoarse and nearly causing three separate accidents, he screeched into the parking garage at 9:26. There was still a chance. He bolted out of his car, sprinted toward the back entrance, and swiped his key card.

Red light.

He swiped again and got the same result. After three more unsuccessful attempts, he took off toward the front. The detour cost him three minutes, but his card worked for that door, at least. Once inside, he ran past the front desk and down the aisle to his station. His boss was waiting there for him.

"I realize it's only 9:32," she said before he could stammer out an excuse. "But you are supposed to be here promptly at 9:00 AM. This is also the sixth time you've been late this quarter. I've given you too many chances already, Mr. Carl. Please collect your belongings and be out of the building by lunch time."

\*\*\*

Brian gathered everything from his desk into a box; just like every clichéd 'fired office employee' he'd ever seen on television. He then walked out to his car, threw his things into the back seat, and unsuccessfully tried to start the engine. After a few more futile attempts, he looked down to see that the knob for the lights was still in the on position.

After being turned down by three of his former co-workers, someone from the next office building over gave him a jump. He drove back home in a fog of anger and depression, which caused him to completely miss a red light—and the police cruiser at the next intersection, resulting in his third traffic ticket in the last two months.

Brian wasn't sure how the day could get much worse. He found out after coming home and opening the door. His girlfriend was seated on the couch with another man, their hands and mouths wandering over each other. Before the rage hit him, Brian had an exceptionally brief moment of clarity. It wasn't fair to be angry with Jennifer. He'd cheated on her plenty of times. But he didn't give a shit about fairness. Nothing about this day or his life was fair.

Brian unleashed a torrent of expletives. Jennifer responded in kind. The other man awkwardly excused himself and ran from the room.

"What the hell are you doing home this early, anyway?" she screamed.

"I got fired, all right!" Brian shot back. "And now, I come home and find out you're screwing around on me!"

Jennifer went silent. Then her eyes softened as a grin spread across her face. "So get the hell out. The only reason I put up with your shit is because I needed help with the rent. Now you can't even do that, anymore."

More shouting and swearing followed. It continued while Brian packed up his belongings and didn't end until the door slammed behind him. He got in his car and drove back towards town, calling anyone he thought might take him in along the way. Every one of them had an excuse for why it was a 'bad time' or they 'just didn't have the room.' He was eventually forced to rent the cheapest hotel room he could find, which would last him two days at the most before his bank account ran dry.

Brian checked in, flopped down on the bed, and rested his head against the flat, cigarette-stained pillow.

"Hell of a day…"

"*Indeed, it wassss,*" hissed a voice in his ear.

Brian shot up and turned to his right, where a large snake slithered along the bed—and somehow spoke.

"*In fact, up until you died in that car wreck, it wasss the worsssst day of your life. But at leassst your death wasss quick, unlike the family of four that you killed.*"

"W-what are you talking about?"

"*You died inssstantly. There wasss no pain,*" the snake replied, curling around his arm and drawing its head up next to his. "*Ssso during your ssstay here, you will relive thisss day…forever.*"

"Here? Where am I?"

"*Guessssss…*"

Before Brian could respond, the snake snapped forward, sinking its fangs into his neck and plunging him into darkness.

*Tires squealing. Metal crunching. Glass shattering.*

# THERE WILL BE DAMNATION

### Christopher Hivner

June 15, 2015, South Carolina

The body hit the floor with a wet screech as it slid across in a slick of blood from its own side. Still unconscious, the naked man lay in a heap, his head buried in scratched and punctured arms, his broken nose pressed against the concrete. The man was burned, sliced, shot, and cut; blood ran over him like Indian war paint.

The cage door clanged shut, the lock moving into place with a harsh click. His jailer stood with his hand still on the bars of the door, the nub of a cigarette burning his lip. In his right hand, he held his hunting rifle. On his belt were three sheaths that contained knives of various sizes. There were smaller blades in each of his boots and a Sig Sauer handgun shoved into his belt in the back.

Henry Barlow had gone to war well armed and was still surprised he'd survived. This wasn't the first vampire he'd captured, and he'd learned from each skirmish, but he knew what he was up against: superior strength and speed with supernatural mental abilities. Henry had taken the Viking approach of attack first. If he put enough holes in the creatures, they'd eventually fall, just like a man.

Henry had an impressive collection of his own injuries. He'd lost enough skin the past six months to cover a sofa. If it weren't for Ginny, he'd quit, sit in his kitchen drinking Southpaw beer, and waste away until it was all over. He couldn't let her memory go like that.

Walking to his left, Henry's hand found a round dimmer switch on the wall. He turned it clockwise, and the inside of the cage was bathed in dull, ethereal light. On a rickety table under the switch, Henry picked up a three-foot long cylinder of metal. He took his place in front of the cage before sliding the metal pole between the bars and touching the vampire on the buttock.

Five thousand volts of electricity arced through the cattle prod into the unconscious creature. The body rose up for a moment before falling back to the concrete. Henry also saw one eye open briefly. He jabbed the prod harder into the vampire's backside, holding it against the skin. The electricity shot through to the brain, and he was awake. Rolling onto his back, mouth opened, he revealed chipped, bent fangs. He howled in pain. Before he could orient himself, Henry Barlow placed the prod's tip against the vampire's balls and zapped him once more.

The howls turned to pitiable cries as the creature curled into a fetal shell, trembling hands holding onto his groin. His eyes, fully open and watering, darted in all directions to take in the surroundings.

"I guess you're awake now," Henry slurred, while laying a new cigarette between his lips. "Get ready to talk, or you die. Choice is yours."

Henry lit the Marlboro and took a quick drag. The vampire's body had stopped shaking, but he still held himself. Long, dirty hair fell over his face. Two red eyes burned through to meet Henry with hatred.

"Who are you?" the vampire said, causing a cut on his lip to re-open, which sent a fresh stream of blood over his chin.

"Now, now," Henry replied, balancing his cigarette while sucking deeply from the tobacco. "You don't need to know who I am. What's important is I know who and what *you* are, Jonathan."

Henry Barlow accepted all the anger emanating from Jonathan, relishing the man's confusion. He finished his cigarette, dropping the butt to the floor. He walked back over to the dimmer switch, placing two soiled fingers on it.

"Where can I find Kessler?" Henry asked.

Jonathan looked away, but asked, "How do you know him?"

"Where is he? That's all I want to know."

"I don't know where he is, and I don't care."

Henry didn't hesitate. He turned the dimmer switch until the lights in the cage turned bright white. Jonathan's skin immediately burned, smoke rising, crackling filling the air. The vampire skittered from one corner of the cage to the other, searching for any darkness in which to hide, finding only pain. Curled into a ball, Jonathan screamed his throat raw before Henry finally dimmed the light.

"Where's Kessler?"

"I . . ."

"Where?"

"Kes . . . gone, don' know . . ."

"Wrong," Henry growled. He had barely moved the switch when Jonathan howled.

"No, no, no, no!"

"Where is he?"

"He's gone!"

"Where?"

"He'll know I broke. He'll hurt me."

"It's him or me, son. And I've got my hand on the switch. Where is he?"

Jonathan crawled across the cage, his fingers digging into the concrete floor. He owed allegiance to Ivan Kessler, fearing and loathing him at the same time. Could he turn his back on the man who made him? He pushed himself up to his hands and knees, wanting to face his abuser with dignity.

"Jonathan?"

The vampire stood up on wobbly legs. His whole body shook, blood pooled around his feet. He brushed hair from his face and looked at Henry Barlow.

"I can't," Jonathan said. "I won't. Ivan Kessler is my lord. I can't betray him."

"You know, the rest all said the same thing. Until they gave up."

Henry flicked a switch that sparked spotlights on the ceiling of the barn. Each one highlighted a cage, duplicates of Jonathan's prison, and in each was a pile of ash still in a human outline. He let Jonathan stare for a moment before turning the dimmer switch to the right again.

The light in Jonathan's cage flared, and he dropped to the floor in agony. His skin turned crimson, fissures forming that opened into deep cuts. Acrid smoke filled the cage. Jonathan screamed until he had no breath left. His scalp burst into flame, the fire crawling through his hair like it was dead wood.

"I can make it stop, Jonathan!" Henry yelled.

The skin on Jonathan's chest opened up. The blood beneath bubbled, hissing with steam. He looked at Henry with a face contorted into an abstract shape.

"Pennsylvania!" Jonathan cried. "He's gone home to Gettysburg. It's where he came from. He was a soldier . . ."

Henry nodded with satisfaction before easily moving his hand away from the dimmer switch. Jonathan tried to say something, but no sound came out. The light bore deeper into his body. Blisters rose on his skin, quickly bursting and spraying pus into the air. His boiling blood caught fire until his whole body was aflame, consumed by an inferno.

Henry Barlow lit a cigarette, resting it between his lips but not breathing it in. He watched the vampire burn as if he were watching a family campfire. In the past four months, he had caught, questioned, and eventually killed four of the creatures and all had given him the same answer to Kessler's whereabouts.

"I'll make him pay, Ginny," Henry said. "I swear it."

\*\*\*

July 2, 1863, Gettysburg, Pennsylvania

"I cain't believe how longs we been away," the soldier said as he stared at his pocket watch, rolling the instrument in his hand. "My Tammy gived me this watch. I shore does miss her. Ya know what I misses the most?" he asked, turning to the man next to him, who was trying to sleep, propped against an oak tree.

Ivan Kessler didn't acknowledge the kid. He kept hoping if he ignored him long enough, Billy whatever-the-fuck-his-name-was would just shut up. But the rambling went on and on. He missed his ma and his pa and the farm and the chicken dinner on Saturday night, blah, blah, blah.

"Ya knows what I misses most?" Billy Whoever repeated. Kessler tilted his hat back and finally looked at the kid.

"What?" he growled. "Pray tell, what do you miss the most about your life before you became a soldier in the mighty Union army?"

"My wife's titties."

Kessler burst out laughing. The kid was so earnest in his admission; it was if he had spilled an ancient secret.

"Well, hell, son," Kessler nearly shouted. "I've never met your wife, and *I* miss her titties, too."

"What?"

"I bet every man here misses little Tammy's titties." Kessler stood up. "Hey," he shouted through his cupped hands. "Who here would like to see Billy the Kid's wife's titties?" A boisterous shout went up from the 28th Pennsylvania infantry as they waited on Culp's Hill for morning and the re-start of the war.

"What tha hell's wrong wit you?" Billy said angrily as he stood to confront Kessler. "Why is you talkin' 'bout ma wife like that?"

"Because I want you to shut up and leave me alone." Kessler pressed forward. Being over six feet tall, with arms and shoulders made tight from physical labor, Ivan was the biggest man in the group. Billy was several inches shorter and as thin as a sapling. The boy backed down quickly.

"Sorry, mister," he said while turning away. "I jus wanted to talk ta someone."

"Find someone else," Kessler said. The kid gave him a last, sideways glance, shook his head, and then put his pocket watch back in his hand.

"I need to take a piss," Kessler sneered before walking away. He made his way through the trees to put some distance between himself and his fellow soldiers.

Ivan Kessler was born not far from Gettysburg, in Lancaster County. His father had taught him how to work, and his mother had taught him how to think. Both had contributed to keeping him alive after two years of getting shot at for a cause he cared nothing about.

Farm work was rote, but he liked the physical activity. His mother had taught him to read and write, though he never found much use for either. Kessler found himself to be smarter than most people he was acquainted with, and he sometimes took advantage. Other times, people bored him so much; he would rather disappear into the woods to be by himself.

When he found a clearing inside a circle of pine trees, Ivan Kessler unbuttoned and relieved himself. He wanted to survive the war, although he didn't have much to return to. He didn't particularly miss his family. The country had grown; maybe it was time to see more of it.

Kessler reached to button his trousers when a hard, thick arm wrapped itself around his throat. The arm was attached to a heavy body that pressed him against the tree. As he pulled at the massive arm that was stealing his breath, he felt a huge, scabbed hand wrap around his cock.

"Did you get this out just for me?" the man said, with a throaty chortle. Then he stroked Kessler until he started to harden. Ivan continued to fight. He thrust his elbows into the man's gut, but he was as big as a mountain. Nothing Kessler did made an impact. He tried bracing his arms against the tree and kicking backward. He struck the man's knees, his shins, his groin; the beast laughed all the louder.

Kessler exhausted himself and accomplished only in getting the arm to slip tighter over his throat. He could do nothing while the rough hand stroked his prick until he came. Embarrassed and scared, Ivan Kessler clenched, when the tip of the man's tongue ran across his neck. Without warning, the arm was taken away, and Kessler was released. He lost his balance from the sudden shift of weight, dropping to the forest floor. He scrambled to his feet, pulling a bowie knife from his boot.

The man in front of him was immense: half a foot taller than Kessler, himself – with shoulders wider than a barn door. A red beard consumed the man's craggy face. Blue eyes peered out from under hooded lids. And he wore a gray, Confederate uniform.

"How the hell did you get here?" Kessler asked.

"Where am I?" the man asked back with another rumbling laugh.

"Behind enemy lines, surrounded by three hundred Union troops. How did you get past everyone? You're as big as a damned house."

"I can be anywhere I like, soldier."

"Yeah, well, I'm gonna gut you for what you did."

"What did I do? Don't you like my rough touch?"

In the middle of the behemoth's questions, Kessler charged him, plunging the knife into the mid-section. He expected to feel resistance when the blade punctured flesh. Instead, he punched the air, falling flat on his face.

Jumping up quickly, Ivan Kessler spun around, knife at the ready. The Confederate was standing where Kessler had been, arms akimbo, and a gashed smile on his face.

"Don't you like me over here?" the Confederate asked. "Maybe you like me better behind you."

He was gone. Kessler couldn't breathe. The man had just disappeared.

"If you still want to gut me, I'm back here."

Kessler turned around to see the beast of a man standing behind him; his own knife pointed at his face. Kessler backed away.

"How did you do that?" he asked.

"I told you. I can be anywhere I like."

"How?" Kessler asked again, anger rising in his voice.

"Do you know what a vampire is, boy?"

"I'm no boy."

"To me you are. I've walked this ground for five centuries. You're a pup."

Ivan Kessler smirked. "Right. Give me some of what you've been drinking, giant."

"Ah ha," the Confederate laughed. "A nonbeliever." He sat down on a tree stump, took an apple from his jacket pocket and began slicing off pieces with his knife.

"My name is Svein, born to a Norwegian father and an Irish tart for a mother, in Dublin, 1321 the year of our Lord. I fished, I farmed, I fought, and I fucked. A normal life for a lad. Until I was turned."

"Turned?" Kessler repeated. He had relaxed some, but his knife stayed ready in his sweaty palm.

"To a vampire, son. I met a man who called himself Trinket. A silly man, tall and spindly, with long, wavy hair. Told stupid jokes and drank whisky all night long without getting drunk. Trinket and I had our times together. I enjoyed his company after a long day of work. Then, one day, he told me he had to be off, and he wanted me to come along, only I wasn't interested. That's when he did something unexpected."

Kessler took a few steps back to lean against a tree. The knifepoint fell to the ground. The big man's story was unbelievable and yet, the longer he talked, the more fascinated Ivan Kessler became. The blue eyes penetrated him, dug into him like fingers, to hold him in place.

"Trinket and I were walking on a road back to my family farm when he asked me to travel with him. After I said no to his proposal, he picked me up and threw me to the ground. Do you understand? I weigh over three hundred pounds, and Trinket was barely half that, but pick me up, he did. Once I was on the ground, he pinned me so I couldn't move. I had never been scared of anyone, never had to be, because no one was as big as me. But on that road, when Trinket's mouth opened to reveal his black fangs, I pissed my pants.

"Once I was turned, I left with Trinket. I couldn't stay with my family anymore; they wouldn't understand. I have to give the man credit; he stayed with me for a century, teaching me how to choose my victims, allowing me to grow stronger. It was during his birthday celebration in France in 1430 when I ripped his heart from his chest for making me what I am.

"That, soldier, was Trinket's mistake. He let me become more powerful than he was. I won't make that mistake with you."

"With me? No. You're not 'turning' me, whatever that means." Kessler immediately tightened, his hunting knife poised to strike.

"That's why I chose you, lad. You're a fighter. I can't stand piss pots. Give me a man who knows he's beat but still won't lie down."

"I won't lie down for you or any man," Kessler said. "I don't know how you did your trick, but that's all it was. This knife . . . is no trick."

Kessler blinked and Svein was gone. He turned quickly, to protect his back, but the big man wasn't there. Kessler started to run. His legs were cut out from under him, and he fell, face first, into a slab of slate rock. Before he could recover, Svein was on top of him, a serrated blade at his throat, and Kessler's own knife cutting into his groin.

"Should I geld you, boy? Or do we play nice?"

Kessler tried to push his body up, but it was no use. He looked over his shoulder. Through the blood running into his eye from the wreckage of his face, Kessler saw Svein open his mouth. Ivan Kessler had never screamed in his life, but he wailed like his mother when the fangs pierced his neck.

\*\*\*

August 20, 2015, Gettysburg, Pennsylvania

He had the girl tied down to a metal table. To Henry Barlow, she looked to be no more than twenty years old. Kessler stood behind the table, stroking her long, auburn hair. The skin of his hands was gray, the blood vessels underneath so thick, they pressed against the flesh like shifting mountain ranges.

The girl was gagged, but Henry could hear her mewling. They were in an abandoned industrial park on the outskirts of town. Kessler was holed up in a warehouse filled with broken-down farm machinery. The windows were devoid of glass, so Henry had to be quiet in his spot crouched down on a wooden crate.

Kessler moved aside of the girl, running his crooked fingers in circles around her nipples. He placed one hand, palm down, on her stomach as her breathing sped up. He took his index finger and held it over her belly button, twirling it slowly like a pendulum. Outside, Henry shifted position to better see. He almost missed the crusty black talon emerging from Kessler's finger. Henry jumped when the vampire plunged it into the girl's stomach.

Her scream was piercing, even as the cloth in her mouth absorbed it. Kessler pulled his claw up her midsection, making a slice from groin to breast. Blood bubbled to the surface, forming a vermiform line. Kessler bent down, putting his face against the girl's skin. With the tip of his tongue, he tasted a drop of her blood. He laughed, pressing his nose to the red stream and snorted the blood into his nostril. Kessler went from the balls of her tits to the top of her groin taking her into his body.

When he finished, the vampire stood up with blood running from his nose over his lips, threw his arms back and howled into the ceiling. Henry watched as Kessler stripped naked, turning back to run a finger over the bottom of her foot as though they were lovers playing sensual games.

The girl was still alive, barely. A thin stream of blood ran down the side of her mouth as her body bucked, fighting Kessler's violation of her. Barlow said a prayer for the girl to die before she suffered any further. He had just re-opened his eyes when he saw the vampire climb onto the table and enter the dying woman. She tried to cry out but emitted only a gurgling from her throat. The vampire rode her hard, slamming himself inside of her. The smile on his face was repulsive.

"Sweet Jesus, I have to end this," Barlow whispered out loud. He wasn't prepared for his confrontation with Kessler yet, but he couldn't allow the girl to suffer, either. Henry pulled the Sig Sauer from his boot, checked that the magazine was full, and pulled back on the slide. He eased his hands above the ledge of the window and took aim.

"When is it my turn?" a female voice said, from the shadows. Barlow froze. He *knew* that voice.

"Ginny," he said.

\*\*\*

Ivan Kessler, emboldened by the young girl's life force, pounded his cock into her, pushing her body back and forth on the shaky table. Vanessa was her name. A local college student looking for adventure, strayed too far from home, and found the wrong man. Kessler wasn't handsome, but in a century and a half, had developed a powerful mind. Minutes after meeting, Vanessa looked at him with moon-pie eyes, waiting for his first command. This small town girl was merely a diversion on a dull night, sustenance for the next few weeks.

The vampire continued to smear the girl's blood on his face as he raped her; snorting it, swallowing it, pulling the rusty scent into his nose. Vanessa was hanging on, sucking in harsh breaths while her lungs filled with fluid.

"When is it my turn?" a soft voice asked from against the wall. Kessler tilted his head.

"Are you ready to feed, my pet?" he asked.

"Please, master."

"Come here."

The woman was older than Vanessa by twenty years, but phlegmatic, with pale, lustrous skin and red hair that fell in coils around her face. This one, he had stolen months ago, and he was keeping her around. She reminded him of a girl he had lusted for growing up. Esther Mathers never liked Ivan Kessler, the tall, gawky, teenage boy. But now, Ginny Barlow would do anything to make Kessler, the vampire, happy.

Ginny walked up to the dying girl with lust in her eyes. She ran her tongue over her lips, letting the tip stick out, trembling.

"Ready?" Kessler asked again, enjoying his lover's excitement.

"Yes, master," Ginny replied, without taking her eyes off of Vanessa.

Never breaking rhythm with his hips, Kessler reached up with one claw, raking it across the girl's throat. Blood spurted into the air and Ginny gleefully thrust her face in the middle of the fountain. She stuck out her tongue to catch a stream and lap it into her mouth like a dog. Kessler finished inside Vanessa as Ginny enveloped the slit of her throat with her mouth, swallowing the girl's blood in gulps. Jumping to the floor, Kessler looked at the window.

"Henry, would you like to join us?" he said.

***

When Henry saw Ginny, he started to cry. She was still so beautiful, even though she had lost weight. *Too skinny*, was his first thought. Only when he was able to calm down did he see how she looked at Kessler. Henry's chest tightened. That was **his** look. She saved those eyes for him, her husband – the man who had swept her off her feet when she was just out of high school. The gun wavered in his hand. When the girl's throat was cut, Henry Barlow vomited down the front of his pants. He never saw his wife bathe herself in blood and drink it like she was starving. Then he heard his name.

***

Kessler waited until the tobacco farmer lifted his head in the window frame. Henry Barlow was medium height and wide shouldered. His short brown hair was showing gray at the sides. Moderately well off, he had hired Kessler as temporary help on the farm and Kessler took it to get close to his wife. When he left with a freshly turned Ginny at his side, Kessler believed he would never hear from Henry again, but the man had proved resilient and sadistic in his pursuit. The things he did to the vampires he had caught surprised Kessler. Then again, he had never been in love.

When Henry was present in the window frame, Kessler reached out a hand and closed it. Henry was lifted off the ground, his body flying into the room, crashing to the floor.

"Welcome, Henry. I've been expecting you." Kessler took a long, red robe off the wall, slipping it on and cinching the belt. He sat down on a high-backed chair to put on a pair of black leather boots. As he locked the buckles, he watched Henry Barlow catch his breath.

"What do you have in mind for me, Henry? Hmm? Torture? Cutting off limbs? Or will you just kill me straight out?"

Barlow had managed to push himself to his knees. He looked over at Kessler, knowing he was in trouble. He had dropped his gun and had no other weapons on him. Whatever his plan had been, it was gone from his mind now. Henry heard movement behind him. He turned to see his wife.

"Ginny," he said, getting to one knee. Ginny's hair was plastered to the sides of her face by the blood that covered her cheeks. It ran down her neck, over her breasts. She looked at her husband curiously.

"Henry? What are you doing here?"

"He's here to kill me and take you home," Kessler said.

Ginny looked down at Henry. "I love you," Henry said to her, not able to stop his tears. Ginny stepped closer. She bent down, balancing on the balls of her feet. Taking Henry's face in her slick, blood-soaked hands, she ran the backs of her fingers across his cheek. Then she kissed him, first lightly on the lips, followed by a peck on his forehead.

"Go home, Henry," she whispered. "Before you get hurt."

"I can't go without you."

"You have to. I'm staying with Ivan."

"Ginny, I can . . ."

"No, Henry. You can't kill him. And I don't want you to. I belong to him now."

"What's happened to you? What about us?"

"Henry, if you would somehow kill Ivan, you would have to kill me too . . ."

"No."

". . . Because I would slice your belly open with a razor blade and pull your insides out to feed to the pigs."

Henry pulled away from his wife's touch. He looked into the same, sparkling blue eyes he had said good morning and good night to for almost twenty years. She smiled, blood dripping from her teeth. Ginny stood and walked to her master. She turned to look at Henry again.

"Go home," she said. Turning back to Kessler, she dropped to her knees. She opened his robe and took his cock into her mouth.

Henry stayed on the floor, staring at the concrete. Drops of Vanessa's blood had splattered next to his hand. He had watched a girl be murdered and done nothing.

His own wife. . .

When he thought of Ginny, Henry flinched. She was gone. Everything he had done for the past months, all the scars he had collected, the depraved acts he had committed; it was all for nothing.

The sounds she was making assaulted him as loudly as if it were cannon fire. Each smack of her lips was a stab at his balls. Henry looked around the room. It was mostly rotted, rusted junk, but leaning behind him was a long, metal pole. The top end had been sharp at one time, although age and use had blunted it. Henry didn't know what the implement was and wished it had a point, but there was nothing else within reach. He chanced a look at Kessler. The vampire's eyes were closed, in full enjoyment of Ginny's ministrations. Henry felt another kick to his groin.

Inside his head, Henry Barlow counted to three, then jumped up and grabbed the pole. He turned to charge Kessler. The vampire was holding out one hand, pointing a finger. Henry took two steps and was lifted into the air. He hung there, his feet kicking wildly. He threw the pole at Kessler. The vampire blew a puff of air and the pole flew across the room, clanging off the wall.

"Was that it, Henry? All these months planning revenge and that was it?"

Henry Barlow danced in the air. Eventually, he stopped struggling. He looked at Kessler with resignation, the skin drooping from his face like saddlebags.

"I will say; I was impressed by what you did to my former traveling companions. There are a few vampire hunters in the world that I would have thought capable of it, but you were not on that list. Let me show you what *I'm* capable of."

Kessler stood, pushing Ginny away from him. He released Henry, who fell to the floor. The vampire wrapped an iron-hard hand around Henry's arm and dragged him down a dark hallway, into another room. There was a fading, low-wattage bulb in the overhead lamp. Along the walls, there were sets of chains. Wrapped up in the chains were four men, although, Henry wondered if he could call them that anymore.

"Take a close look, Henry, and tell me what you see," Kessler said, throwing Henry at the feet of the first man. Henry looked up and saw translucent, yellow flesh, hanging on a skeleton. The man wheezed when he breathed in. Wisps of gray hair flared off his head in all directions. When Henry dared to stare into the man's face, he saw the fangs protruding from the mouth. This was a vampire. He looked into the man's eyes and was sure he recognized them. Henry glanced back at Kessler.

"You remember this creature?" Kessler asked.

"It can't be him."

"Who?"

"Trevan."

"And how do you know Trevan?"

"He was the first vampire I captured. The first I questioned about your whereabouts, and the first I *killed*."

"Correct."

Henry turned back to Trevan. "But, he was dead," he said.

"Look at my next display," Kessler said.

Henry hesitated. Finally, he stood and took a few steps to the next man. He was taller, but his body was in the same condition: Sallow skin, clinging to bone like parchment. When he looked at the face, into the eyes, Henry knew it was Francisco. Another vampire he had tortured. And killed.

Before being told, Henry moved on to the third prisoner. The chains were holding this one up, as he was too weak to stand on his own. Henry was not surprised to see Igor, who had been a thick, barrel-chested man. Now, he leaned against the wall with his tongue hanging out the side of his mouth, breath escaping in gasps. Henry turned away, instead looking into the eyes of the fourth vampire he had killed. Jonathan stared at him. There was still fire in his eyes, but no strength in his body.

"I don't understand," Henry said. "I know I killed them. You monsters are not indestructible."

"That's true," Kessler conceded. "We can be killed, and you did just that to these men."

"Then, how?"

"Because I am not these men," Kessler boasted. "They followed me for a reason: to learn my powers. To gain from my strength. You defeated my minions and thought you could get me as well, but I am like nothing you have ever seen, Henry Barlow. I brought these men back."

"But . . . why?"

"They betrayed me. I take loyalty very seriously. I brought them back to do this to them." Kessler swept his arm around the room. "They're suffering, Henry. It's what they deserve."

"I didn't know . . . your kind could do something like this."

"Most can't. I was turned myself, by one of the most powerful vampires walking this earth. Svein is still out there, somewhere. We traveled together for one hundred years, country-to-country, town-to-town, and I spent the entire time watching, learning, and growing my abilities. Svein could crush me, but I can do things even he can't. There is no limit to our power if we use it."

Kessler walked over to tower over Henry Barlow. "Now," he snarled. "I have to get rid of you, Henry. I'm going to show you just how *powerful* I am."

\*\*\*

The humidity of a Pennsylvania summer night hung in the air like wet clothes on a line. Kessler had knocked Henry out cold, and with Ginny in tow they marched like soldiers to Culp's Hill. There, Ginny stripped Henry and re-dressed him in a Union soldier's blue uniform that they had stolen from a gift shop. When she was finished, Ginny slunk away. Kessler took over, lifting Henry to his feet. Kessler woke him up with a hard slap to the face.

"Time to pay the price, Henry. You wouldn't want to sleep through it, would you?"

Barlow's head rolled forward and back as he came to. He felt Kessler's immense grip on his shoulders as the vampire leaned down to look into Henry's eyes. His dry, scaly hands moved up to brace either side of Henry's face.

Henry tried to pull away, but it was no use. Kessler held his face tight, forcing him to look into the vampire's eyes. At first, he saw only black orbs, but slowly, they changed. The color began to swirl until a line of red snaked through. It twirled around Kessler's eyes like a ribbon. Henry felt weak. Only Kessler's grip was keeping him on his feet. The red ribbon of color jumped from Kessler's eyes into Henry's.

Henry Barlow could no longer see clearly. His vision was a blob of floating black, cut in half by a dancing red line. He felt sparks from the color. Heat from his eyes burrowed deep into his head until his skull was on fire.

Ivan Kessler leaned down, and with one long hand, he exposed Henry's neck. "Time to go," he said before plunging his fangs through the skin.

"No," Henry shouted. "Nonononono!"

Kessler drank Henry's blood, sucking deeply from the wounds. When he'd had enough, he pulled away, grabbing Henry by the neck.

"Goodbye," Kessler said with a laugh, before throwing Henry Barlow head first into the trunk of a tree.

*** 

"Come on, get up. The rebs is comin'."

Henry felt two hands trying to lift him. His head ached, and there was a knot under the skin. He was dragged to his feet.

"What happened to you?" the voice asked.

"Where . . . am I?" Henry asked.

"Where are you? You're in the middle of a shit storm, mister. The rebs broke through our lines. Come on."

Henry felt something being put into his hands. When he looked down, he saw a long rifle. "What the hell?" he mumbled. He looked at the man who handed him the gun. He was about thirty, black, greasy hair sneaking out from under a blue cap. He wore a military uniform, blue wool with gold buttons. Henry heard an explosion and shouting. More men in uniform ran by, some stopping long enough to shoot in the direction they were running from. Suddenly, a bullet chipped into the tree trunk just above Henry's head.

"Jesus Christ!" he shouted, while ducking.

"I done told you, mister. We got to go," the soldier said, starting to move away.

"Wait," Henry said to him. "What year is this?"

"What year? I don't know what's wrong with you, but I don't want to die. You're on your own." Again, the soldier started to run.

"Are we in Gettysburg?" Henry asked.

"We'll be in our graves if we don't run! The south is comin'.'"

"No," Henry said. "He *couldn't*." He heard another bullet pass by. He looked and saw men in gray uniforms running his way. More explosions rocked the ground. Henry finally stared down at himself, seeing for the first time the clothes he was wearing.

"No," he repeated.

"Mister?"

"No," Henry said, shaking his head. He bent back and shouted into the sky. "NO!"

The soldier with him blanched when he saw the fangs protruding from the edges of Henry's mouth.

# PENICILLIUM PERICULUM

### Lisamarie Lamb

It was the third day and Anthony's throat was burning. Still. It would never end, he was sure of it. Water did nothing, food was impossible, and now swallowing caused a fire to ignite that spread through his neck and head and down to his toes, making them crackle and crunch.

His wife had suggested he visit the doctor. "It's gone on too long, Anthony. It's too much. You'll make yourself ill with this not eating."

Anthony shook his head, which also shook lose the pain and bounced it around his skull, his joints, his poor, sore throat, like a pinball. "I won't make myself ill," he croaked. "I'm *already* ill. That's the problem." And he refused to go. "Witch doctors, that's all they are. With their drugs and their ointments and their surgery. Cut, cut, cut, that's all they want to do. Or sell, sell, sell. Do you know how much it costs the country for me to visit the GP? *Do you*? Too much. No, I won't go. I'll never go."

His wife shrugged, brought him another cup of whiskey and honey and lemon, and left him to it. Let him suffer. Let him hurt. It was his own fault for being pig-headed. She hoped he choked on his toddy. And, when feeling more charitable, she was quite sure he would call the doctor in the end. She hoped he would.

It was on the fifth day that he almost succumbed. He almost phoned, he had, in fact, dialed the number and was preparing his speech about not wanting to be a bother, not wanting to be a pain, but really, perhaps he should see someone after all, when he realized that what he was doing could not be undone and he slammed the phone down into its socket just as the receptionist answered in her well-practiced and overly kind voice.

So close.

But it wasn't worth it. The prodding, the needling, the subtle little jokes at his expense which would come because he had given in and done the terrible deed of making an appointment at the doctor's. When he was so adamant that he would never do such a thing. That he *could* never do such a thing.

Better to suffer. Better to be in pain. Better to keep drinking his drinks, his head swirling because now they were more whiskey and less honey and no lemon at all. And they were becoming cooler, colder – icy. And soon it was just whiskey because the honey did nothing and the ice was better at numbing him. But even that wasn't perfect. Even that wore off after a while.

No one noticed.

No one cared.

And his throat still ached and burned. He couldn't eat without gasping out loud from the pain. It felt, he said to no one listening, as though there were shards of glass embedded in his gullet, as though every time he swallowed he was jangling them all straight onto his nerves, the pain blinding him for a moment, the agony killing him for an instant. The torment strangling him with a blanket full of needles.

He grew thin. His eyes became dark and tired and so very, very haunted.

He could no longer speak and took to writing instructions on a pad of paper, tearing the top sheet off and shoving it in the face of anyone who dared come near. Not that many did. His wife, of course, because she lived with him, and she thought she ought to make an effort. His daughter, on occasion, when she required some cash, or wanted to see how ill her father looked now, fascinated by the transformation, but other than that… No one.

Anthony cried to himself as he sipped his whiskey and tried to stop or numb or forget about the pain. Nothing worked. He half wrote a note asking his wife to call the doctor, declaring that he could no longer stand it, could no longer bear this and the jesting and joking would simply have to be endured. And then he ripped it to bits and threw it on the fire. Gone. Forgotten. Much like him.

On the tenth day, when his stomach was an untamed beast, clawing and snarling within, he lifted his pounding head from his pillow and decided that he would have to eat. He would just have to. If he didn't, he would die, and he couldn't die, not now, not from a sore throat. That would be embarrassing. That would be excruciating in all possible ways.

He made his way down to the kitchen, a room he hadn't seen for a week or so now. A note on the table, taken, he saw, from his own pad, a fact that made him angrier than it should have done, told him that his wife had gone shopping. *There's just no food in the house. Back soon.*

He had wanted soup. He had thought soup would be all right; he could suffer his way through it, if he had to. If it stopped him from dying, it seemed worth it. And maybe it would give him his voice back. And maybe, if that happened, he would get round to phoning the doctor, to making an appointment. To being seen. He'd have to try it first, though.

But there was no soup. His wife wasn't lying when she wrote that there was nothing. But the hunger was shredding him, tearing at him, and he was mad with it. Cupboard after cupboard was bare, Miss Hubbard's house tenfold, until Anthony, proud (stubborn) man that he was, was reduced to sifting through the rubbish. The smell was terrible, but the idea that there might be something edible in there was irresistible.

He pulled the bin from under the sink and plunged his hand into it, rummaging around, his fingers coming into contact with slimy, rotting, repulsive things. Cat vomit, brown and soggy lettuce leaves, hair pulled from somewhere, a drain perhaps, it was all in there. His arm was deep in the detritus now, deep in and swirling around, fingertips brushing against this or that putrid thing.

Until he found the bread.

He knew the feel of it, the crumbly, soft texture of days old white loaf, medium sliced, thrown out because of some reason or another that he did not care to know.

Bread was good. Bread was life.

Anthony pulled his arm free, his shirtsleeve hanging wet and orange with unwanted Bolognese sauce. Chewed and discarded food and rotten things clung in clumps to him. He didn't mind it. He didn't even mind the smell now, the sweet scent of decay.

The bread was not too badly damaged. It was relatively free of muck and it seemed, to Anthony's delirious eyes, all right. Just about. So he ate it. He folded it in half and stuffed it into his open mouth as quickly as he could, chewing, swallowing, again, and again, his throat screaming out, his stomach churning, and still he swallowed, swallowed, again.

When it was gone, Anthony felt a little better. Not entirely better, not done and back to work better, but less light-headed, less on the verge of death. He wondered whether, perhaps, there was another slice in the bin. Although he was almost himself again, it didn't stop him from delving in deep once more, searching, seeking for another slice. And why, he wondered, when he found one, and pulled it out of the bin, spraying rotting vegetables over the kitchen floor, had it been thrown out in the first place?

He ate that one too.

But he kept the last little bite in his hand, wanting to enjoy that piece, wanting to savour the final mouthful before his wife returned with real food. Clean food. Proper food that a man was expected to eat.

Anthony sighed.

He had, for a mad and intensely exciting moment, been a hunter-gatherer. He had foraged for food and found it, albeit dead bread in a bin in his own kitchen.

And that final corner of the loaf in his hand, held gently, was ready to be eaten. It was his prize, his reward. But as he brought it to his mouth, he noticed something. A musty smell, a fragile, frail layer of green dust that left itself on his fingers. And now he could taste it, knowing that he must already have eaten some of this, lots of this. He burped as his stomach tried to reject the filthy food, but he refused to let it go.

Because it had made him feel better. It *had*. There was no doubt about that.

Disgusting as it was, and he knew that now, now that his brain had been fed and his body was building itself back up once more, he thought it had done him good. Wasn't mouldy fungus on bread just penicillin anyway? And wasn't that a good thing to use on a sore throat? Surely it was. The doctor would have prescribed it for him anyway. Anthony felt smug, felt that he had been right all along, and now he had the proof.

He poured himself another toddy, without the honey, without the lemon, and drank it bravely, no sipping, down in two, the first swallow hesitant, the second less so when he realized it didn't hurt.

Homemade penicillin. Good work, Anthony. He was a genius. A genius on the mend. He popped the final little square of mouldy bread into his mouth and chewed, swallowing the dusty mixture with as much control as he could.

And as he cleared up his mess, put it all back into the bin from which it came, he whistled to himself. He smiled.

On the eleventh day, his sore throat was back, worse, if anything, and he wept when he awoke. He hadn't thought that he might have a relapse. He hadn't considered that at all. But of course, he was aware of the dangers of antibiotics, which is why he didn't like to take them in the first place. He knew that if the course was not completed, only the weak bacteria died. The stronger stuff hung around, analyzing the fungal extract that was being thrown at it, until it knew how to beat it. And then it came back, with reinforcements.

Damn it.

Why hadn't he thought of that the day before?

Why hadn't he planned for this?

Angry with himself, he strode from the bedroom, rubbing his tongue against the back of his throat, making clicking noises, soothing the pain as best he could. He clearly needed more mould. He'd have to search for it.

He'd have to go outside and see what he could see, find what he could find.

It was raining, a dark and dismal day, but what else could he do?

He dressed, vaguely, and pulled on his coat and boots. "I'm off out for a bit!" he called up the stairs, wondering whether there was anyone there, wondering if anyone was listening to him anyway. There was no response.

So he left.

Anthony trudged up and down the road, afraid to look inside the dull green wheelie bins that sat, squat and full, pregnant with waste, on the pavements. Someone might see him. Someone might *know* him and ask him what he was doing. And although he knew he was doing the right thing, saving money, it could be said, for the greater good, he understood that no one would appreciate his efforts, that they would think him vile, dirty, possibly even insane. And so, even though he knew that his treasure, his special medicine, would be inside – it always was, people had no sense of importance, of society and the bigger picture – he kept walking.

His fingers were itching, twitching to lift a lid and dive in.

But he could not. Despite the ragged saw-teeth whizzing around in his sore throat, despite his tingling fingers, he refused to give away his secret. That was his real fear. That was his worry. Because, if he told people what he was doing, if he explained his actions, they would all want a piece. They would stop throwing their mouldy old bread away; they would keep it for themselves.

Which wasn't fair.

He did have a plan though.

Anthony walked on stinging feet, pins and needles now jabbing at his soles. All part of the same disease, he had no doubt. All part of the same problem, which the fetid bread would fix. Once he got to it. If he got to it before anything else did.

The park. That's where he was heading. The pond in the park, to be precise. Where the ducks were, and where the children fed the ducks; throwing old bread, bread that was surplus to requirements, complete with fungus, all green and blue and greyish white, all the goodness, at dumb ducks. Wasting it.

Forget about the crusts being the best part… It was the mould. Anthony knew that for a fact, and his numb fingers and his tired body, all the aches and pains, were telling him it was true.

By the time he arrived at the pond, he was frozen, chilled all over, the cold stabbing at his skin and letting itself in through his pores, down to the blood, down to the bone. Taking him to the edge of sanity, making him wish he were someone else doing something else. For now. But the bread would save him.

He could see torn off, jagged squares of white and brown and beige lying on the ground, growing damp and soggy, and he pounced on them, scaring off the startled, madly quacking ducks that waddled towards him as he fell. On the ground, he crawled from one piece to the next, taking only those that were mouldy, only those upon which the fungus had taken hold. The rest he left. There was no point in being greedy.

Shocked and sickened mothers grabbed toddlers' hands and backed away, ignoring the disappointed wails of their children, seeing only the madman, the one with the blackened nose, the bleeding eyes, the leper, perhaps, as he snuffled and sniffed around on the ground, snorting the bread their children had thrown down for the ducks. A childhood memory now sullied by insanity.

Anthony didn't see them. He couldn't see much. A veil of dripping, melting flesh was covering his eyes, sloughing from his forehead, from his skull and off, onto the ground in great bloody lumps.

Fingers, too. They went, snapping away as he reached for the sodden, milky bread, rain-dampened and mushy, melting as he touched it, just like his skin, and he left them where they fell. Because, what did he care about skin or fingers? He was feeling so much better. His throat wasn't hurting anymore. The penicillin was perfect, was working so well, that he wasn't bothered by anything.

He knew that he had lost his toes. He could feel them rattling around in his boots, but there was nowhere for them to go, trapped inside his thick woolen socks. He would deal with them later. He would empty them out and get his wife to sew them back on, or throw them away. Whichever option was the best one. He didn't know. He didn't know much anymore.

His nose split away from his face, if it could be called a face, and hung, loose, dangling on one side, blood spilling from the wound, the dead, gangrenous skin gradually, slowly flit-flitching away, as though the stitching was coming loose, until it landed on the ground. It splashed into a puddle, a shallow one, and lay there, the nose that he remembered, that he recognized from some far away place and some far away time.

Anthony tried to stand, but his legs were unfeeling, anaesthetized, desensitized. They buckled at the knees and he crashed to the ground, falling on top of his nose, his fingers, his face. He couldn't move. He couldn't breathe.

He couldn't live.

But at least his throat didn't hurt anymore. And for that he was grateful.

# ABOUT THE AUTHORS

**James E. Coplin** has been a freelance writer and journalist since the 1970's, having appeared in dozens of mainstream publications, newspapers and as a columnist for the Examiner news website. Yet, growing up as he did reading such authors as Robert E. Howard, Algernon Blackwood, Arthur Conan Doyle, Rudyard Kipling, E.R. Eddison, Bram Stoker, H.G. Wells and others, his not so secret hobby has been writing atmospheric tales of suspense and the supernatural. This is his second appearance in EMP's Creepy Campfire Quarterly with a collection of his Gothic and Period ghost stories entitled *Creaking Staircases* due out by the same publisher this fall.

In her alternate reality, **Morgan Griffith** and her rat companions live in an obsidian tower in the heart of an uncharted forest. Ravens perch on stone gargoyles. Silent rain coaxes iridescent petals from black earth. Around her desk, pale ghosts gather, whispering dreams of the dead, and songs are moaned by the wind through skeletal ribs of a long-dead dragon.

Her most recently published tales appear in anthologies available on Amazon: "Secrets of the Sargasso" in *Fright Mare--Women Write Horror*, edited by Billie Sue Mosiman; "Sticks and Stones, Skin and Bones" in *A Mythos Grimmly*, from Wanderer's Haven Publications; and "Hellaway Bridge" in the charity anthology *In Creeps the Night*, benefitting Mothers Without Borders.

**Vincent Salvati** was born and raised in New Jersey. He is a graduate of Pratt Institute, Montclair State University and William Paterson University. A visual artist, poet and author, he strives for creativity in his work and his life. He has previously written and performed poetry in the New York City area and has been published in *The Paterson Literary Review*. Among his many solo and group exhibitions is his inclusion in the New Jersey Arts Annual at the Montclair Art Museum. He is currently on the board of directors for the Jersey City based non-profit, Pro Arts.

He is an avid traveler and loves learning about different cultures. When he isn't creating he can be found trekking around one continent or another. Vincent currently lives and works in New Jersey.

# David Neilsen is the author of *Dr. Fell and the Playground of Doom*, and several other odd, weird, supernatural, and occasionally slightly disturbing books and stories. David is also a classically trained actor who works as a professional storyteller up and down the Hudson River Valley and in New York City. His one-man performances based on the work of H.P. Lovecraft have sent many screaming into the hills in search of their sanity. Visit David online at http://www.david-neilsen.com.

# Howard Rachen is a writer and editor of horror fiction, particularly involving supernatural and body horror. *The Monster Next Door* is his first publication under this name. When not trying to twist the knife, he works under a separate name on a fantasy trilogy.

# Nancy J. Hayden is a writer, artist, and organic farmer from northern Vermont. She also has a keen interest in World War I and has published several WWI short stories including "Unknown Soldier" (*Kneeling in the Silver Light: Stories from the Great War,* a Horror/Dark Fantasy Anthology, Alchemy Press, 2014), "No Man's Land" (*Enter at Your Own Risk: Dreamscapes into Darkness,* Firbolg Publishing, 2015), and "Coffee Break on the Western Front, 1918," in (*Storm Cycle: The Best of,* Kind of a Hurricane Press, 2015). The story in this issue of CCQ takes place during the Battle of the Somme, one of Britain's deadliest battles ever.

Nancy had two other stories published in 2015 and two in 2016. Her horror/noir WWI short story collection is due to be out at the end of 2016. She is also working on a novel. She has an MFA in creative writing from the Stonecoast Writer's Program at the University of Southern Maine. She also has degrees in English and studio art, biology, and environmental engineering. She is a member of Horror Writers Association. Her website, www.northwindarts.com, has a link to her WWI Collage Blog where she regularly writes about art, stories, and research related to WWI.

**Jack Lee Taylor** is an author based in Tennessee. His many works are directly influenced by his love of reading horror, science fiction, and the *just-plain-weird*. His stories have been published in anthologies, online, and in magazines, including the forthcoming volume of long-running *Weirdbook Magazine.* Jack is currently working on his novel, *Mortals*, a sci-fi thriller that is the first installment of his *Deathless* series.

When not trying to squeeze as much writing as possible in what little time he has, Jack spends the rest of his time hanging out with his wonderful wife and two children. To help support his writing habit, Jack goes through the weekdays overanalyzing data and works the weekends being a rockstar. You can visit his personal blog at www.jackleetaylor.com.

**Daniel Schuette** (most often known by D.J.) is an author, blogger, and freelance editor residing in the northern suburbs of Minneapolis, Minnesota. His work covers a wide variety of genres—from dark thrillers, to horror, to YA Fantasy and beyond. He is a published and award-winning songwriter and poet and the creator of enterthemaelstrom.com, a fictional blog written from the perspective of Aleksandr Zorin, the serial killer featured in his first novel *Chaos*. Daniel's personal blog, a comprehensive list of works in progress, features on some of his friends in the Minnesota writing community, and pictures of his adorable dog Pogo can all be found on his author's page at djschuette.com.

**Tom Breen** is the author of *Orford Parish Murder Houses: A Visitor's Guide*, the first of several anticipated publications from a nonexistent historical society serving an imaginary town. His short fiction has been published in several anthologies and periodicals including, *Once*, a fanzine devoted to the late GG Allin. A former newspaper and wire service journalist, he lives and works in eastern Connecticut. You can catch up with him on Twitter @TJBreen, and follow the goings-on in *Orford Parish* at facebook.com/opdowntown.

# Ryan Neil Falcone's short fiction has appeared in various

prominent horror, sci-fi, and fantasy themed markets including *Stupefying Stories* and *Macabre Cadaver*. His stories have also been featured in numerous print anthologies commercially available on Amazon and at bookstores. He currently serves as a story editor for Dark Moon Books and *Dark Moon Digest*, and is an active member of Cornell University's Irving Literary Society. His platform of work is summarized at: www.ryanneilfalcone.com

# Jim Cort has been writing since God wore short pants. He is

currently President, CEO, Corresponding Secretary, Administrative Assistant, and Chief Cook and Bottle Washer at Deaf Dog Press. The Deaf Dog Press catalog is available at Smashwords:
https://www.smashwords.com/books/view/337106 and
https://www.smashwords.com/books/view/527874.

# Dale W. Glaser is a lifelong collector, re-teller and

occasional inventor of fantasy tales, and has yet to meet a bottle that doesn't have a demon at the bottom of it. And he has met a lot of demons, some fun-loving, some tormented, some both. His short stories have been included in such anthologies as *Twice Upon a Time* from Bearded Scribe Press; *Under a Dark Sign* from WolfSinger Publications; *King of Ages* from Uffda Press; and *Eldritch Embraces* from Dragon's Roost Press. He currently lives in Virginia with his wife and three children, and can be found online at https://dalewglaser.wordpress.com.

# Fredrick Obermeyer enjoys writing science fiction, fantasy, horror, and crime stories. He has had work published in *NFG*, *Electric Spec*, *Newmyths*, *Perihelion SF*, *Acidic Fiction*, the *Destination: Future* anthology, and other markets.

# Ambrose Stolliker lives in the Pacific Northwest with his wife and son. He is a former newspaper reporter and magazine writer and currently works in marketing at a global technology company. His work can be seen in *Ghostlight Magazine*, *Sex and Murder Magazine*, *Hungur Magazine*, *Sanitarium Magazine*, *The Tincture Journal* and Charon Coin Press' *State of Horror: Louisiana, Volume II* anthology.

Upcoming publications include his story *Reckoning in Spotsylvania*, which will appear in Rampant Loon Media's *Nightcrawlers*; his novella, *The Death Chute*, which was recently selected for publication by Strigidae Publishing; and his story *Six Miles to Bastogne*, which will be published in *Muffled Scream I: Corner of the Eye*, a new horror anthology from DAOwen Publications.

You can keep up with the latest news about Mr. Stolliker's writing via his blog, A Darkness More Than Night. You can also follow him on Twitter at @horrorwriter74.

# Jeffrey Todd, 37, resides in FL. He has written about fifty short
stories, seven of which have seen publication. Two novels (one occult, one a vagabond memoir) are in the making.

# Christopher Hivner writes from a small town in Pennsylvania surrounded by books and the echoes of music. He has recently been published in *Illumen, Night to Dawn* and *Yellow Mama*. A collection of short stories, "The Spaces Between Your Screams" was published by eTreasures Publishing. website: www.chrishivner.com, Facebook: Christopher Hivner - Author, Twitter: @Your_screams.

**Lisamarie Lamb** started writing in her late teens but it was only with the birth of her daughter that she decided to write more seriously, with the aim of publication. Since that decision in 2010, she has had over 40 short stories published in anthologies and magazines.

In November 2012, Dark Hall Press published a collection of Lisamarie's short stories with a twist, entitled *Over The Bridge*. In November 2013, J. Ellington Ashton Press released a second short story collection entitled *Fairy Lights*. April 2014 saw the publication of her first children's book, *The Book of Mandragore*, (J. Ellington Ashton). And in February 2016, J. Ellington Ashton published her adult horror, *Trip Trap*. These are all available from Amazon.

Lisamarie is the features and online editor for insideKENT (www.insidekentmagazine.co.uk) and insideSUSSEX (www.insidesussexmagazine.co.uk).

She is also a freelance writer who has ghost-written hundreds of blog posts, articles, reviews, fiction, and more.

She lives with her husband, daughter, and two cats in a centuries old cottage in the Kent countryside, in between two farms and next door to a field full of horses.
http://www.lisamarielamb.co.uk
http://www.facebook.com/lisamarielambwriter
http://www.twitter.com/lisamarie20010

# Acknowledgments

EMP Publishing and Creepy Campfire Quarterly would like to thank the following in no particular order. Each and every one of you has supported the CCQ and you are all responsible for helping every issue come into being.

**THANK YOU.**

Jeremiah Thompson, Søren Skøtt, Marlena Frank, Jenny Koenig, Bruce Galbraith, Jessica Hogue, Lewis Crown, Damian Stout, Ashley Spychalla, Jaime Metoyer, Ashwini Reddy, Rachel Blackburn, Michael LaPointe, Kristin Giglio-Baldi, Dale W. Glaser, Theresa Huffman, Kimberly King.

Visit the Indiegogo InDemand page today to order books from EMP Publishing, including one and two-year subscriptions to the CCQ!!

One-year Subscription is $55.00

Two-year subscription is $100.00

https://www.indiegogo.com/projects/a-house-but-so-much-more--3/x/10793111#/

www.ingramcontent.com/pod-product-compliance
Lightning Source LLC
Chambersburg PA
CBHW021706150626
46549CB00016B/562